"Stay away from me, de Burgh!

"If you think to do anything here but sleep, you had better prepare to die," she warned.

He snorted. "Yes, Elene, I rode miles from the manor simply so I could have my way with you on the cold, hard ground instead of the comfortable bed in our chamber."

His snide comment stung. Her mouth felt suddenly dry as she pictured him, dark and virile and warm. "I mean it, de Burgh," she whispered. "I'll slit your throat as soon as you move."

"And if you don't be quiet, I'll stop your mouth!" he warned.

"And just how will you do that?" she asked, contempt fueling her anger once more.

"I will kiss you."

Elene caught her breath at the threat, but instead of shock or horror, she felt a slow, insidious heat creep into her. Anticipation? Yearning? She parted her lips to curse him…!

Dear Reader,

The de Burgh Bride by Deborah Simmons is the entertaining sequel to her 1995 release, *Taming the Wolf,* a steamy adventure that earned her a 5★ review from *Affaire de Coeur.* This book is the story of the scholarly de Burgh brother, Geoffrey, who has drawn the short straw and must marry the "wicked" daughter of a vanquished enemy, a woman who reportedly murdered her first husband in the marriage bed!

A city banker forced to spend a year recuperating in the country goes head-to-head with a practical country widow and learns that some of life's greatest pleasures are the simple ones, in Theresa Michaels's next book in her new series of Westerns, *The Merry Widows—Catherine.* Corruption, jealousy and the shadow of barrenness threaten the love of a beautiful Saxon woman who has a year to produce an heir, or be separated forever from the knight who holds her heart, in Shari Anton's stirring medieval tale, *By King's Decree.*

In *Devlin,* by author Erin Yorke, an Irish rebel captured by the English is rescued from prison by the young Englishwoman whose life he saved, but the two must battle distrust and betrayal before finding the happiness they both deserve.

Whatever your tastes in reading, we hope you enjoy all four books this month. Keep an eye out for them, wherever Harlequin Historicals® are sold.

Sincerely,

Tracy Farrell
Senior Editor

Deborah Simmons

The de Burgh Bride

Harlequin Books

TORONTO • NEW YORK • LONDON
AMSTERDAM • PARIS • SYDNEY • HAMBURG
STOCKHOLM • ATHENS • TOKYO • MILAN
MADRID • WARSAW • BUDAPEST • AUCKLAND

ISBN 0-373-28999-5

THE DE BURGH BRIDE

Copyright © 1998 by Deborah Siegenthal

Books by Deborah Simmons

Harlequin Historicals

Fortune Hunter #132
Silent Heart #185
The Squire's Daughter #208
The Devil's Lady #241
The Vicar's Daughter #258
Taming the Wolf #284
The Devil Earl #317
Maiden Bride #332
Tempting Kate #371
The Knights of Christmas #387
The de Burgh Bride #399

DEBORAH SIMMONS

A voracious reader and writer, Deborah Simmons began her professional career as a newspaper reporter. She turned to fiction after the birth of her first child when a longtime love of historical romance prompted her to pen her first book, published in 1989. She lives with her husband, two children and two cats on seven acres in rural Ohio, where she divides her time between her family, reading, researching and writing.

For Jenny Barber Witherspoon,
who once lived with me Two Doors Down

Chapter One

Geoffrey de Burgh looked down at the short straw in his hand with a numbing horror. Around him, he was aware of the responses of five of his brothers, their swift gasps of surprise, their relieved sighs and their mumbled condolences, but he did not reply. He could only stare at the small stick, unable to believe that he, of all the de Burghs left unmarried, had drawn it.

He had lost. And now he must wed the Fitzhugh.

Glancing up finally, Geoffrey met his father's concerned gaze. If the earl of Campion was startled that the most scholarly of his sons was to marry the renowned hellion, he did not show it. Gentle understanding at Geoffrey's dismay was evident, along with pride, for the earl obviously knew that Geoffrey would not disappoint him.

Geoffrey felt the weight of that faith and the responsibilities that flowed from it more heavily than ever before, but he could not deny it. King Edward had decreed that one of the de Burghs take the wench to wife, and so he must do his duty, for his king, his father and his brothers.

Straightening, Geoffrey carefully masked his alarm. "Very well. I will have her," he said.

There were no congratulations, for no one in the solar harbored any delusions that Geoffrey would be happy with his bride. And for once, none of his siblings engaged in their usual teasing and taunting. All were grateful that they had escaped his fate and would not make light of it.

Mumbling excuses, the five bachelors, fearless warriors all, fled the room, eager to forget their cowardice when it came to marriage. And Geoffrey could not blame them, for who would not flinch at the idea of such a wife? He watched them all go, leaving him alone with Campion.

"Sit," his father said, tilting his head toward a nearby chair. Geoffrey settled himself to face the man he respected more than any other, unflinching under his sire's intense scrutiny. Campion rubbed his chin thoughtfully. "I would have hoped for another, Simon perhaps, though he is so hotheaded that he might have killed her before the ceremony was finished," he said with a wry glance.

Geoffrey allowed himself a slight smile at the jest. Campion's second son, Simon, was a fierce knight who had no use for women. No doubt, he would easily have cowed even the Fitzhugh, but he had a temper that sometimes clouded his judgment.

Campion nodded, as if in agreement with Geoffrey's thoughts. "Aye, perhaps 'tis better that you, the most skilled negotiator, take on this task. I am proud of all my sons, but you, Geoffrey, are the most like me."

Geoffrey glanced at his father in surprise. Although Campion made his affection for his sons apparent, he was not overly generous with his praise. This was high acclaim indeed, for Geoffrey knew of no other he would better strive to emulate.

"You have the strength that they do, but wisdom, too. Use your head and your heart, along with your sword arm, to deal with the woman who will be your wife," Campion advised. "We have heard many tales of her, but you know as well as I that such rumors are often exaggerated. People are not always what they seem, and I would ask you to keep an open mind when you marry. You, of all the de Burghs, are capable of heeding such advice."

Geoffrey nodded silently, though he held out little hope that the Fitzhugh creature was anything other than what she had been painted: a she-devil who was known for her rude outbursts, foul speech and wild behavior. 'Twas a fact that she had murdered her first husband in their marriage bed, an act that the king had seen fit to excuse because of the circumstances surrounding the wedding. Still, the cold-blooded deed gave a man pause, especially one who would follow in the dead knight's footsteps.

As if reading his son's thoughts once more, Campion cleared his throat, his expression turning somber. "Use your good sense and your compassion in the days ahead, but, my son," Campion warned, "don't forget to watch your back."

Geoffrey carefully placed the volume in his hands next to the others lined up in the trunk. He had more books than any at Campion Castle, even his father. Although all the de Burghs could read and write, only Geoffrey had studied with a traveling scholar, in an effort to quench his thirst for knowledge. And still he expanded his library whenever he could, for he had not given up his interests, even after his tutor moved on.

A knock came on his door, surprising him, for his brothers had made themselves scarce this day. Geoffrey understood, even if they did not, their reluctance to see him. They were all brave men and strong, who stood together when challenged, but the Fitzhugh was an enemy they did not know how to confront. His impending marriage could not be fought off with swords and axes, or routed by an army, and so they were at a loss to aid him.

"Enter," he called, thinking it was a servant, come to do his packing, but to his surprise, his eldest brother, Dunstan, filled the doorway. Geoffrey did not blink at the great knight's ferocious scowl, for he had learned that Dunstan often hid softer feelings behind gruff words and expressions.

Right now, Dunstan looked distinctly uncomfortable as he nodded a greeting and stepped inside. Campion, larger and more luxurious than most castles, boasted many private rooms, and Geoffrey shared this one with one of his brothers. Smiling ruefully, he swept aside a pile of Stephen's carelessly tossed clothing and bade Dunstan take a seat.

Perching on a large chest, Dunstan looked at him soberly. "I would rather your lot had fallen to another," he said. "Simon, perhaps."

The echo of his father's sentiments annoyed Geoffrey, but he merely shrugged. "We shall deal well enough, I expect," he said, folding a fine woolen tunic.

"By faith, Geoff, I—" Dunstan growled out another, fouler oath before beginning again. "I feel responsible. I'm the one who killed her father."

Geoffrey halted his task and eyed his brother directly. "Because he made war on you. Fitzhugh was a greedy bastard who would stop at nothing to gain your castle and lands. Have you forgotten how he waylaid your train, slaughtered your men and imprisoned you in your own dungeon?"

Dunstan's jaw tightened. "Nay. But 'twas my own knight, Walter Avery, who betrayed me to Fitzhugh and then wed his daughter."

"Luckily, she put an end to him before he could continue the battle against you," Geoffrey said lightly, avoiding his brother's gaze. Although what he said was true, he did not care to pursue that line of thought too closely, especially when he was next in line to wed the wench.

"By faith, Geoffrey, I am grateful that my brothers came to my aid, but I would not have any of them, least of all you, suffer for it. Blast the king's edict!" Dunstan muttered.

Geoffrey continued his packing. "You cannot fault Edward for seeking an end to the feuding. He wants to be assured of peaceful borders, and none better to provide that than one of your own brothers."

"Aye, but you, Geoff..." Dunstan said, his dismay evident.

Glancing at him sharply, Geoffrey bit back a reply. Although he was not as bloodthirsty as Simon, he could hold his own against a woman, murderess or no, and he was beginning to resent the implication that he could not. He sent his brother a challenging look, but Dunstan glanced away, as if embarrassed. "I only regret that you are required to form a loveless union," he mumbled.

Geoffrey's hands stilled at their task, his ill feelings fading at Dunstan's admission. Of all his brothers, only Dunstan would raise such a concern, for the rest would scoff at such romantic notions. Indeed, not too long ago, Dunstan would have laughed longest and loudest of the lot, but he was married now and recently had come to admit his feelings for the woman he had wed in haste.

Marion. Geoffrey tried not to compare the gentle, nurturing woman he treasured as a sister with the hellion he was to marry, but he could not help it. Too well he recalled his stay at Dunstan's castle, Wessex, where he had watched the couple with no little envy, longing for such affection in his own life.

Now it would be denied him. Silently Geoffrey returned
to his packing, unable to mouth some platitude that would
exonerate Dunstan, for his tongue felt thick and useless,
his heart heavy and hard. He wished his brother had never
broached the subject, for it settled around him like a stifling gloom, making the future look dim beyond his reck-
oning.

Suddenly, his sacrifice loomed before him very great
indeed.

Christmas passed quickly, a bittersweet celebration
made special by the presence of Marion, who was expecting the first de Burgh grandchild. She and Dunstan
lingered, even after the holiday was over, as if they could
forestall the grim reality of the next de Burgh wedding.
The state of the winter roads also conspired to put off the
impending nuptials, but finally there was a break in the
weather, and all but Campion set off for Wessex.

The earl, suffering from a winter chill, remained behind, and Geoffrey was relieved that he had talked his
father out of going with them. Although his brothers
thought of their father as little older than themselves,
Geoffrey had noticed that Campion was moving more
slowly of late. He rarely left the castle, and Geoffrey did
not want him making a journey in such temperatures. His
fears were well-founded, for they reached Dunstan's demesne only after nearly a week of struggling along sodden
roads through cold rains. There they left a vigorously protesting Marion, for Dunstan did not want her traveling any
more in her condition.

Although it went unspoken, Geoffrey was aware of another concern—that the Fitzhugh, infamous as she was,
might well be dangerous. No one, including Geoffrey,

wanted Marion exposed to violence, or anything that wasn't fine and good.

To what would soon be his life.

Geoffrey tried to force aside the unusually maudlin thoughts, but his accustomed optimism had been fading ever since they passed through the village near Fitzhugh's manor and saw the sorry state of the houses. Poor. The people he was to govern were poor. It was not something Geoffrey had expected, and it had taken him aback, striking at his very heart. Obviously, the Fitzhugh's father had spent his resources on war, instead of improvements. Geoffrey's contempt for the man grew apace with their progress to his home.

Although no one commented on the shoddy huts, Geoffrey had been aware of the glances of his brothers, swift and startled. Only Dunstan, whose finances had but recently improved, had seemed unaffected by the squalor, and Geoffrey found himself grateful to his eldest sibling. He had never been close to Dunstan, who had left home many years ago, yet now he felt bound by more than respect to the man they called the Wolf of Wessex. The tie would make his new life easier, for Dunstan would soon be his liege lord, as well as his brother.

Unfortunately, Geoffrey could hold out no great hopes for other aspects of his future. Already he had a job ahead of him—rebuilding what Fitzhugh had neglected and destroyed. As they marched past the outer wall, Geoffrey carefully assessed the granaries, workshops and stables clustered in the bailey. The old stone barrier needed to be moved, extended to make room for all who served the manor. And everything looked in need of repair.

Biting back a sigh, Geoffrey glanced at the house itself and knew a measure of relief. It was larger than he had expected, and the knowledge sat well with him, for after living at Campion, he did not relish cramped, over-crowded quarters. Another wall surrounded the inner bailey and protected the entrance to the manor, but it looked paltry to Geoffrey, accustomed as he was to an impregnable castle. He made a mental note to shore up the defenses, as well.

They were met at the doors by the steward, a nervous-looking little man with a balding pate. Although he bowed and scraped before them, no amount of fawning could make up for the absence of the lady of the house. Geoffrey felt his heart sink further, for the Fitzhugh should have greeted them at the gate, as was the custom when higher-ranking visitors arrived. The baron of Wessex and his brothers would definitely merit such a greeting, yet there was no sign of her even in the hall.

The room itself was spacious, but not very clean, and Geoffrey wrinkled his nose at the odors that could accumulate all too quickly during the winter months. The rushes on the floor were old and deteriorating, while the walls were covered with soot and grime. Although Geoffrey had grown up in a predominantly male household that had its share of dirt, Marion had changed all that, and even after her departure, the servants had continued her practices.

Now Geoffrey found the sight of an untidy hall less than appealing, and his opinion of the Fitzhugh wench dropped even lower. With a woman in residence, the place ought to look and smell good, at least. What kind of chatelaine was she? The question brought on a host of others surrounding the mysterious creature he was to wed, and Geoffrey wondered if she even bathed. Abruptly he had a vision of a hideous Amazon, fully armed, tall and fierce and filthy, with greasy hair and missing teeth. He did not even know her age.

Geoffrey shuddered, steeling himself for anything, but no one came forward, and he saw no crones in the nearly deserted room. Releasing a low rush of breath, Geoffrey stood waiting expectantly until he realized that his brothers were looking to him, as the future master of this holding, for welcome. The knowledge startled him, for he was accustomed to deferring to his father and his more outspoken siblings.

Yet he knew as well as the rest of them how to run a household, probably better, since his brothers had little patience for accounts or for managing servants. Stepping forward, Geoffrey called to the frightened steward. "Set out ale for me and my party, and bring the lady of the house to us, please."

"I shall see to your refreshments at once, my lord," the man said, backing away while bowing. "But... Mistress Fitzhugh is...unavailable at present. She bade me tell you to return at a later date."

Geoffrey sighed at the slight, only the beginning of many, he was certain. Glancing at his brothers, he saw that they were not taking the news well, either. Grimly Geoffrey noted the vicious set of Simon's face, the muscle working in Dunstan's jaw, and the insolent look on Stephen's handsome visage that portended trouble.

When he heard the rattle of mail behind him, Geoffrey moved swiftly between his siblings and the poor steward. The man was obviously not to blame. Geoffrey frowned. He knew all too well who was responsible. "And where is the lady?" he asked.

The steward glanced frantically toward the stairs at the back of the hall and then to the imposing knights flanking Geoffrey. Apparently, the man feared his mistress and the visitors with equal vigor, which boded ill for Geoffrey's future happiness. "Perhaps she is in her room," Geoffrey said, with forced cheer. "I will try to coax her into joining us."

"Geoff, don't go up there alone. She's liable to have a crossbow ready and waiting!" Simon warned.

Although the same thought had flickered through his mind, Geoffrey was determined not to treat his future wife as some kind of criminal until he had had a chance to judge for himself. Nor did he intend to cower in fear in his own home. Ignoring the warning, he looked to the steward, "She has a chamber, does she?"

"Yes, my lord, to the right at the top of the steps," the man said. And then he fled.

Geoffrey kept one hand on his sword hilt as he climbed the curving stairs. He had been in worse situations than this, but his natural caution would not allow him to discount the possible danger. The she-devil might be armed, and it was obvious that she did not want to marry him.

When visions of her first wedding taunted him, Geoffrey told himself that situation had been totally different. Walter Avery had been a rogue knight intent upon stealing her birthright, while any woman in her right mind would welcome an alliance with the de Burghs. But then, that was the question, wasn't it? Geoffrey thought grimly. Was the Fitzhugh in her right mind or not?

The answer awaited him ahead. Moving past what appeared to be the great chamber to a smaller door close by, Geoffrey knocked softly.

"Go away!" The shout was fierce and throaty. A woman's voice, but low and husky, it warned him to be-gone in no uncertain terms. Was it the Fitzhugh who spoke? Judging it wiser not to reveal his identity, Geoffrey simply knocked again, gently.

"Get thee gone, and disturb me no further!"

Geoffrey hesitated for a moment, then tried again, no louder, but with a firm persistence.

"I warn you, Serle, you imperil your life! Send the bastards away, as I told you, and cease to bother me!"

Geoffrey smiled. She thought him to be the steward, who had introduced himself to them as Serle. Perhaps she would venture out, if he kept at his task. He did so, and this time, her shout became a roar that resounded even behind the heavy door. It swung open abruptly, and Geoffrey stepped inside, shutting it with a swift kick. Having no love for the public antics for which his bride-to-be was known, he intended to hold this first meeting with her in private.

Keeping the door at his back, Geoffrey prevented escape, while facing whatever enemies the room might hold. Servants, soldiers, guards of some sort, he anticipated, but to his surprise he found himself in a tiny space, barely big enough to hold a small bed and a chest. It was neat and clean, so the Fitzhugh must have a personal servant who kept her chamber better than the rest of the manor. And Geoffrey suspected he was looking at her.

"Where is your mistress?" he asked of the lone woman who faced him. She was dressed in a dull-colored wool of better quality than most servants', but it was poorly crafted and far inferior to his own rich tunic.

"Mistress?" she sputtered. "I have none! I am the Fitzhugh, and I answer to no one, knave! Now get thee gone before I carve my name upon your liver!" Her hand closed around the hilt of the dagger conspicuously lodged in her girdle, and Geoffrey stared at the woman he would marry.

She was tall for a female, but no Amazon, and slender, as far as Geoffrey could tell. His assessment was hampered by a wild mane of hair that hung over her bodice and past her hips. Of an indiscriminate shade, it looked in sad need of combing, and fell over her face, as if to hide a scarred visage.

Keeping one wary eye on her knife, Geoffrey steeled himself for the worst. And yet her fingers were slim and clean, the nails even and pale. At least she bathed. Geoffrey comforted himself with that knowledge as he studied her features through the heavy hair that obscured them.

Surprised, he sucked in a sharp breath, for he saw no sores or marred flesh. Indeed, instead of being marred or ugly, the Fitzhugh appeared rather…comely. Her eyes, flashing fire at him, were amber, like a cat's, but there the wildness ended, for nothing of a feral creature was in her countenance. Her complexion was a light golden color, her cheekbones were gently curved and her mouth was small, evenly formed and seemingly incapable of spouting the curses she was leveling at his head.

Geoffrey's heart began to pound erratically as he focused on her lips. Finally he forced his gaze away and looked her up and down in amazement. This was the woman who inspired such fear and revulsion? She was no hag, no monstrous creature, but a simple female, albeit a foulmouthed one.

"Who the devil do you think you are to gape at me, fool? If you are come on behalf of that foul pack of jackals called the de Burghs, you can begone!" she shouted.

"Wolves," Geoffrey said, absently. He was still reeling from the realization that his bride was not some gruesome crone. There was the hair, of course, but Geoffrey found himself fascinated, rather than repelled, by it. His hands itched to reach out and crush it between his fingers, to brush it free of its tangles and pull it back so that he might get a better view of that intriguing face.

The Fitzhugh stared at him as if he had lost his wits,

and he explained softly. "The de Burghs. Their device is a wolf, not a jackal."

Her eyes narrowed. "I care not, for I shall have nothing to do with them. Go back and tell them that I spit upon them, lackey!"

"I don't think that would be wise, for some of them are of a violent nature," Geoffrey advised. "Come, serve as mistress of your hall, and you shall soon be rid of them."

"Ha!" she shouted. "And how am I to accomplish that?"

"Easily enough. As soon as the wedding is over, I can promise you they will go," Geoffrey said. And it was true. Indeed, he was as eager to rid himself of his watchful relatives as the Fitzhugh. He would get the household and its mistress in order himself, without any assistance from his sometimes overbearing brothers.

"Wedding! Ha! I will marry no one, especially not a de Burgh!" she cried.

Her casual slight struck him oddly. "Am I so repulsive?" he asked softly. She was a termagant, a volatile creature whose opinion should mean nothing to him, and yet Geoffrey found himself waiting expectantly for her answer. He had not the glib tongue and seductive ways of his brother Stephen, who dallied with many a maiden. Nor was he well versed in the ways of wooing, although he had eased himself upon willing flesh. Suddenly, the lack of such arts seemed a sore neglect, and he wondered how to win a woman's favor, most especially *this* unusual woman's.

The Fitzhugh stared, shock apparent before she masked it, and twisted her lovely features into a fearsome grimace. "You? You are a de Burgh?"

"Geoffrey," he said, seized with an absurd desire to hear his name upon her lips.

Instead, she let loose a string of foul oaths that would have impressed even Simon. "I should have suspected some such trickery!" she snarled, her fingers closing around the hilt of the long, wicked-looking dagger at her waist.

Geoffrey frowned to see her face transformed so evilly, and he wondered if the outward comeliness he had fleetingly glimpsed hid a black and bitter core. It was only to be expected, he thought grimly. Her pleasant looks had unnerved him, but he would be wise to remember the nature of the beast. The Fitzhugh was no ordinary maid.

"Perhaps you've heard that I was married before," she said, as if echoing his reservations, and her eyes glittered dangerously. Cat's eyes, Geoffrey thought again, as she gripped the hilt of her blade. "Do you court his fate?"

Geoffrey sighed, shaking his head at her implied threat. He had hoped to appeal to her intelligence, but perhaps the Fitzhugh was as a wild animal, mindless and vicious, despite her even features. His heart slowed and steadied its abnormally raucous beating. "'Twill do you no good to kill me, mistress, for there are five below who could take my place. Resign yourself."

The gentle words, meant to comfort, seemed only to enflame her further. "Resign myself! I resign myself to nothing, de Burgh! Fair warning, *lord*," she said, pronouncing his title like a curse. She lowered her chin to fix him with a frightful glare from behind her mass of hair. "Marry me, and you shall be the one regretting your fate."

She pushed past him roughly to throw open the door, and Geoffrey leaned back against the wall. Already he felt as if he had spent the afternoon jousting, and he had yet to take her to wife. She would wear him out, with her sharp tongue and wild ways, if nothing else. But would she really try to kill him?

Loosing a long, low breath, Geoffrey watched her leave, fascinated by the sway of those long, tangled locks as she moved. They would cover a man, like a blanket, he mused, and then he pushed away from the stone with a curse. The wench was a crazed killer, not a lady to be admired, he told himself.

And yet there was something about her, about the way she hid behind that mass of hair, about the Spartan neatness of her room and her haunted amber eyes, that did not jibe with her reputation. Geoffrey had seen that look before, and for a moment, he lingered, his scholar's mind puzzling over the problem, until he sighed at his own folly and hurried after her.

Vicious and untamed as she might be, he would not throw her to the wolves that waited below.

Chapter Two

Elene Fitzhugh stamped down the stairs, eager to escape the man who taunted her. His ingratiating manner, although foreign to her, did not fool her one whit. Geoffrey de Burgh was a man and, as such, not to be trusted.

In fact, she thought, swallowing hard, her intended was more man than she had ever seen before. He was bigger than her father, larger even than Walter Avery, who had been short and compact, though heavy with muscle. This de Burgh looked as if he could toss Walter around like a child's ball.

Damn. Damn the de Burghs. Damn the king. Damn every man who ever lived! Elene thought wildly. All her life she had struggled against them, and now, when she finally had something of her own, they would take it from her! Never, she swore to herself.

She had known of their arrival, of course. That was why she had taken to her room, though she should have known that they would not be so easily deterred. She had never dreamed that the man himself would come to her door. The memory drew her up short, for she would have expected him to hammer it down, chop it open, but never to knock. Softly. Politely.

Elene blinked, refusing to let de Burgh's confusing behavior cloud her thinking. Obviously, her initial plan to wait them out had failed, but she was not done yet. By the time she was finished with them, the whole family would be glad to be gone!

Confident, Elene marched into the hall, only to stop in her tracks, frozen by the sight that met her eyes. There were more than five of them. Six, by her count. And all unmistakably related to the man who had come to her room. They were huge, dark-haired knights, some even taller than the one who called himself Geoffrey. And they were eyeing her with a mixture of curiosity and revulsion. It was a look Elene had come to know well, and it spurred her to action.

"What are you staring at?" she shouted. "Get out, and take the other one with you! There will be no wedding here!" She spat on the floor in front of them, taking pleasure in seeing six pairs of eyes swivel toward the spot.

But then those eyes all returned to her, and Elene took a step back. The biggest de Burgh looked positively brutish, as if he would kill her where she stood, and he was not the only one. Another tall one was mumbling and swearing, but Elene held her ground. There was always a danger; she had come to accept it as part of her life. And so, she faced them, refusing to flinch even when she felt a hand upon her arm.

It was Geoffrey, the one who would use his soft voice and gentle eyes as others did their fists—to subdue her. Shaking off his hold, Elene backed away, her hand drifting down to her knife, gripping the hilt with ready fingers. She was prepared for anything, but, to her surprise, the knight ignored her threatening stance and gestured toward the others.

"Mistress Fitzhugh, may I present my eldest brother

Dunstan, baron of Wessex," he said, and the big bully stepped forward. So this was the Wolf of Wessex! He looked like a predator, Elene thought, scowling at the man who had long been her father's nemesis. Then, to her astonishment, he bowed, though his expression told her it pained him to do so.

He acknowledged her through gritted teeth. "Mistress Fitzhugh."

Elene blinked. What nonsense was this? Why were they playing at courtesy? She sent a startled glance to Geoffrey, but he held himself as though all was as it should be, bewildering her further. Were they all mad, these de Burghs?

Elene stepped back, gathering her wits together for another assault. "I care not who you are, de Burgh. Take your brothers and get you gone from my home, all of you!" she shouted. "There is nothing for you here, you scavenging bastards!"

The Wolf grunted and stepped forward, as if he would strike her, and Elene braced herself for fight or flight, but even the bully was halted by just a word from Geoffrey. "Dunstan," he said in a low voice, "please excuse my bride-to-be. She is feeling out of sorts."

Elene turned to gape at him. Was he a lunatic? She had just insulted them, and he acted as if she had said nothing! Why didn't he storm away in disgust? Why didn't they all? Panic edged along her spine as they held their ground, unmoving, while she heaped curses upon their heads.

It was the king's foul edict that kept them rooted here, Elene thought angrily. They wanted her land, although why the rich and powerful de Burghs cared anything about this sorry little manor was beyond her. Like all men, they grasped for every last acre, with not a thought for anything else.

"Since you do not care to meet my brothers, you must be anxious for the ceremony to proceed. I shall call for the priest and see to it at once," Geoffrey said. Ignoring her oaths, he held out his arm to her, and Elene stared at it dumbly. She could not remember the last time someone had treated her with courtesy, even if it was feigned. She blinked, confusion muddling her senses, and then shook her head, denying the lure of his civility.

There were all types of snakes in this world, including some she did not yet know. This Geoffrey undoubtedly was one of them, and Elene had no intention of letting him slink into her life. Glancing back at the rest of them, she saw violence, barely suppressed, and hatred, boldly displayed on some of their faces. She ducked her head, eyeing them evilly, for she knew their kind well enough. Perhaps it had been better if she were faced with one of them, instead of this more cunning brother.

Geoffrey remained still, his arm outstretched, and Elene was wont to wonder why he had come forward. Pausing, she studied him more closely, taking in the shiny, walnut-colored hair, the eyes that matched it, warm and deep as the earth itself, and the features that were so like, yet somehow softer and cleaner than, the others'.

With a start, Elene realized that he was the best-looking of the lot. Surely, they did not think she would be...taken by his beauty? The very notion would be laughable, if it were not so frightening. People did not treat her like a woman or assign to her a female's sentiments, and she certainly did not want the de Burghs to do so.

She turned on Geoffrey. "Why you?"

He smiled, displaying even white teeth such as she had never seen, and despite herself, Elene stared. "We drew straws," he answered with a rueful shrug.

Her relief at his admission was tempered by her instincts for survival. And those instincts told her that this one was dangerous, more dangerous, perhaps, than any of his menacing brothers. Elene felt cornered, backed against a wall without an escape, as time ticked by and he waited, patiently, with his arm outstretched.

Again, she glanced back at the rest of them, formidable knights all, big men who would use their strength against her. And they were not as stupid as they looked. They would not be driven away, for she had pushed them to their limits with no success. Stubborn wretches.

Well, she could be just as stubborn, but for now she had no choice except to play for time in which to scheme anew. Feeling the eyes of every one of the de Burghs upon her, Elene lifted her hand from the hilt of her knife and placed it firmly upon Geoffrey's sleeve.

But for the first time in years, her fingers trembled.

Geoffrey sat watching his bride-to-be move restlessly about the hall. It was a bit like studying some alchemist's concoction, waiting for it to shift, change or catch fire. And this particular volatile substance had been quiet far too long for Geoffrey's peace of mind.

Her submission had left him both amazed and wary. Of course, it had been the only reasonable option, but Geoffrey did not think her reasonable. The Fitzhugh had acquiesced too easily, and now he studied her as one would a wild beast that might turn upon its captor at any moment. Although normally the most patient of the brothers, Geoffrey found himself wishing that the ceremony be completed before she exploded into some new tantrum. Unfortunately, there could be no wedding without a priest, and he had yet to arrive.

Although Serle said there was a priest on the premises who ministered to the villagers and in the manor's small chapel, the fellow was certainly taking his time making an appearance. Geoffrey tried to relax, but every muscle in his body was tense with waiting. It seemed the steward had been gone forever, and his brothers shifted restlessly, refusing to meet his eyes.

Where the devil was the priest?

The situation was difficult enough without this new delay, Geoffrey thought, and then he stiffened, seized with a dark suspicion that made him turn slowly toward his bride-to-be. She was standing with her back to him, staring out one of the long windows, and he rose to his feet to join her. Silently he approached, until he was near enough to ensure some privacy between them. Then he leaned close, whispering the question that had driven him to her side.

"What did you do with him?"

She whirled at the sound of his voice, her hand going to the dagger that Geoffrey was heartily sick of already. He was tempted to take it from her, but did not want to force such a confrontation. Schooling himself to patience, instead, he watched her carefully as she glared at him from behind that veil of hair.

"What are you babbling about, de Burgh?" she snarled, stepping back from him.

"The priest. What did you do with him?"

"I did nothing with him, you lousy, putrid whoreson!"

"If I find out that you harmed an innocent priest to avoid this marriage—"

"Then what? Shall you beat me or kill me, de Burgh?" she shrieked, drawing everyone's attention. Geoffrey groaned. Obviously, her brief period of quiet was at an end. "I would advise you to fret not over the holy man, but over your own fate!"

Simon leapt to his feet at the loudly voiced threat, but

Geoffrey stopped him with a look. Then he rubbed his eyes with his palms, trying to drive away the headache that was coming on. The gesture was not missed by the Fitzhugh.

"Are you suffering, de Burgh?" she hissed evilly. "Let me prepare a potion to ease you! I am quite adept at combining certain herbs."

"I'll just bet you are," Geoffrey answered, wondering how he could ever have thought her pretty. From behind that mass of hair, she resembled a witch, ready to present him with some foul recipe of newts and toadstools. And she was bragging about her skills with poison! Geoffrey felt as if he had drifted into a nightmare.

"This is just the beginning! Flee while you can," she warned, like some village idiot who knew only one song's refrain.

Geoffrey's head throbbed, but he refused to lose his temper. "Look, you little fool, if you think that one of my brothers will treat you better, then take your pick!" he said, waving a hand toward where his siblings lined the massive table.

The words were out of his mouth before he considered them, and Geoffrey felt an odd sort of pang as he anticipated her response. Still, he forced himself to continue. "Do you prefer another?" he whispered heatedly. He glanced toward his brothers, all fine and strong, and he tried to decide who would be the best man for her. Nicholas was too young, and Dunstan already wed. But what of carefree Robin? Somber Reynold? Geoffrey stared at his bride-to-be, willing her to answer quickly and be done with it.

Instead, she drew the moment out, as if taking pleasure in his wait. Then she ducked her head and grimaced foully. "Nay. I want none of them," she said. At her words, Geoffrey released the breath he hadn't realized he was holding, but she was not yet finished. "Nor you, either!" she cried, taunting him.

"The feeling is mutual!" Geoffrey said, turning away from her to fold his arms across his chest. Immediately he regretted the childish outburst, for, headache or no, he refused to descend to her level. His father has raised him to be an honorable man, a worthy knight, not some petty squabbler. Just as he was considering how to treat her, Geoffrey saw Serle enter the hall. Finally! He straightened as the steward came forward slowly, but his initial optimism faded when he realized that the man was alone— and looking more frightened than ever.

"Where is the priest?" Geoffrey asked.

Serle threw up his hands in despair. "He is nowhere to be found, my lord!"

Geoffrey heard the low murmurs of his brothers, but ignored them to focus on the steward. "Was he not aware that he had a ceremony to perform?"

"Yes, my lord. 'Tis common knowledge that you are to marry the mistress, although we were not certain when you would arrive. But he is gone! One of the servants said he went into seclusion, to fast and pray!"

Geoffrey stared in astonishment. It was the middle of winter. What kind of idiot took himself off into the wilderness? He pressed the bridge of his nose, where the pain seemed to have centered, and forced himself to speak evenly. "And did this servant have any idea where the priest might have gone?"

Serle shook his head and backed away, as if anticipating retribution. Not for the first time, Geoffrey wondered what the man had suffered under his previous master. Obviously, Fitzhugh had been an evil man with a worse temperament, to leave such a legacy behind him.

But then, one had only to look at his daughter to judge the Fitzhugh blood, Geoffrey thought grimly. By faith, she was enough to drive anyone away—even a priest! And now the ceremony that he was anxious to see concluded would be delayed even further, while he sent someone to track down the man. He could have done it himself, of course, but he didn't dare leave his brothers with the Fitzhugh. They were restless and easily goaded into violence, and someone might get killed. More than likely, his bride-to-be.

And despite his misgivings about the upcoming marriage, Geoffrey did not care to return only to find his fiancée dead. It would be a scandal unworthy of the de Burghs. Besides, he was determined to see this wedding through. Without examining the reasons behind his resolve too closely, Geoffrey glanced at his siblings. His first thought was to ask Dunstan to head the search, but he could hardly assign errands to his prospective liege lord. He looked next to Simon, who was probably just as capable, and was more ruthless than his elder.

"Simon, would you take a party of soldiers and look for the priest?" Geoffrey asked. Although the secondborn de Burgh usually was eager to head an expedition, he did not immediately answer. Instead, he stared menacingly at the Fitzhugh, as if he would like to accuse her of murdering the priest and hiding the body. Geoffrey sighed, unwilling to waste more time while his brothers voiced their unwelcome opinions of his bride-to-be.

"Simon, round up some men and look for the fellow," Dunstan said, coming to Geoffrey's aid unexpectedly. "'Twill be quicker and easier than going back to Wessex to fetch Aldwin." He shot a glance, laced with significance, at the Fitzhugh. If she thought to escape her fate, she was well warned. There were other priests, and her tactics would only serve to delay the inevitable.

"Aye, I'll do it," Simon said, grudgingly.

"I'll help," Robin said, jumping to his feet. "I've an urge to look about your place, Geoff." Geoffrey saw the Fitzhugh jerk around sharply at the words, but she said nothing when Simon was joined by Robin and young Nicholas.

"The rest of you stay here," Dunstan advised, with an eye toward the Fitzhugh, and Geoffrey stiffened. Did his brother think him unable to handle the woman? So far, he had accomplished more with soft words and reason than they could with their hot tempers and ready sword arms. Resentment surged through him at the lot of them. Did they plan to protect him indefinitely? Sleep in his bed? Join him at his bath, as if he were a babe, helpless to protect himself from his own wife?

Biting back the sharp retort that came to his lips, Geoffrey glared at Dunstan. "The more men, the sooner the task would be completed," he noted, forcing himself to speak evenly.

Dunstan, although he appeared uneasy, met Geoffrey's gaze and held it. "I would not have us divide too readily, for she may have set a trap for us," he explained.

A trap? Geoffrey turned slowly toward the Fitzhugh, to find her eyeing them evilly, a sly look on the part of her face that was visible. "You do not trust the soldiers quartered here?" he asked Dunstan.

"I trust no one these days, Geoff, least of all the men of my enemy."

"But Fitzhugh is dead, his war upon you over months ago," Geoffrey said. Although many of those now serving the manor had fought against Dunstan under the Fitzhugh's father, she had ended the struggle. And since then, she had shown no interest in battling Wessex—unless she thought to murder Dunstan and his kin in her hall. The thought had never crossed Geoffrey's mind before, but now it burst upon him like a catapult. He had been naive not to see the opportunity for treachery this wedding afforded the bride-to-be.

He felt stupid, he who prided himself on his great knowledge, for when he glanced at his brothers, they all looked away. Even Stephen, who rarely emerged from his wine cup long enough to note anything, seemed to be aware of the risk. Had they all known they might be walking into an ambush?

"There are probably not enough men left here to pose a threat, Geoff," Dunstan quickly assured him. "But I would be cautious."

"Yes, of course," Geoffrey said, swallowing his resentment. Dunstan had learned to be vigilant the hard way, at the hands of a friend who betrayed him. He could not be blamed for being wary. And the welcome they had received, together with the priest's disappearance, was not heartening.

Slowly Geoffrey turned his attention once more to the object of their suspicions. She positively glowered at them through the veil of her hair, until he felt like yanking it back from her face himself. Taking a deep breath, he kept his hands at his sides as he walked toward her, close enough to hold private conversation. "Is this some trickery, mistress? Do you think to have Wessex?"

"I share not my father's folly," she hissed. "I want only to be left alone!"

"That I can't grant you, as yet, but as soon as the priest is found and we are wed, I promise you that you will be undisturbed."

"Don't bother to lie to me, de Burgh. Your wiles sicken me to death!"

"Well, try to hang on until after the ceremony," Geoffrey said. He grinned when she blinked at him in astonishment, her amber-colored eyes widening almost imperceptibly. She had plainly been caught unawares by his retort, and her expression was almost comical, making it hard for him to believe her the despicable schemer that Dunstan suspected.

"Go on, Simon," he called over his shoulder, more confident now. "Fetch the priest," he said, watching her face as he spoke, "for Mistress Fitzhugh is most anxious to marry me."

Supper was laid out and twilight approaching by the time the search party returned, Nicholas bounding ahead of the others with the good news. "We found him, Geoff, holed up in a cave!" the youngest de Burgh called.

"A cave?" Geoffrey asked in surprise. He had no idea why a man would leave his warm hall for a cold, dank crevice, but the ways of holy men were beyond him. Monks and friars routinely made oaths that he could not keep, silence and chastity among them. Abruptly Geoffrey glanced toward the Fitzhugh, who was sulking in the corner. Then again, he might take those vows himself—this very night.

"A cavern," Simon affirmed. "We found more than one tunneled beneath the rocks."

"I think he picked this particular one because of the outcropping above. It looked rather like a cross, if you looked closely."

Simon grunted, obviously at odds with that bit of whimsy. "Come along now," he said, turning to those who followed behind him. When he moved, Geoffrey saw that between Robin and an anxious-looking Serle was a tall, skinny fellow dressed in priest's robes. He sported a thick shock of white hair and pale eyes.

"This is Edred," Robin said, eyeing his charge curiously.

"Edred," Geoffrey said with a nod. "It seems you picked a poor time for solitude, for you are sorely needed here. I would have you perform the ceremony as quickly as possible, since supper is waiting, and we are all tired after the long journey."

"What ceremony, my lord?" the priest asked. Geoffrey would have thought him insolent, but for his serene expression. Perhaps he was slow-witted, for what other manner of priest would stay with the Fitzhughs?

Geoffrey sighed. "The wedding," he said. "Mistress Fitzhugh and I are to marry."

"Nay," the priest answered, shaking his head solemnly. "It cannot be."

For a moment, stunned silence reigned. Then a raucous burst of noise erupted, as all the de Burghs began talking at once. Out of the corner of his eye, he saw a grim Reynold cross himself, while Stephen burst into laughter. Geoffrey ignored them as best he could, thinking that perhaps Edred had not understood him.

"I wish to marry Mistress Fitzhugh, and you are to perform the ceremony," he said slowly and distinctly, looking into those pale eyes. They were so light a blue as to be almost translucent, giving the strange-looking man an otherworldly countenance. Perhaps that air of mysticism had saved him from Fitzhugh's brutishness, but Geoffrey saw no use for it now. "Surely, you knew of the union?"

The priest remained unmoved. "I cannot join this woman with any man."

Puzzled, Geoffrey looked toward the Fitzhugh, who flashed him a fiendish-looking smile of victory. At least her teeth were good, he thought idly, before returning his attention to Edred. "And why is that?" he asked, the dull throb of his headache returning.

"Why? You ask me why?" The priest's high-pitched voice rang out through the hall, silencing the de Burghs with its force. "Because she is the spawn of Satan, unfit to join with a man."

Geoffrey felt his jaw drop open.

"All women are, by birth, evil, but this creature is among the worst of her kind, an instrument of the devil! Care you not what happened to the last knight who took her to wife? Heed thee well the lessons of those who have gone before you! Only through the intervention of God's own can this female be turned from sin."

Stunned, Geoffrey shot a glance at the Fitzhugh, whose mulish expression appeared to confirm the priest's opinion. For a moment, he wondered if she had compelled Edred to spout such nonsense, but she did not appear easy in her triumph. And one look into the priest's eyes confirmed his passionate conviction.

Sighing, Geoffrey pressed his fingers to his temple and vowed to replace Edred as soon as possible. In the meantime, however, they needed a priest. "I understand your reservations, but the union has been ordered by the king himself," Geoffrey said.

Impatiently Dunstan strode forward. "As baron of Wessex and a knight duly sworn to uphold King Edward's commands, I order you to preside over this wedding."

Although Edred paled, Geoffrey thought he might yet refuse, until Dunstan put a hand to his sword. When the five other de Burghs took their places behind their brother, the priest swallowed, his consideration for his own hide

obviously overcoming his twisted beliefs. "Very well, but
be warned. This marriage is doomed, as is your soul,
Geoffrey de Burgh, if you would fornicate with the devil's
daughter," he said.

Geoffrey's long-suffering patience snapped at the
man's pronouncements. It was no wonder that the Fitzhugh was full of bitterness and hatred, if this was the way
of the household. Geoffrey could not imagine anyone
growing to adulthood under the tutelage of such a priest,
let alone a father who plundered his neighbor without
compunction.

Stepping forward in one swift motion, Geoffrey gripped
the man's tunic, dragging him off his feet. "No. *You* be
warned. Holy man or not, I'll have you speak no more ill
of my wife, or I shall cast you out. Do you understand?"

Geoffrey saw the man's neck move as he gulped and
nodded, his eyes wide and startled. "Good. Now get on
with it," he said, releasing his hold on the rough wool.
Then he walked over to the Fitzhugh, who was staring at
him as if he had lost his wits. He had to admit that he
had never threatened a priest before, but he would have
no one treat her thusly. He was in charge now, and things
were going to change. Stepping closer to her, Geoffrey
took a deep breath—and reeled with surprise.

Clean. Underneath all that hair, she smelled clean. The
soft, gentle scent of a woman drifted up to him, coupled
with just a hint of some spicy musk. It had been a long
time since he had known such an enticing fragrance, and
Geoffrey's heart started pounding rapidly. Those thick
locks of hers were so close he could reach out and touch
them—or grip them in his fists. They were not an indiscriminate brown, as he had first thought, but shot with
light streaks and darker ones, including a ginger color that

made them seem vibrant. Alive. And Geoffrey could not tear his gaze away.

Until she whirled around to face him. "What are you staring at?" she hissed, just as Edred began to speak. In the wavering torchlight, her hidden features took on a shadowed cast, making her appear as evil as the priest had claimed, and Geoffrey's momentary fascination fled.

Edred's pale eyes flared at the interruption, but he went on, his tone deep with foreboding. The whole room seemed to pulse with it, and when Geoffrey caught a glimpse of his brothers, their expressions were grim at the union they were witnessing.

For once, Geoffrey felt more courageous than the lot of them, and he was grateful for the vast and varied education that had enlightened him. One look around the aging hall, darkness encroaching outside and portents of doom abounding inside, was enough to make even a brave man pause. It inspired thoughts of the black arts, death and destruction, and when more than one of the de Burghs crossed himself furtively, Geoffrey loosed a low sigh.

All in all, it did not bode well for his wedding night.

Chapter Three

The evening passed too swiftly, as Elene knew it would. She drank some wine, hoping that the liquor would dull her overwrought senses, but it only upset her stomach. Now that the wedding was over, she could do naught except watch and wait.

She glanced with contempt toward the trestle tables, where the de Burghs lingered, still alert and wary. What was the matter with them? They did not swill down their ale and carouse as other men did. She had laid open stores aplenty, hoping they would eat and drink themselves into a stupor, but neither hospitality nor the lack of it seemed to sway them. Strange creatures! For the most part, they looked like great warriors and acted like monks—all except the one they called Stephen.

He drank more than his share. And he, Elene understood. She recognized the hungry look in his eyes, the glimpse into a haunted soul that told her he was uncomfortable in his own skin. But the rest of them carried themselves with an arrogance that defied all her efforts. Instead of slumbering in their seats or groping the female servants, they remained vigilant, especially the Wolf. Elene had caught him watching her more than once, his green gaze burning with hatred and threats.

He did not voice them, however, for Geoffrey had made it clear that no one was to malign her. She might have been amused by the very notion, had his warning to Edred not been so forceful. For a man who moved slowly and quietly, seeming to cultivate the patience of a saint, he had astonished her, both with his words and with the speed of his sudden violence. That had reminded her, all too swiftly, that he was a man of great strength, though he tried to lull her into forgetting it with his soft voice and fine manners.

He was clever, far more than the rest of them, for he sought to confuse her with his bizarre behavior. Defending her. Treating her politely. Teasing her. Elene flushed. At first, she had been stunned speechless by such comments, tossed off with a grin and a twinkle in the boundless depths of his brown eyes. Now, she would arm herself against him and his…charms.

She scowled. Never before had a man dared to try such foolishness with her. No doubt it worked well upon the ladies he was wont to woo, but she was immune to that…female nonsense, and wise to his trickery. Angrily she kicked at a small stool, sending it spinning across the tiles. *Take that, de Burgh, right in your perfect teeth*, she silently swore.

"Mistress Elene!" Glancing up sharply, Elene was amused to see her father's steward dance around the stool before approaching her warily. Although younger than her father had been, Serle seemed older, because of his small stature and bald pate. He was a short man, compact but not frail, with the malicious eyes so common to the household. Elene would have dismissed him if she was more certain of her own ability to keep the accounts. The knowledge of her own lack irritated her, as did his presence. "What do you want?" she snapped.

His brows drew together. Although accustomed to her father's ill-treatment, Serle did not bear up under her own temper as well. Nor could he seem to flatter her as convincingly. "I came to speak with you, to plead with you to...behave." *Behave?* The little weasel had the effrontery to advise her! Elene ducked her head and fixed him with a fierce glare that made him step back.

"'Tis only th-that I would hate to see another rule at Fitzhugh Manor," he stammered. Although he tried his best to look stricken, Elene knew all too well that fear for his position had prompted this sudden display of loyalty, and she laughed in derision.

Serle flushed. "For the sake of us all, use your wits, mistress. 'Tis one thing to kill a landless knight who forces you to wed, quite another to murder a de Burgh, one sent by the king to marry you."

Elene grimaced. Had she not pondered her quandary often enough since receiving the king's edict? She knew that Edward would show her no further leniency; it was one of the reasons she had assented to this absurd union. Yet she had vowed not to be used again by any man, so what was she to do? Her thoughts twisted and turned until she became aware of Serle's intense scrutiny. She whirled upon him.

"Begone!" she shouted, her hand moving to the sharp dagger she kept in her girdle. It was the very same that had killed that knave Walter Avery, and it gave her comfort as her fingers closed around the hilt.

Bowing rapidly, Serle backed away, but Elene felt another's presence. For a moment, she froze, stunned by a feeling of warmth, of solid roots, of a deep, earthy strength. She shook it off, bristling. How the de Burgh managed to radiate such intangibles was a mystery to her. *He* was a mystery to her, a dangerous unknown that she must protect herself against.

"Is there a problem, Elene?" he asked softly.

She blinked, hating his casual use of her name. Ever since the ceremony, he had called her by it, the way none had since her mother's death. She grimaced, her hand tightening its grip upon the knife. "'Tis not your business, de Burgh," she said.

His face registered something, Elene was not sure what, exactly, but she thought he would dispute her claim. He was her husband, and she knew that men liked to lord their power over others. Yet he only sighed, as if weary. She wondered if his head pained him still. She hoped so, and smiled evilly at the thought.

"'Tis time to retire, Elene," he said.

Her smile faded into a scowl. "If you are weary, then find your bed, de Burgh. I will stay here."

"No."

Elene glanced at him in surprise, for his voice held an unaccustomed heat. Did he gainsay her? She opened her mouth to berate him, but he leaned close, whispering quickly. "We will continue this discussion upstairs, away from the others. In the meantime, I suggest it is to the advantage of both of us if we make this look like a real marriage."

She blinked up at him, torn. He spoke reasonably enough, but her instincts for self-preservation warned her not to believe him—or any man. He straightened, and now she had to tilt her head to look up at him. He was not the largest of the seven, to be sure, but he was tall and muscular. She grasped her dagger, aware of the eyes that were upon her. Surreptitiously servants ogled her from across the room, while the de Burghs…the de Burghs waited and watched.

"Let us go, then!" she said, certain that whatever she must do, it would best be done away from the rest of the brood.

"First, give me the dagger. There is no need of it, Elene." Geoffrey spoke softly, in that coaxing voice of his—the kind a clever man might use to tame a wild beast or a horse to his hand—but Elene would have none of it. She laughed in his face.

"The dagger, Elene." Geoffrey held out his hand, palm upward, and she felt a bloodthirsty urge to slice right through it. She shuddered at the violent thought. What was happening to her? Had she become her father? Her mind rebelled, even as her body felt aflame, gripped by sensations beyond her control—an urgent need to strike out, to protect herself before it was too late. She teetered, her wild emotions in a precarious balance, until he leaned close. "Make a big show of surrendering it," he whispered, "else my brothers will surely follow us to chamber."

Elene blinked. For a moment, she had felt as if the demons that Edred claimed possessed her had, indeed, taken over her mind and body, but the feeling was past now. She loosed a breath and stepped back. "Take it, then! I need no blade to handle the likes of you!" She had others secreted about her person that she could use if need be, so let the poor fool think he had bested her!

Pulling the blade from its sheath, she tossed it across the floor. It skidded across the tiles past Geoffrey's feet, but instead of berating her or calling for a servant, he simply went to retrieve it himself. After giving it to one of his siblings, he turned toward her, holding out his hand again, as if nothing untoward had occurred.

"Come," he said.

Elene loosed a breath. For a long time, she simply stared at his palm, big and callused and radiating heat. He waited, as if he had the patience of Job, until Elene finally gave in with a low, angry hiss. Better that she do so, or they all might be standing here come morning! Placing her palm in his, Elene let him lead her to the stairs. His hand was large, like the rest of him, and warm and dry. He clasped hers loosely, without force, and her surprise at such carried her to the top of the steps.

When he opened the door to the great chamber, she balked. "This is not my room! Loose me, de Burgh." He did at once, and Elene would have fallen backward at his unexpected cooperation, if he had not steadied her immediately by lightly grasping her shoulders. Angrily she threw off his touch.

"I told the servants to prepare this chamber," he whispered.

"Nay."

He sighed, lifting a finger to the bridge of his nose. It was long and well shaped. "Inside. Then we will talk."

Liar! Did he think her a fool, to imagine he would chat with her amiably this night? She laughed aloud, but she went into her father's chamber, her thoughts on the other dagger strapped to her leg.

He followed her in, bolting the door behind him, and Elene backed to the wall, prepared to fight, if she must. But, to her astonishment, the man ignored her totally, striding gracefully to a heavy chest, where he sat down and rubbed his hands over his eyes.

Silence reigned for a long time as she waited for him to make a move, but he remained still and quiet. Finally, without even glancing up at her, he spoke. "I suspect you have additional weapons hidden about," he said, and Elene stifled a gasp at his perception.

"I'm guessing that's why you gave up the other so easily," he explained. Would he search her? Would he put his hands on her? Rage and other hot, violent emotions surged through her, but he made no threatening gestures. Instead, he lifted his head, letting the dark pool of walnut hair fall back from his face, and smiled wryly at her.

"I shall let you keep them, and I shall bed down here by the hearth. In exchange, I expect no foul deeds from you during this or any other night."

His brown eyes lifted to her, and Elene felt as if she might drown in them. She stepped back, coming into contact with the rough wall behind her, unwilling to believe the patience that she saw there. An illusion, no doubt. Perhaps this de Burgh was the sorcerer of the family.

"I do not begin to understand what led to murder in this room," he said. "But I know that Walter Avery was the lowest sort of knight, a man who would betray his own lord and his honor for money. Although I cannot say I condone the manner of his death, I will not judge you by it." Judge her? What was he babbling about? Elene had never known a man to speak so much and say so little!

"Let me only warn you that I married you at the king's behest, and he would not be able to excuse any further blood shed by your hands. You may be hot-tempered, but I do not think you are stupid, Elene. Don't let your distaste for marriage make you do something foolish."

Elene gaped at him, dumbfounded, as he rose to his feet, a good six feet of powerful male, and made a bed upon the floor. He stretched out upon it, fully clothed, and crossed his arms behind his head as if had not a care in the world. Before her very eyes, his lashes drifted shut, as if he would find his rest.

What trickery was this? Did he think to lull her into docility? Ha! He did not know the Fitzhugh well! Although she moved to the bed, Elene had no intention of sleeping. No doubt, the moment she slumbered, she would find her dagger gone and the foul whoreson atop her. Shuddering at the thought of his weight, she sent him an evil glance.

If he saw it, he paid no heed. Well, two could play his game, Elene decided. Without removing any of her garments, she stretched out upon the mattress, covering herself with a thick fur. Turning onto her side, the better to watch him, she reached down and felt for the weapon hidden beneath her gown.

And she waited.

Geoffrey kept to his elaborately casual pose, striving to relax his muscles and his breathing while remaining alert. Despite his gentle words to his wife, he had no intention of letting down his guard. He had a healthy regard for his own skin, and that she-devil was not going to slit his throat while he slept.

The fire gave off just enough light for him to see the flash of a blade, should she try to strike, and Geoffrey trusted his hearing to warn him of her approach. As the minutes wore on, gradually his tenseness eased, and his thoughts traveled back over the events of the day. Although he had made the best of a bad situation, while managing to keep his brothers and his wife from coming to blows, now that the darkness settled around him, Geoffrey felt his chest constrict.

Since their arrival, he had been too busy to consider his fortune, but now it was all too clear. This was his wedding night, and he must spend it on the floor, wide awake. Geoffrey cursed the ill luck that had caused him to draw the short straw. Surely any one of his brothers might have been better suited to this task, for none of them possessed even the remotest hint of a hidden romantic soul.

Geoffrey sighed, trying to come to grips with his fate. At least there was no other woman he wanted to marry. Although he had bedded more than a few in his lifetime, he had never met a lady he aspired to take to wife. Still, he had often imagined what such a woman would be like, and his breath caught as he conjured up his ideal.

Aisley de Laci.

He had seen the heiress once, and she had been beautiful, piercing-bright as a star, and calm and intelligent, too. Soft-spoken and elegant. Unreachable. Geoffrey pictured himself entwined with her cool, pale limbs, her straight blond hair flowing over him, but somehow, without his volition, the vision changed. Instead of white, the long locks that covered him were various shades of brown and so rich and thick a man could get lost in them. Groaning, Geoffrey turned over and tried to banish the image from his mind.

It was going to be a long night.

Geoffrey awoke with a start, then lay perfectly still as he looked out from under lowered lashes, immediately alert. God's bones, he had dozed off! He was lucky to find himself in one piece, he thought ruefully. Although morning light streamed through the narrow window, around him the room was still and silent, except for the soft sound of breathing coming from across the room.

Had the she-devil slept, too?

Slowly he sat up and looked toward the bed. There was

no movement from it, so he rose silently, stretching muscles that always protested a hard berth, and made his way toward where his wife was lying, fully clothed, across the covers.

What a wedding night.

Leaning over, Geoffrey realized she wasn't awake, and then he sucked in a sharp breath at his first opportunity to study her, unguarded. The hair that was so ill-kept spread like a blanket around her, tumbling over the fur that covered her. Rich and heavy, it called to mind spices, expensive and exotic, like ginger. No, cinnamon.

That was what she reminded him of, Geoffrey decided. Stifling an urge to touch those tempting tresses, he forced himself to look at her face, and stared in surprise. With her hair spread away from it, he could see her, really see her, for the first time, and his initial impression had not been wrong. She *was* lovely.

Short cinnamon-colored lashes rested against gently curved cheeks that led to a stubborn little chin. Her nose was straight and pert, her skin flawless and clear right down to her throat. Geoffrey's heart began beating faster as his gaze lingered, arrested, on the smooth expanse. Was it soft to the touch? His fingers itched to discover the answer, to explore the soft column, and he might well have given in to temptation, if the throat and all that was attached to it had not suddenly lurched upward. Abruptly Geoffrey felt the prick of a small blade against his own neck.

"Get off me, de Burgh!" his wife snarled. The face that he had thought so intriguing was twisted into such a frightful grimace that Geoffrey wondered if he had imagined her beauty, envisioning only what he wanted to see in his new bride, instead of the ugly reality.

"I'm not on you, Elene," he said tiredly. Ahead of him,

his life stretched forward, an endless battle, full of threats and noise and public brawls. Sighing, he pulled away, while she scooted back against the wall, hurling invectives at his head.

Without even listening, he marched toward the door and made his escape. Peace and quiet had never seemed so desirable or so far out of his reach. But before he could seek some solitude, he must bid farewell to his brothers, a task he did not relish.

Geoffrey was nearly to the bottom of the stairs when he realized that he had not changed his clothes. He paused on one of the final steps, unwilling to let his brothers draw the correct conclusion when they saw him wearing yesterday's garments. Briefly he considered returning to the great chamber, but the thought of facing the she-devil again this early in the morning made him reject that idea. Better to brazen things out with his siblings.

Before he could take another step, however, Geoffrey heard Simon's loud voice mention his name, and he hesitated. Uncomfortable at the prospect of listening unseen, but unwilling to come upon them when they were discussing him, he waited.

"I say if he's not down soon, we should go up and check on him! Likely she's slit his throat and escaped through the window."

"Impossible," said Dunstan. "I stationed a soldier beneath it." At the casual declaration, Geoffrey stifled a grunt of outrage. A guard, in his own home, where he should be master!

"And I waited outside the door all night, like you told me," Nicholas said. "There were no screams, or sounds of any kind."

Stephen snorted. "Well, what did you expect? You can't imagine poor Geoff would actually do the deed. That wench is the most hideous-looking creature I've ever seen. Even a blind man couldn't get it—"

"Enough!" Dunstan said, and Geoffrey seethed in the silence that ensued, furious at their unwelcome intervention and at Stephen's insults. By faith, Elene wasn't that bad to look upon!

"Poor Geoff," Robin muttered.

"That hair!" Stephen spoke again, joined by a chorus of groans and agreements, and Geoffrey found himself stiffening. Certainly, Elene could take better care of herself, but perhaps she had no servant who would put up with her long enough to aid her. Once groomed, her hair would be lovely. As was her face. Although not classically beautiful, her features were pleasing, her eyes that unusual clear amber color.

Could they not see past their own noses? Geoffrey bristled. How dare they malign her when they knew nothing of her? Had even one of them spoken to her? Suddenly, his brothers seemed like meddling, unfeeling oafs who had outlived their welcome. Steeling himself, Geoffrey entered the hall, ready to hasten their departure.

Immediately he felt their eyes upon him, the startled glances that told him they wondered what he had heard, along with curious gazes that looked for signs his wife had sliced him to ribbons—presumably while he lay docile, frightened by the mere sight of her! He forced a smile.

"As you can see, I live, and no longer need nursery maids to watch over me," he said, surveying the bread and ale that littered the table. "I am glad to see that you broke your fast. Now you can get on the road without delay."

Six faces registered startlement, five of them swiveling first toward him and then Dunstan. "But I thought," Nicholas began, only to close his mouth as everyone waited for the eldest to speak. Geoffrey, too, turned to the Wolf with lifted brows.

"Geoff," Dunstan said, a bit uneasily, "you've seen the accommodations here. Although I would not call Wessex luxurious, it is bigger—and cleaner. I just assumed that you would come stay with us."

"And what of my wife?" Geoffrey asked, standing firm. Despite his trampled pride, he still had his honor. He knew what he had to do.

Dunstan looked uncomfortable, and Geoffrey recognized his answer well enough. They all expected him to leave her here while he went to live off his brother! Geoffrey's stony expression must have given some of his thoughts away, because Dunstan quickly spoke up.

"'Tis common enough, Geoff! Even lesser nobles are wont to live at the castle of their overlord, and as my brother, you are doubly welcome." Geoffrey had no doubt of that, but he knew, also, that his wife would be just as unwelcome as he was welcome. The addendum was there, implicit in his words, though unspoken, as well as the reason for it. Dunstan was bound to protect Marion from the madwoman his brother had married.

However, a night of undisturbed rest had altered Geoffrey's point of view. So far, Elene had done nothing worse than shout and swear and fail to brush her hair. He was not going to leave her unacknowledged. Nor was he going to abandon this manor. It might not look like much to his brothers, but it was his. Could any of them, except Dunstan, claim as much?

Campion would expect him to do his duty, and that was here, righting the wrongs that Fitzhugh had forced upon his people, improving their lot as best he could and trying to make peace with his volatile wife. Geoffrey felt a now familiar stab of annoyance at their thoughtlessness.

None of them would turn away from a challenge. Why would they expect any less from him? He had made his decision when staring down at the short stick; he would not shirk it now.

As if to confirm his choice, Elene came hurrying from the stairs. Her hair was in more disarray than when she had slept, and Geoffrey wondered if she had actually done something to make it look worse. After hearing his brother's foul opinions of her, Geoffrey found himself touched by her stubborn little chin and her fierce grimace. A surge of protectiveness welled up in him that made him clear his throat in dismay. He could not think of anyone less in need of protecting than his wife. Nevertheless...

He turned back to Dunstan. "No. I must put Fitzhugh's house in order first," he said.

Elene, standing near enough to hear, but far enough to be apart from the group, as was her wont, hurriedly voiced her disagreement. "There is no need for you to stay here, de Burgh," she said, forcefully. "I shall keep the place for you."

"Nay. 'Tis mine now, and I would see that all is well within its borders," Geoffrey said. Without giving Elene a chance to anger his brothers further, he continued, facing Dunstan. "Let us know when the babe is born. We shall pay our respects then."

For once, the Wolf looked uncertain as he cast a dubious glance toward Elene. "You are welcome anytime, Geoff. I hope you know that," he said gruffly.

"I do," Geoffrey said, smiling at his brother's rare show of affection. Dunstan recently had come to appreciate his siblings, but for Geoffrey it was time to declare his independence. He waited, knowing that, as his overlord, Dunstan could force the issue, but hoping that, as his brother, the Wolf would not.

"Very well." Dunstan nodded grimly, his disapproval obvious. "It shall be as you wish." Then, striding past Geoffrey, he stopped before Elene, his expression cold. "I warn you, woman, if anything should happen to my brother, I shall hunt you down until you beg for death."

Before Elene could erupt into a fit of temper, Geoffrey stepped in. "Dunstan, do not threaten my wife," he said softly. He moved to stand beside her, allying himself with her—against his brothers. This was his life now; let them realize it, and get on about their own business.

Six faces swiveled to him, their astonishment obvious. No one ever reprimanded Dunstan, the eldest, strongest and most powerful of the de Burghs, but Geoffrey held his ground. Better that he make his position clear now than later. Silence reigned for a long moment, the tension so palatable that even Elene kept quiet, but then Dunstan nodded brusquely. Geoffrey loosed a sigh of relief as the rest of his brothers trooped past, muttering their farewells in an unusually subdued manner.

As Geoffrey watched them go, he noticed the eyes of the servants upon him, furtive and sullen. And near the doorway, several of Fitzhugh's old knights lounged against the wall, their faces grim, their postures vaguely threatening. Even Serle, for all his groveling, gave Geoffrey an ominous look that made him wonder if he was right to send his family away so soon. And beside him, Elene, obviously displeased with his decision, muttered a stream of foul curses from behind her tangled mane.

Suddenly, Geoffrey was acutely aware that the departure of the de Burghs left him surrounded by enemies, not the least of whom was his wife.

Chapter Four

Steeling himself against his own doubts, Geoffrey turned toward his steward. "Serle, I would like to view the manor, the kitchens, and the buildings in the bailey. Afterward, you may call together all those who reside here, so that I may speak to them." Without waiting for the steward's reply, Geoffrey turned to Elene. "Will you join me?"

Instead of acknowledging his request, his bride glared at him ferociously. But she followed. Geoffrey sighed as he maneuvered himself behind her. Although he didn't think Elene particularly dangerous, he had no desire to present his back as a tempting target for her assorted blades.

When they trooped into the kitchens, Geoffrey quickly discovered that the cooking areas resembled the rest of the place, ill-kept and unsavory. Ordering the servants to wash down the room, he promised a reward for a job well done, so that he engendered no hard feelings. He glanced at Elene to gauge her reaction, but could see nothing except that annoying veil of hair. If she was insulted by the changes he demanded, she did not show it. Eyeing her sharply, Geoffrey wondered whether she even served as

chatelaine. The workers looked to Serle, giving Elene a
wide berth, their eyes downcast as they backed away from
her.

But, then again, they treated Geoffrey little better,
watching him with wary expressions that made him uneasy. He was accustomed to enjoying a good relationship
with the servants at Campion. Here, he felt like the enemy.
He opened his mouth to deny it, but only cleared his
throat. Obviously, Fitzhugh had ruled with an iron hand;
it would take time and effort to change things.

Geoffrey's determination to be patient lasted until he
saw the stores. Staring at the pitiful supplies, he swore
aloud. "Is this all there is?" he demanded, rounding on
the steward. "Who is in charge here?"

"I am, my lord," Serle said, backing away and cringing.

"But there is more winter ahead! How are we to feed
everyone?"

"I'm sorry, my lord. The war depleted our supplies,"
Serle explained. "As the ransoming of knights emptied
our coffers."

Geoffrey bit back another oath. The battles against
Wessex had done even more damage than he had first
thought. His plans to rebuild and restore prosperity would
have to begin with basic survival. Releasing a low sigh,
he realized he would have to ask his father for help. Although ill pleased by the prospect, he knew that Wessex,
albeit closer, did not have the extra to spare.

Sighing, Geoffrey felt the weight of the responsibilities
that Dunstan had struggled under, and knew his brother's
frustration. For the first time in his life, all eyes looked to
him, not his father or his siblings. But he did not falter.
"I will need an inventory of what we have, along with a
list of all people residing at the manor."

Serle appeared to balk at the task, but then bowed his head in agreement. His reluctance made Geoffrey wonder about the state of record-keeping in the household. "And, Serle," he added, "tomorrow, I want to go over the accounts."

The steward ducked his head in curt obeisance and then led the way outside. Geoffrey stepped back, allowing his wife to go ahead of him, even as he wondered why she did not serve as chatelaine. Had she been found wanting? It was hard to imagine worse management than what he had found so far, but perhaps Elene was too wild, too unreliable, for the task.

As he followed behind her, Geoffrey's gaze fixed on the thick fall of her hair. She was married now, and supposed to cover it, but, as usual, she was not adhering to custom. He tried to envision it caught up in a caul, but could not. There was just so much of it. A braid, perhaps. Geoffrey thought of braiding it himself, of taking the thick tresses in his hands, and his heart began to pound. His attention traveled lower to where the ends were swaying gently as she walked and brushing the back of her gown just below her...

Swiftly Geoffrey jerked his head away from the sight and drew in a deep draft of cold air. He turned his attention to the brewery they were entering, but even as he listened to the workers speak, his mind wandered back to his wife. Tasting the ale that was presented to him, Geoffrey found it rather flat, but adequate. He wondered if its flavor reflected something unwholesome, or if there was a foul wind about his new home that affected a man's mind.

The notion would explain much, he mused, especially his recurring interest in his wife.

* * *

Elene brooded in the corner, watching her husband from narrowed eyes, as she often had in the past few days. Although he spoke little to her, she felt his gaze upon her every so often, as if to make sure of her. No doubt he was taking care not to find a dagger suddenly embedded in his back, she thought, smiling evilly. But the grin quickly faded, along with her thirst for his blood.

Things were not so simple anymore.

Geoffrey de Burgh had managed to confuse her even further in the week since their wedding. She had expected him to leave with his brothers, and had been sorely grieved when he had not, as well as puzzled by his motives. Perhaps he intended to do like her father and make war upon the Wolf; other men had fought their siblings for less.

Yet he seemed to have little interest in his army. Indeed, he seemed more concerned about the foodstuffs! Unlike any man she had ever known, he pretended to care about the welfare of the people and the state of the manor. Obviously, it was some ploy to divert her attention, but from what? The man had called for the accounts days ago, and now appeared to be utterly engrossed in them.

That, too, astounded her, for her father had never even glanced at the manor's records. Not willing to be bothered with such mundane tasks, he had left them to his steward, or so he had said. Elene had always suspected his reading skills were too poor to make sense of them. She glanced back at her husband, wondering just how well he was deciphering Serle's scribbling. He was still bent over the books, so deep in concentration that he had not even noticed the lock of dark hair that fell across his forehead.

Elene shifted in her seat, glaring at him. At least she had understood her sire. Greed and ambition had fueled Fitzhugh. He had married Elene's gentle mother only to acquire her dower lands, and they had never been enough. Through fair means or foul, he had gained nearby estates, but he had not been satisfied. He had coveted a castle. He had wanted Wessex.

Elene understood her father's knights, as well. Greed and fear had driven them to follow him blindly. Faith, she even understood Walter Avery, whose avarice had spurred him to betray the Wolf to her father. All of them were angry, grasping men, questing for more.

Geoffrey, by contrast, lived as Spartanly as a monk. He did not swill ale or gobble his food like a glutton. He did not speak coarsely or loudly or cruelly, and he rarely swore. He treated everyone, even the lowliest serf, with respect. He did not belch or break wind in the obnoxious fashion of her father's men, nor did he harry the women.

Abruptly Elene wondered if he possessed the same bodily functions as other men, then blushed hotly at the thought.

One thing he did, and frequently, was bathe. Alone. Elene had caught the fresh, clean scent of him more than once, seen that dark hair falling damp across his forehead. Moving restlessly, she pushed aside those visions. Rarely had her father or his henchmen seen fit to wash, and baths at the hands of the few female servants had ended in squeals and splashes. Indeed, one poor girl had died trying to birth a whelp that she claimed was sired by Avery himself during one of his visits.

Elene shuddered.

Glancing across the room at Geoffrey, she told herself that he was no different. Only his tactics were unusual, and, perhaps, worse, for he pretended to be kind and gentle, lulling them all, before he would strike. But he had not fooled her with his careful manners. Elene kept the dagger he had returned to her close at hand, fondling it

whenever he tried to come too close. And yet he continued to make up a pallet on the floor each night, putting
it all to rights in the morning, so that the servants would
not know of his bizarre habits.

Stranger still was the activity she had caught him in
last night. Waking, with some alarm, to see a candle burning, she had reached for her knife, only to see him lying
on his side, holding a book! At first she had thought it
was full of drawings, the kind she had once seen Avery
studying avidly, but this morning she had found it lying
near the window. She had wasted no time inspecting it,
only to find it was a real book, the first she had seen
outside of the few religious volumes that Edred brandished to emphasize his speeches.

Could Geoffrey read so well?

The discovery made her wonder what else he had secreted away in the trunks he had brought with him. Sitting
up suddenly, she eyed her husband warily, but he was
absorbed in the accounts. Briefly Elene speculated upon
what held his interest so closely. Her resentment stirred,
but she pushed it aside, for his preoccupation would serve
her well.

Rising quietly, Elene slipped upstairs and into the great
chamber. Shutting the door firmly behind her, she knelt
before the largest of his chests and lifted the lid. She was
greeted by a whiff of the scent she had come to associate
with her husband. It seemed to reach into her senses—
clean, warm and solid—and for a moment she hesitated
to invade his privacy.

Choking back a guffaw at such fancies, Elene looked
in at the pile of garments and drew a breath. Neatly folded
were a dizzying supply of clothes in rich fabrics the like
of which she had never owned. Elene felt the strange bite
of jealousy as she compared this colorful array to the drab

gowns she wore year after year. Fingering the soft material of a green linen tunic, she tried to imagine herself dressed in such finery.

They called her Lady de Burgh now, but what would it be like to really be a lady? Dreams that had died long ago, at her mother's bedside, returned to haunt her, and Elene felt a shaft of pain so intense that she nearly doubled over. Scowling, she reburied the memories with haste and pushed the clothes aside. Beneath them, she found a small wooden ball, a child's toy, and lodged beside it was an old set of jousting puppets. Elene's brows drew together in puzzlement. Why would a grown man keep such possessions? Shrugging, she lifted up an elegant, thick fur, and stared at what lay below. Lining the entire bottom of the trunk were books, fat ones, thin ones, small ones—more volumes than she had ever seen in her life.

He could read.

Not only could her husband decipher the accounts and the one book she had seen, but many more, and well. Better than Edred. Better than anyone. In addition to all else, Geoffrey was a scholar.

Elene rocked back on her heels, feeling angry and threatened by his knowledge. Her hand closed into a fist as resentment rose and crested, and without bothering to rearrange his things, she slammed down the lid of the trunk.

He had just given her another reason to hate him.

Elene ordered her supper brought to the great chamber. She had often eaten alone when her father and his men were about, in an effort to escape the noisy carousing in the hall. Now she would keep her distance from the man who had turned it into a peaceful, orderly place.

She had just taken her first bite of watery stew when the door opened. Annoyed at the interruption, she looked

up to find Geoffrey standing in the archway, filling it with
his height and breadth, and nearly choked on her food.
Damn the man! Why couldn't he just go—and stay away
forever? Twisting her wrist so that her eating knife
pointed toward him, she waited, poised for fight.

"What are you doing, Elene?" he asked, in the low,
coaxing voice that somehow managed to both draw her
and irritate her.

"I was eating, but something repulsive has taken away
my appetite. Get out!" she shouted.

"Are you feeling ill?"

"I am now! The very sight of you sickens me!"

"Your place is in the hall," he said softly.

Her place? What did he know of her place? She had
no place here. She never had anything but the scraps she
needed to survive! Her father's contempt for women had
prevented her mother and herself from ever serving as
chatelaine or in any capacity in his hall. Fitzhugh had only
married her mother for her money and her birthright, and
he had stolen both, along with so much else.

Just as this one would steal from her.

Shakily, Elene rose to her feet. The blade was ready in
her fingers, but she heaved her supper at him instead. To
her surprise, he moved swiftly, so fast, in fact, that the
trencher meant for his chest only grazed his arm. It slid
to the floor, leaving a thick trail of stew down his expensive sleeve. Staring at the mess, Elene wondered if she
had pushed him too far. Although that had not been her
intention, perversely she wanted to see him explode. Then
she would have her proof that he was nothing more than
a man, no better than her father or his minions, no cleverer
than Serle and his ilk.

But he did not lose his temper—if, indeed, he possessed
one. He simply sighed and turned his back on her to walk

away, leaving Elene to stare after him, her fury unabated. Rising to her feet, she ran to the doorway and shouted down the stairs.

"Are you turning the other cheek, my lord? Who do you think you are, some kind of saint? We shall have to get Edred to canonize you, good Saint Geoffrey," she taunted, and heard a muffled snicker from a servant at the bottom. For a moment, she froze, unaccustomed to the novel experience of sharing a joke with another. Then she smiled, enjoying the strange sensation, until she remembered the puddle of stew that lay waiting for her inside the chamber. And none of it edible. Stepping back inside, Elene slammed the door loudly behind her and went to bed hungry, cursing the de Burghs with a lifetime's worth of hatred.

She was still dressed and awake when Geoffrey returned to make his pallet on the floor. He might act the saint, but Elene didn't trust him, and she never relaxed until she heard the even breathing that marked his slumber. Tonight, when she was already angry, he seemed especially late and inordinately loud. She heard each of his sighs and every one of his movements as he turned this way and that. So what if he was lying on the hard tiles? At least he had a full belly, Elene thought.

Abruptly the thought of his flat stomach made her flush, and she rolled over herself, making a great noise as she plumped her pillow and settled down once more. But the silence did not last long. On the floor, Geoffrey still rustled his blankets, until she thought she would scream. Then she heard him sit up and move about. Annoyance turned to wariness as she opened her eyes. She could see him poking at the dying fire and then leaning over to light a fat candle. As she watched, curious, he pulled out the book she had found earlier. Then he lay down once more, resting one muscular arm behind his head, and opened it, focusing all of his attention upon it.

Resentment flooded Elene as she stared at him. He held the volume easily in his big hands, a lock of dark hair falling forward as he concentrated effortlessly. He still wore his garments, as did she, but there was something about the way his long body stretched out on the rumpled pallet that seemed to tease her sharpened senses.

Elene scowled. And now the room was awash in light. How was she to rest at all? She sat up suddenly, hating him for all that he possessed and for the way he lay there, casually relaxed in front of her, as no man had ever been before. Why wasn't he cringing in fear or fleeing in revulsion, as did all the others?

"What do you think you're doing, de Burgh?" she shouted. "Is it not enough to harry me all day? Now must you keep me awake all night, as well?"

He didn't even bother to look at her. "'Tis only a candle, Elene. Go back to sleep."

"No! Quench it, or you'll be sorry, de Burgh!"

"Elene…" he began, and his low, coaxing tone offended her. It spoke of a familiarity that no one had ever dared. Enraged, she lunged to the side of the bed and blew out the candle. The ensuing semidarkness gave her a rush of triumph, but it was short-lived. Before she could move away from the edge of the bed, she felt Geoffrey's hands on her, dragging her down on top of him. In an instant, she was beneath him, her wrists pinioned above her head in a strong grip.

All too swiftly, Elene was reminded that the man she taunted was two hundred pounds of pure, muscular male. The speed with which he moved that big body astounded her, so much so that she did not struggle when she realized he was atop her. She was distracted, too, by his un-settling heat, so pervasive and startling that her instincts were momentarily befuddled.

She blinked, adjusting to the dim light of the fire, and when she lifted her lashes, Geoffrey was staring down at her with a similar astonishment. His dark eyes were wide, his breath was coming as rapidly as hers, and against her chest, his heart pounded as fiercely as hers. While she gaped at him, his eyes seemed to become even darker, taking on a strange, dreamy cast, while his full lips parted as though he were hungry. Stupidly Elene wondered if he had gone without supper, as she had. The thought made her lick her suddenly dry lips, and she saw his gaze follow her movement.

Something flared deep inside her when she felt his at-tention upon her mouth, an unnatural heat that made her want to forget that his body bore down on her, heavy and solid, pushing her down. It spread within her for an in-stant, before panic took its place and she pushed wildly at him, thrusting his bulk away.

And then she was fighting with the very air, for just as suddenly as he had struck, he released her, rolling off her with a low groan. For a moment, Elene simply stared at him, lying full length beside her, as her chest heaved with her efforts.

"Fair warning, Elene," he whispered, his eyes shad-owed and intense. "Don't come at me in the darkness, because I will defend myself."

His words sent her to her feet, and Elene leapt for the bed, unable to find a voice to answer his threats with her own. Silently she reached for her dagger, but, for once, the deadly weapon gave her no comfort. She realized that during all those long minutes while she was at his mercy, she had never once even thought of it.

Worse yet, she suspected that it mattered not, for Geoffrey presented the kind of menace that could not be fought off with a sharp blade. A bleak sense of unease enveloped Elene as she considered the strength of her defenses against such an unfamiliar arsenal as her husband's appeal.

Geoffrey pinched the bridge of his nose, fighting off another headache as he pored over the accounts again, trying to make sense of them. He would have suspected his wife of plying her poisoning skills upon him, if his pains were tied to food, but they were not. They were brought on directly by her behavior.

He had taken to rising and leaving the great chamber before she awakened. Otherwise, he was treated to her shrieking threats with every movement he made. As if he had any desire to climb into bed with her! He would rather lie down with a she-goat!

Or would he? Unbidden, memories returned of the other night, when she had been prone beneath him and he had discovered that under those shapeless clothes was a woman's body, supple and gently curved. With a groan, Geoffrey threw his head back. The last thing he needed was to start looking upon his wife as a woman!

It was not that he thought Elene repulsive, as his brothers did. He had to admit that she had lovely features, those amber eyes, and, of course, the hair that was coming to obsess him. But the woman herself was as volatile as Geoffrey was stable. She possessed a wild, careening personality so at odds with his own that she made his head throb.

Geoffrey frowned. He was letting her disturb his demeanor, and he had sworn that he would not. So far, he had met every one of her rude insults with courtesy, each of her foul curses with calm indifference, as he tried his best to emulate his father. But his patience was wearing thin, especially since he had heard the servants calling him Saint Geoffrey behind his back.

Yes, as if she weren't bad enough, he had the recalcitrant staff to worry about. Despite his own gracious behavior, they continued to eye him warily, and sooner or later, he was going to have to deal with the soldiers, whose loyalty he questioned. Although he wanted to embrace his new home, he was alert and cautious at all times, suspicious of all except Serle and the priest. And even the holy man gave him a few strange looks!

Mad. He was going mad, Geoffrey thought, pressing the heel of his hand against his eyes. He was seeing menace in everyone and everything. Although he knew he would never have gained the trust of his people if the de Burghs remained en masse, he often wished he had not been so eager to send his brothers away.

Putting Fitzhugh's legacy to rights seemed nearly an impossible task for him to accomplish alone. Geoffrey had always thought himself more capable and clever than most, but even he couldn't make sense out of the manor's accounts. Discrepancies were everywhere, with sums of money simply assigned to Clarence Fitzhugh or Serle, without any explanation. Meanwhile, the winter supplies were dwindling. He had sent a man to Campion to borrow some stores from his father and hoped fervently for an early spring. But from the looks of the records, Geoffrey would be hard-pressed to pay his sire back for some time.

He wondered if Dunstan got headaches, too. But no. Dunstan's books were finally in order, and thanks to Marion's considerable fortune, Wessex would soon be thriving. Dunstan's troubles were over because of his marriage, while Geoffrey's were just beginning.

Geoffrey sighed. He preferred not to think about Elene. Although her taunts about murdering him had lessened, she still found plenty to shriek about. And she glared at him, with those cat's eyes, from behind that veil of hair, until he wanted to yank it out of her head. His hands itched to do the deed, but along with the thought came a thudding in his chest and a peculiar tightening elsewhere. He had never been attracted to violence, as were some men, but where his wife was concerned, who could blame him?

Glancing dispiritedly at the pages, Geoffrey leaned his head back and massaged his neck. All this time poring over columns had left him tired and stiff, and he needed a breath of fresh air to clear his mind. Rising to his feet, he stretched and donned his cloak for a walk in the bailey.

Outside, the coolness felt invigorating, but the unfamiliarity of the place struck him, as always, and he gravitated to the one thing that reminded him of all he had left behind. Walking toward the stables, he stepped into the dim, close building to check on the horse he had brought with him from Campion.

Majestic was his name, and although he was no longer in the prime of life, he was still a fine animal. More than that, he had been a good companion for years. Geoffrey was just about to step toward the destrier's stall when he realized he was not alone. At first he thought it was a groom who stood at the other end of the room, but the thick mane was instantly recognizable as Elene's.

The voice was not. While Geoffrey stood staring, he heard her talking to one of the horses, not in her usual strident screech, but in a soft, husky tone that made his pulse quicken. This was his wife?

Winter sunlight peeked through the cracks, illuminating her hair and bringing out the gingery highlights. She seemed shorter and daintier in the large stable, and when Geoffrey saw her gently stroke the beast's head, he realized he had never seen her use her hands so gracefully. They were smaller than he had thought, and slender, and he suddenly wondered what it would feel like to have those hands on him, running down his arms, touching his chest, stroking his sex... He must have made a strangled sound, because she whirled to face him, and immediately the spell was broken. Lovely features that had looked so angelic in the filtered light now twisted fiercely.

"What do you want, de Burgh?" she shouted. "Can I not have a moment alone without you at my heels, dogging me like the veriest hound?" Her voice rose to that abominable shriek, and Geoffrey could see the horse beside her becoming agitated. It snorted in warning, but Elene was too busy railing at him to notice.

"Cease your ranting, Elene!" Geoffrey warned, but she paid him no heed. Over her strident curses, he could hear the animal pawing the packed ground, and then it surged forward. At the same moment, Geoffrey dived at his wife, pulling her down into the rushes that littered the dirt floor of the stable and rolling her away from the beast's sharp hooves. For a long moment, they lay entwined together, both of them breathing harshly at the narrow escape.

Shaken, Geoffrey rose above her, preparing to give her the tongue lashing that she deserved, but she looked so stricken that he said nothing. Her hair was spread away from her face, her amber eyes were wide, her lips were parted as she took in shallow swallows of air. She looked...vulnerable.

For once, her features were not hidden, and her skin was so golden and flawless that Geoffrey could hardly believe it was real. Slowly, gently, as if he were coaxing a trembling doe to his palm, Geoffrey lifted his hand and rubbed the back of his knuckles against her cheek. Smooth. Finer than silk, and he watched as her mouth formed a small "Oh" of surprise at his touch.

It looked luscious—rich and spicy and exotic—and he had to have a taste. Just once. Lowering his head, Geoffrey brushed a kiss upon her lips. And another. Unable to help himself, he let his tongue trace the delicate outlines. She was so supple and surprising. And not just her mouth. The body cushioning his was gently curved and firm, the twin mounds of her breasts pressing into his chest, stunning him with their heat. He felt a bizarre urge to rub himself against them, to roll over and wind himself in her wild mane.

Lifting his head, Geoffrey looked down at her again. Her lips were moist and poised for him, and he wanted entry. Some small, still-rational part of his brain warned him of the risk. She could do serious damage, if she decided to bite him, but absently he decided it would be worth it. Just this once. Burying a hand in her thick tresses, Geoffrey kissed her again, more deeply, urging her to open for him, and when she made a low, gasping sound, he took advantage and eased his tongue inside.

Cinnamon. She tasted of it. And damp heat, so erotic that he grew hard instantly. Geoffrey licked her teeth, stroked the hidden recesses of her mouth, and groaned out his pleasure. He forgot where they were, who she was, even his own identity, in a hot rush of desire such as he had never experienced. Unable to help himself, Geoffrey moved slightly, pressing his groin into the crux of her thighs, needing that pressure so desperately that he shuddered.

It was a mistake.

Abruptly she pushed at him, rolling out from beneath him and struggling to her feet. Dazed, Geoffrey lay on his

side, watching her. For a long moment, she stared back
at him, her eyes wild. Warily he waited for the earsplitting
harangue that would surely follow, but she only wiped her
mouth with the back of her hand and spit on the dirt floor
beside him. As Geoffrey sat up, she turned and fled, giving him a glimpse of shapely calf in her haste. Lifting a
hand to push a lock of hair from his forehead, Geoffrey
released a low, shaky sigh as he tried to understand just
what had occurred.

With a rueful smile, he realized that at last he had found
a way to stop his wife's constant shrieking.

Chapter Five

Elene stood beside the window, watching her husband work his soldiers on a small piece of packed ground in the bailey. After a fierce beginning, March had turned surprisingly warm, and Geoffrey had taken advantage of the mildness to exercise what remained of her father's army. He had focused his intense concentration on them, just as he had upon the all-important manor records, and Elene stared in amazement as he directed them as easily as he did everything else. Idly she wondered what it would be like to be the object of that powerful interest.

"I see the weather is holding."

Elene nearly flinched at the sound of Serle's voice, low and surly, beside her. She had been so intent upon Geoffrey that she had not heard the steward's approach, and now she scowled, annoyed at her vulnerability. It was just another example of how her husband managed to affect her, and she did not like it.

"It looks like Saint Geoffrey will get the early spring he wanted," Serle said. Elene, absurdly annoyed by his use of her husband's nickname, studied the steward through narrowed eyes. Recognizing the contempt in his voice, she puzzled over his motives. Although she had good cause to despise Geoffrey, Elene could not understand why the rest of the household had not taken to him. Their enmity seemed not only unjustified, but unjust, she thought, before catching herself.

Unjust? Her life had never been just. Else why had death taken her mother, leaving her adrift in a frightening household without an ally, without *anyone?* She had stood at the graveside, listening to Edred's rants about eternal damnation and wondering where in this world or the next, was there justice.

So what if Geoffrey was taunted by the people he tried so hard to win? Telling herself she cared naught for anyone's opinion of her husband, Elene glanced back out the window. "Perhaps good Saint Geoffrey has influence over the seasons," she said, only half in jest. Although he had yet to win over his new people, her husband seemed possessed of frightening abilities.

"Blasphemy, my lady? Edred would not be pleased."

Elene laughed shortly at Serle's jest. The priest was always railing about something—herself, more often than not—but she had learned to ignore most of his tirades. Although Elene fostered no illusions about herself, she knew that her gentle and innocent mother had not been the evil creature Edred claimed all women were by birth. The priest who served the manor before had not spouted such venom, but then, he had been a godly man, who stood up to her father one too many times and died for it, like everything else good in her life.

Pushing aside that bitter truth, Elene forced her attention back to the field outside, where Geoffrey and the foremost of her father's knights were facing off with quarterstaffs. She had seen such practice often, but never had it involved her husband. To her surprise, suddenly Geoffrey looked different, stronger, deadlier....

"Maybe Montgomery will kill him," Serle said, with a jarring degree of relish. "Then you would be a widow, my lady."

Elene was startled by a swift stab of alarm. What did Serle mean? Was someone at the manor plotting murder? Although Elene had no love for her husband, she knew that if he died, she would soon be bartered off to another. An insidious panic made her swing toward Serle, her hand on her dagger. "I will do the only killing around here, and watch your tongue, else I start with you," she hissed.

Bowing insolently, Serle backed away, and Elene turned once more toward the window. Her palms were wet, her fingers tense as they curled protectively around the hilt of her blade. Compared to some new, unknown threat, Geoffrey suddenly looked very, very good.

In more ways than one.

He wore no mail, only a light tunic, for the exercise, and Elene found her gaze drawn to his body. Although she had seen him dressed thusly many times, today he appeared different, for he had worked up a sweat, making the dark green material cling to him.

As she watched, Elene realized she had never really noticed the clean, hard lines of his torso. He was not bulky, like Montgomery, but he was strong and swift. Although his opponent outweighed him, Geoffrey's leaner arms wielded the quarterstaff with agility and finesse, keeping him in control of the weapon. Elene rarely paid any attention to the knights, but there was something fascinating about the way Geoffrey struck and parried, his movements lithe and graceful. As the mock fight grew more intense, the tunic became plastered to his skin, and Elene could see his muscles bunch beneath the material.

Enthralled, Elene could only stare as that which normally repulsed her now drew her like a moth to a flame.

Men, warfare, knights and their shows of strength, were repugnant, and yet she remained where she was, as if rooted to the spot by the sight of him, the sweat gleaming on his forehead and throat, his forearms straining when the staffs came together.

Since that first night when he left her alone, Geoffrey had grown less intimidating, to the degree that she could mock him as a saint, but now, viewing him alongside hardened soldiers, she saw anew just how big he was, how virile and male. He stood out among the crowd, not only by virtue of his birth, but through superior skill, agility and intelligence.

Geoffrey threw back his head, his dark hair falling thickly behind him, and Elene's nostrils flared, as if to take in the masculine smell of his struggle. She licked suddenly dry lips, puzzled by the strange feelings coursing through her. Her body felt heavy, weighed down by some foreign ailment, her breasts full and ripe. Her breath came shallow and quick, while her heart increased its pace.

Abruptly, the scene Elene had forced from her mind for the past two weeks returned in vivid detail, and she was once more lying beneath Geoffrey in the stables, feeling the weight of him. He did not crush her, but cushioned her, his hard muscles protecting her, cradling her, as he lowered his mouth to hers.

He had tasted like nothing she had ever known, heady and warm and wonderful....

Cursing loudly, Elene swung away from the window and lifted her fists to her face. What was happening to her? She felt wholly unlike herself, as if she were changing into someone else, and it frightened her far more than any outside threat could have. She turned on her heel, determined to leave the disturbing sight of her husband, but a shout drew her back, and she was trapped, her attention pulled by some unseen force to the fighting men.

Elene saw the reason for the excitement immediately. The mock battle had become brutal. The ranks of the soldiers filled with grim-faced freemen and villeins, watching avidly, as if the two men were struggling for dominion over the manor itself. Elene's eyes narrowed as she saw Geoffrey nearly go down when tripped by his opponent.

She muttered an angry oath at Montgomery's treachery. He had been one of her father's own, the most prominent knight left after the battle for Wessex. Although many soldiers had been killed in the fighting, knights were too valuable to slaughter. They brought much-needed funds when ransomed, and though Elene would have decried the cost, Walter Avery had ordered Serle to barter for the missing men before meeting his fate. Too late, Elene had discovered the price paid for warriors she did not want, and she had eyed them warily ever since, all too aware of their capabilities and how swiftly they could turn against her.

Now, it appeared that Montgomery was eager to overthrow his new lord, for what had begun as an exercise obviously had turned into a real battle. As Elene watched, the blond knight fell, only to surge upward, giving the staff a vicious thrust toward Geoffrey's throat.

Elene heard a muffled cry, and was startled to realize it was her own as Geoffrey barely dodged the weapon. He recovered quickly, lodging his staff against Montgomery's chest and calling a halt to the practice. For a moment, Elene was not sure whether the knight would comply, and her hand tightened on her knife. By faith, she would not let Montgomery kill her husband! She shuddered, a tremor going through her body as the beaten knight finally assented, sending Geoffrey a black look filled with hatred.

Still Elene waited, her eyes fixed on Montgomery, her fingers grasping the hilt of her dagger. Only when she saw the knave rise and walk away did she relax her grip, but she remained vigilant while Geoffrey dismissed the soldiers and headed back to the manor. Her heart continued its frantic pace as he weaved through the crowded bailey. For all his strength, her husband seemed vulnerable. Anyone could slip a knife through his ribs, Elene thought wildly as she moved toward the door.

Suddenly, it was imperative that she prevent that from happening. As she watched his approach, Elene told herself that protecting him was in her best interest. Whatever his dark motives, Geoffrey was far easier to handle than another man. Better that she be wed to him than to some unknown.

He strode into the hall, and she opened her mouth to shout at him, berating him for his reckless folly. But as he grabbed a swatch of linen from a servant and wiped the sweat from his face, Elene found that her tongue was stuck to her dry mouth. She stared, her throat tight, as he called for a bath. He strode toward the stairs, seemingly oblivious to her presence, and Elene was forced to chase after him, because she did not trust her voice. She followed him up the steps and into the great chamber, only to halt in the doorway as he lifted his arms and stripped off his sodden tunic.

Elene's breath caught and held as she eyed the gleaming muscles of his back. He was strong and broad and golden, his skin taut, and so beautiful that Elene could not look away. She felt as though she were burning up with some strange malady. Her eyes began to water as fear swept through her, accompanied by something else, as dangerous as it was inviting.

He turned, and Elene's knees nearly buckled at the sight of his bare chest, covered with dark hair. It was thickest at the center, fanning out to cover flat male nipples, and Elene knew the strangest urge to reach out and touch him, to run her fingers through the thickness of it. Surely he had done something to her, put an herb in her ale, cast some spell over the household! Dragging in a deep breath, she finally managed to wrench her gaze up to his face.

"Elene?" His dark eyes, deep and warm, studied her, and she felt foolish to be caught staring, yet she couldn't help herself. When he absently wiped a hand across his chest, her attention was drawn once more to the broad expanse, to the sight of his fingers brushing across the contours, as if compelling her to do the same. Want seeped into her skin, hot and alluring, and she shook it off with effort, along with the bizarre lethargy that had settled over her.

"Montgomery will kill you," she said, a bit thickly. She watched with some relief when his hand fell to his side, but her gaze clung to his fingers, long and slender. Big. Warm.

"Do you think he can?"

The soft question, spoken with typical male arrogance, brought Elene swiftly from her daze. "Whatever they might call you, you are no saint. You are only a man, and just as vulnerable to a knife between your shoulder blades as any other."

He seemed to digest this. "And you have cause to mistrust Montgomery?"

Cause? Need she have cause to mistrust a man? Elene laughed derisively. "He wants you dead," she said. "I can see it in his eyes."

A noise behind her made Elene reach for her dagger, and she turned, only to face servants carrying the old wooden tub up the stairs. They eyed her warily, and she stepped aside so that they might put their burden down before the hearth.

"The water is nearly ready for your bath, my lord," one of the young boys said. Then, they hurried past Elene, giving her a wide berth.

His bath. Elene glanced toward the tub, then at Geoffrey, who caught and held her gaze in his dark one as if he had the same thought. As his wife and lady of the manor, she should bathe him, but she had taken on no such duties. Not only did he continue to sleep on his pallet, but they both spent each night fully clothed. Indeed, this was the first time Elene had seen him without his garments. She flushed, wondering what he would look like stripped down to nothing. How far did that dark hair go? Were his long legs thick with muscle? And his behind, was it golden as the rest of him and...

Shocked at her thoughts, Elene let out a low hiss of denial. She had no interest in this man, naked or not, other than in keeping him alive! Deliberately, she flicked a contemptuous glance over him. He stood patiently before her, as if awaiting her decision, and the sight of him, strong and assured and beautiful, while she was none of those things, made her want to scream.

Saint Geoffrey. Always so perfect. Well, she cared naught for his fine body or his lofty manners! Backing toward the door, Elene opened her mouth to rain curses upon his head, but, to her horror, nothing came out. Her voice, obviously unreliable in his presence, had deserted her once more. Finally, she simply swallowed her oaths, turned, and stalked angrily away.

* * *

Geoffrey watched her go, curiosity furrowing his brow. Was he imagining things or had his wife looked upon him briefly with…interest? And if so, what had brought it on? Since their ill-fated kiss in the stables, Elene rarely uttered a peaceable word to him. Although he saw less of her, when he did, she was more shrewish than ever, making him avoid her as much as possible. Sometimes, he wondered if that was her plan, and then shook his head. Elene Fitzhugh de Burgh long had been known for her foul disposition; she was practicing no special arts on him.

Yet, there had been something decidedly odd about this encounter, especially in the way she had stared at his chest so avidly that his blood thundered in his ears. It was almost as if… No, Geoffrey thought, rubbing a hand over his eyes. He was deluding himself. His wife's only interest in his anatomy was in determining the best place to insert her blade!

But what of her warning about Montgomery? There was no mistaking that as both fiercely rendered and unusual. Elene rarely spoke of household matters, let alone the uncertain loyalties of her people. And why alert him to any danger when she had threatened him often enough herself?

As confusing as he found her behavior, Geoffrey did not easily dismiss her warning. He had not trusted Montgomery from the first, although he was not sure why the knight was so surly. Had Montgomery planned to take Avery's place himself? Geoffrey clenched his fist at the thought of Elene with another. Rarely had he considered his wife's first marriage as anything except a cautionary example, but now that he had kissed her and held her beneath him, he felt a violent, possessive fury. He was glad that Avery was dead, killed by Elene's own hand.

Startled at such uncivilized notions, Geoffrey shook his

head, as if to deny them. Faith, he was turning as blood-thirsty as his wife! With effort, he shrugged away the images he had conjured and concentrated on Montgomery. The knight was obviously embittered by Fitzhugh's loss of Wessex, but what could he hope to gain by lashing out at his new lord?

Montgomery's enmity made no sense unless he planned to overthrow Geoffrey—perhaps with the aid of the lady of the manor? The thought took root, but swiftly died, for Geoffrey could not picture Elene conspiring with any man. Although she was capable of doing plenty of scheming her own, the notion of his hellion wife cooperating with anyone sent a slow smile to his face.

On the other hand, Elene might have her own motives for wanting to be rid of Montgomery, Geoffrey mused. But, again, he discarded the possibility, for he could see no reason for Elene to seek one knight's dismissal, especially when the manor boasted so few. Geoffrey sighed, reluctant to part with such a valuable man himself. Half a dozen of the trained warriors, along with a ragtag infantry, were all that was left of Fitzhugh's fighting force. Did Montgomery really pose a threat? It was easy to see shadows everywhere when Geoffrey was essentially alone at the enemy holding.

Yet he remembered too well the look of hatred on Montgomery's face as they fought. Although a man could often be carried away by these exercises, and injuries were not uncommon, the knight's sudden jab had been deliberate—and too close for comfort. Geoffrey sighed. Better to be safe than sorry, he thought. And, besides, Elene was right. He hadn't liked the look in Montgomery's eyes.

But did he like the look in his wife's eyes any better?

Geoffrey rose before dawn, his instincts awakening him as surely as any servant. Still clad in his tunic, he had only to put on his outer one and strap on his sword to be ready to tackle some business that would best be completed as early as possible. Moving quietly so as to not rouse his wife, Geoffrey strode to the door, but a low sound from the bed drew his attention. Cautiously, he walked to the edge of it and looked down upon his bride.

In sleep she was completely guileless, the tempers that so often twisted her lovely features lost in the peace of slumber. Geoffrey drew in a sharp breath, for she looked sweet and incredibly vulnerable, her cinnamon lashes resting against gently curving cheeks. Her lips were slightly parted, and Geoffrey remembered all too well the pleasures to be found there. Spicy and exotic, they beckoned him to this dream maiden.

She stirred, and beneath the thick fur, her shoulder peeped out, clad in a dull brown gown. Geoffrey frowned. Sometimes he wondered if the two of them would always sleep in their clothes, protected and untouchable. They were both stubborn and wary, he recognized that, but sometimes he had a wistful yearning for...

What? A true marriage? A wife who existed only in a netherworld of his own making? Shaking his head, Geoffrey sighed softly. If she found him standing over her, there would be hell to pay, and he had no time to waste. With one last look at a side of her he saw only in her sleep, Geoffrey headed for the door, calling quietly for the boy who served as his squire.

Osbert was new, for the youth who had done the job for many years had been knighted in the fall. Although his brothers had urged him to find a replacement before he left Campion, Geoffrey had thought it politic to choose one of his new people. Now, as with all else, he had to wonder at the wisdom of his decision, for even Osbert eyed him warily.

Or maybe he just saw enemies everywhere.

Smiling ruefully, Geoffrey bid the boy to his side. "Ready Montgomery's horses, packing all that is his from the stables," he said.

The boy gave him a wide-eyed look, but swallowed hard and nodded before running through the dark hall on his errand. Geoffrey watched him go and readied himself for the coming confrontation. It was best to meet the enemy when he was most vulnerable, and so he had chosen this moment when Montgomery was sleeping to make his move. Stepping over the bodies of servants that lined the hall, Geoffrey followed the stairs to the ground floor, a vaulted cellar that housed the knights. Finding Montgomery in the gloom, he nudged him with a booted foot.

The knight rose swiftly, sputtering angrily. He wore nothing except his braies, but Geoffrey did not give him leave to dress. Quietly, he motioned Montgomery up into the hall where his people were stirring. "Your horses are ready. Rouse your squire, have him pack your supplies and be gone at first light."

Montgomery stared at him, obviously stunned. "You jest."

Around him, Geoffrey saw men rise and glance furtively at the barely clad knight. The hall was cold, and without his weapons and mail, Montgomery looked vulnerable and chilled. "No. I have no need of allegiance such as yours. You will leave the manor, my lands and those of my brother, baron of Wessex."

Montgomery's mouth twisted into a snarl as the force of Geoffrey's words struck him. "You can't get rid of me. You need me, fool! Who else will guard your gate and lead your rabble?"

"Don't be insolent," Geoffrey said, settling his hand upon the hilt of his sword. "As *lord* of this manor, *I* will guard it and lead those who give me their true oath."

If Montgomery had been given a chance to arm himself, doubtless he would have drawn his weapon now, so fierce was his anger, but he had nothing. Geoffrey saw him glance swiftly around the hall, filled only with servants staring at his undress. His squire did not attend him, nor were there other knights to join in a betrayal. Swearing viciously, he turned on his heel.

"Hold," Geoffrey said. "I shall have your man bring what you need." Motioning to the returning Osbert, Geoffrey sent him in to fetch Montgomery's squire and possessions. Although tempted to see if any other knights were inclined to revolt, Geoffrey knew he would be vastly outnumbered, if they did. Better to rid himself of the chief worm and hope the rest of the apple held firm.

When the squires returned, dumping satchels and clothes at Montgomery's feet, he immediately reached for his sword. "No need of that now," Geoffrey said softly.

Montgomery's face turned dark with frustration and loathing. "You think I can't do better than this failing manor?" he taunted as he hurriedly donned his tunic and boots. "I'll find a richer lord to serve, perhaps one of your enemies, de Burgh, and then… Then we shall meet again," he promised. Yelling for his squire to follow, he strode from the hall as the hushed servants looked on.

Determined to see Montgomery off his lands, Geoffrey started after him when a shriek from behind drew him up short. He turned to find Elene standing nearby, her face pale behind the tangle of hair. "Are you mad?" she shouted. "What the devil are you doing?"

"I am ridding the manor of Montgomery, as you suggested," Geoffrey answered calmly.

"As I…" She appeared so stunned as to be speechless, and Geoffrey grinned at the unusual sight. At his smile, her fierce manner returned, and she glared at him as if he had lost his wits. "Fool, you could have been killed!" She threw her arm out in a sweeping gesture. "I see no one here but servants—no knights, no soldiers to protect you, no one even to watch your back!"

So accustomed was he to her tirades, that Geoffrey rarely listened, yet this time, something about her tone arrested him. He studied her closely, astonished to see that her fingers trembled before finding the hilt of her dagger in her usual threatening gesture. "Do you want to die?" she cried.

"Would you care, if I did?" Geoffrey asked softly.

The words appeared to freeze his wife in her tracks, and she looked wildly around at their growing audience, then back at Geoffrey. "Nay, I would rejoice!"

"Then, why are you so concerned about my back?" Geoffrey asked. Although he spoke the question lightly, in a teasing tone, he was aware of an odd tingle of elation at the thought that his life might matter to her—that anything might matter to the hellion who was his wife.

His brief optimism faded quickly. Narrowing her eyes, Elene scowled at him contemptuously and ducked her head. "I want no one else to snatch away my victory by killing you before I do, de Burgh!" she shouted. "And that is all!" Then she turned on her heel and stomped away, her long, tangled locks swinging delightfully behind her.

Although oddly disappointed by her response, Geoffrey laughed aloud at the empty threat, for she had done nothing worse than throw food at him since his arrival. Truly, if a man could manage to ignore her ranting and raving, he could get along with the infamous she-devil.

Then, again, maybe not, Geoffrey thought, as he swiftly dodged a flashing blade. Apparently disgruntled at his laughter, Elene had swung back around and in a blink of an eye, threw her dagger past him to lodge in the wall at his back. Clearly, she had not intended to strike him, just demonstrate her infamous skills, but now silence descended on the entire hall as everyone waited to see what he would do.

Obviously, his people expected him to respond in kind, and Geoffrey wondered if Elene and her father had ever exchanged volleys here in their own hall. To Geoffrey, she looked small and pale behind her hair, though outwardly she appeared girded for battle. He let his gaze sweep through the audience, knowing that his actions would be judged by all those present and passed on to those who were not.

Accordingly, he took his time, turning slowly toward the blade. Then, with one swift jerk, he pulled it from the wall and walked toward his wife. Although Elene stood her ground, Geoffrey thought he saw a trace of vulnerability beneath all that passionate defiance.

"I believe you dropped this," he said dryly, handing her the hilt.

Only Geoffrey saw the slight tremor in her hand as she reached out to take it, and only he noted the rush of heat that came when their fingers brushed. She jerked away, her gaze flying to him with something akin to horror, and he stepped back automatically. Then his attention was drawn to the crowd as the combined breath of everyone in the room hissed out in relief that there would be no bloodshed between the lord and lady of the manor.

At least not this time.

Chapter Six

In April, Geoffrey received the news that Marion had delivered a boy—the first de Burgh heir. Although he was glad that both mother and son were doing well, Geoffrey felt an uneasy sort of resentment at Dunstan's good fortune. It both surprised and annoyed him, for never had he coveted the lives of his brothers. He was vaguely ashamed of himself, and yet it was not the Wolf's castle or his wealth that Geoffrey envied. It was the happiness of his marriage, and his new family.

Glancing across the hall at his wife, Geoffrey knew that he would get no children from her, and he was assailed by an inexplicable sense of loss. He was not the type of man who was obsessed with continuing his line. Nor had he any experience with babies. Yet there it was, a frustration that both puzzled and irritated him when he contemplated the future. He studied Elene suddenly, his eyes roving over the slender figure that he knew was hidden beneath the ugly clothing.

He could bed her.

The thought came out of nowhere, seducing him sharply. She was no ancient hag, but young and supple and possessed of a woman's body. Her face, when not scowling, was lovely, and her lips were spicy and enticing. Indeed, the more he thought about it, the less of a chore it seemed to do his husbandly duty. If he could only keep her mouth too occupied to spout oaths at him, her hands too busy to reach for her dagger…

Shaking his head, Geoffrey tried to slow the thundering of his heartbeat. Rightfully wed or no, Elene would never agree. Despite their vows, they kept to their own berths at night, fully clothed, still wary. Even if he could manage to emerge unscathed after the encounter, how could he take pleasure from it? Never would he force himself upon an unwilling woman, and although Elene had acquiesced briefly in the stable, she had made her feelings known soon enough. She had found even his kiss distasteful.

Geoffrey sighed, disgusted with himself for considering the idea. Was he so desperate to produce an heir that he could contemplate lying with that she-devil? She was a wild thing, who contributed nothing to her own household, cared nothing for her own people, and caused nothing but trouble. He disliked everything about her! Rising abruptly from his seat, Geoffrey sent her a hard look. "My brother has a son. Prepare yourself for a trip to Wessex, as we will go to pay tribute to his heir."

Elene blinked and ducked her chin, glaring at him from behind the hair he was never sure whether he wanted to yank from her head or tangle in his fists. "Go where you please. I am staying here!"

Whether his frustrated longings caused his ill temper, or whether he was simply weary of her constant arguments, Geoffrey could not have said. He only knew that he would not give in to her whims this time. He was not about to leave her here to make mischief in his absence, and he owed his brother a visit. "Nay, you are coming, Elene. Do not test me on this, I am adamant."

Elene laughed bitterly. "Saint Geoffrey takes a stand! I quake in my slippers!"

"I'm warning you, Elene—" he began, taking a step forward.

"Do not threaten me, husband, or you shall find yourself dead!"

Sighing, Geoffrey simply turned away. Although he held himself above such common behavior, the she-devil would incite him to violence yet with her persistent taunts! "Prepare yourself," he called over his shoulder as he sought the relative peace of the bailey.

"I'm not going!" she shouted at him, and for a moment, Geoffrey could have sworn he heard a thread of fear in her voice. He shook his head as he walked away. Obviously, the woman was driving him mad. Else he would not be imagining such things.

Nothing scared Elene.

Elene was terrified. Her hands closed convulsively around the reins as she watched the home she had known since birth fade into the distance. Although she longed to shout her displeasure, she kept her mouth shut, having already startled her palfrey by hurling oaths at her husband's head. Now, she could only glare at him in silence or stare futilely at the familiar walls behind them. She felt trapped and frustrated and longed to strike out at someone, preferably Geoffrey, lest the fear consume her.

She had never left the manor in her life. She hadn't wanted to leave it now, but this time the saint had not given way to her will. For all his gentle manner, Geoffrey had his limits. Elene had discovered them before, and she had no wish to find herself in that situation again. All too well she remembered the night she had dared to extinguish his candle, and the feel of him on top of her as he held her still.

Cursing, Elene forced the disturbing image from her mind. Despite his threats, she doubted that Geoffrey would have dragged her physically to Wessex, and for a time, she had considered disappearing conveniently on the morning of his departure. Or she could have caused trouble, trouble that would make him glad to leave her.

But what if something happened to him while he was gone?

Elene had heard Montgomery's threats. Embittered, adrift and violent, he could lie in wait for Geoffrey, attacking swiftly and suddenly, as was the coward's way. Although Elene had seen enough of her husband's skill to trust he would acquit himself well in a fair fight, Montgomery had already proved himself to be a deceitful wretch. And Geoffrey had no one to watch his back.

Except her.

Ever since the morning she came into the hall and found him standing alone against the dangerous knight, Elene had taken the chore upon herself. Instead of seeking to avoid her husband, she kept him within sight most of the day, and when he was too engrossed in his books or his accounts to pay attention to anything else, she kept watch. Geoffrey was oblivious, of course, and that was to the good, for he would make sport of her efforts, perhaps even prohibit them, should he discover that a female was serving as his guard.

Or he might misconstrue her intentions.

She was protecting her own interests, that was all, for she did not want a third husband, a less tractable male in her household. And that was why she was here, clutching the reins of her palfrey in a wild grip while the manor disappeared behind a hill.

She was here, but she did not like it. Once her familiar lands gave way to new pastures and woodlands, Elene fought against panic. She was in a strange place, alone with Geoffrey and a few servants and guards, and she felt naked and vulnerable, as if the manor were a shield she had held in front of her. It had not provided protection, really, but solidarity. In her bitterly changing world, the building had been her only constant.

In a desperate effort to control that which she could, Elene continually peppered Geoffrey with questions about the road and tried to mark her direction. Still, she was not sure she could find her way back easily, and it gnawed at her, this sense of defenselessness.

What if Geoffrey was leading her off into the wilderness to abandon her there, or, worse yet, murder her? There was no one to stop him. Elene was painfully aware that her father's soldiers had sworn their fealty to Geoffrey, and, anyway, they held no love for her. She felt more alone than ever, but rode grimly on, following and watching the back of the man who might betray her, compelled to protect him, though she trusted him not.

By nightfall, Elene was weary and anxious, and the prospect of sleeping on the hard ground, even under a fancy tent, did little to raise her spirits. She ate sparingly, alert to the undercurrents around her, but the men only seemed eager for their rest. Finally, feeling the creep of exhaustion and the aches of a body that had never ridden so long, Elene went into the tent and made a bed of furs and blankets.

Geoffrey had told her to bring a female servant, but she had laughed contemptuously. She was used to doing for herself, and who would be willing to attend her? She put her faith in no one. So she crawled onto her pallet, alone in the smothering darkness of the tent. Although the furs provided welcome warmth against the chill spring night, Elene could not sleep. She hated being confined. She imagined them all leaving her alone here while she dozed, or creeping in to slit her throat, and she kept a ready hand upon the hilt of her dagger.

Then, suddenly, the flap opened and a tall, broad-shouldered figure ducked through it to step inside. The light of the fire cast his handsome features into relief before darkness descended once more, and for one betraying moment, Elene's heart leapt at the sight of her husband. But she quickly denied her eagerness for his company as the implications of his presence set in.

"What are you doing here?" she snapped.

"I'm sleeping here, Elene."

Elene sat up. Although fully clothed, she clutched the fur to her chest protectively as her fingers tightened around her knife. Suddenly, it was all very clear. He had brought her to finalize their marriage, out in the wilderness so that none but the few around the fire could hear her scream. And who among them would come to her aid?

"Get out, de Burgh! Find another tent!"

He sighed heavily in the darkness. "This is the only tent, Elene, and I am tired, so here is where I intend to rest. But if you do not care for my company, then feel free to go somewhere else!"

Elene heard the weariness in his voice, the rasp that revealed not a saint but a man. Relaxing slightly, she nevertheless eased her pallet closer to the side of the shelter. "Stay away from me, de Burgh! If you think to do anything here but sleep, you had better prepare to die," she warned.

He snorted. "Yes, Elene, I rode miles from the manor simply so I could have my way with you on the cold, hard ground instead of the comfortable bed in our chamber."

Another snort followed his sarcasm, and then she heard the rustling of his covers as he settled in.

His snide comment stung. Of course he did not want her! She was being foolish, and yet she had to protect herself, didn't she? Elene tried not to think of his big body so close, with nothing but a few feet of space between them. Her mouth felt suddenly dry as she pictured him, dark and virile and warm. "I mean it, de Burgh," she whispered. "I'll slit your throat as soon as you move."

"And if you don't be quiet, I'll stop your mouth!" he warned.

"And just how will you do that?" she asked, contempt fueling her anger once more.

"I'll kiss you."

Elene caught her breath at the threat, but instead of shock or horror, she felt a slow, insidious heat creep into her. Anticipation. Yearning? She parted her lips to curse him, but thought better of it, just as unwilling to test his word as she was to try her own betraying senses.

Tired and sore from the unaccustomed travel, Elene was in a foul temper when they arrived at the Wolf's domain. It had rained the day before, a deluge that seemed to seep into her very bones, and she felt the familiar terror at the possibility of growing ill. Sickness meant becoming weak and vulnerable, an easy victim for one's enemies, as she well knew. For Elene had watched her mother fail and fade, prey to her father's whims, until she was unable to protect her interests or others or, finally, herself. Elene's hands clenched the reins tighter, as if a show of physical strength would ward off the memory of her own bitter failure to help, as well as the possibility that some inherited frailty might lay her low. Taking a deep, slow breath, she focused her formidable will upon remaining well.

And upon hating Wessex. Of course, Elene already despised it, for the toll it had taken on her life and her
people, but now that she saw it for herself, she was
stunned. Her father had died for this ugly, old castle? It
was bigger than the manor, and obviously better fortified,
but cold and barren and wholly unappealing in her eyes.

"What a bleak-looking wreck!" she cried. "I'm surprised it hasn't fallen down around the Wolf's ears!" She
laughed loudly, just in case Geoffrey coveted the place
himself.

"Behave yourself, Elene," he said softly. Swiftly,
Elene realized that the saint was back, and she frowned,
for some errant part of her preferred the Geoffrey of the
night before, sharp-tongued but human. Geoffrey the man.

Licking suddenly dry lips, Elene glared fiercely at her
husband, as if to deny his allure. It was easy enough to
do when she looked around her. Although relieved at the
prospect of real shelter and a soft bed, Elene did not want
to be at Wessex, and she had no intention of ever being
dragged here again. She would see to it, too. Unwelcome
visitors were often asked to leave early, she mused, a slow
smile curving her mouth just as the Wolf himself rode out
to greet them.

He was surprised to see her, she could tell, though he
disguised it well. His displeasure was more apparent, but
Elene could match it. Ducking her chin, she eyed him
evilly, until even the Wolf looked away uneasily. With a
gruff shout of welcome to his brother, he led them to his
lair.

They dismounted quickly, and Elene was aware of the
Wolf's scrutiny more than once. Good. Let him be wary,
she thought, as well he should be! Then her husband, saint
that he was, demanded her attention by presenting his arm

politely, and she let him lead her through the tall, heavy doors.

The hall seemed huge compared to that of the manor, and Elene gaped. People bustled to and fro, many stopping to stare at the new arrivals, and Elene felt the force of their curiosity. Old discomforts rose, but she pushed them aside. Were they aware of her identity? If not, she would make herself known soon enough!

One figure, a woman, stepped forward from the small group that gathered, and Elene studied her with interest. She was small, with dark curls peeking out from beneath a hair covering that matched the most beautiful gown Elene had ever seen. It was a brilliant blue, and shimmered as if golden threads had been woven into the fabric, reminding her of some of her father's finery, and Elene suppressed an aberrant sting of envy. What need had she of fine fabrics and rich garments?

As Elene watched, the Wolf strode to the woman and put an arm around her, a look of fierce possession on his face. Blinking in astonishment, Elene knew a healthy admiration for the lady, who did not even flinch at the brute's pawing. Indeed, she glanced up at him with apparent adoration.

Poor creature. She must be his leman, Elene thought.

As if reading her mind, the small, shapely female spoke. "Welcome to our home, Lady de Burgh. I'm Lady Wessex, but since we are sisters now, you must call me Marion." She ended the little speech by smiling, a beautiful flash of white teeth that ended in two dimples.

For a moment, Elene was so entranced that reason fled, but then her eyes narrowed. No mistress, but a wife! And, obviously, this Marion had the kind of charm that Geoffrey possessed. But Elene had much practice in shunning his false friendliness, and she knew very well she was not welcome here. Ducking her head, she spat on the floor at the woman's feet.

A hush fell over the hall as everyone gaped in stunned silence. Then the Wolf jerked forward, as if to strike, and Elene reached for her dagger, prepared to defend herself. Yet the Wolf remained where he was, and Elene blinked in surprise to see that he had been halted by the tiny hand of his wife upon his arm. Faith, the woman dared much! No doubt the Wolf would beat her later for her insolence, poor fool.

Although he made no move against her, the Wolf growled his displeasure. "You will behave in my home, Fitzhugh, or you will rue the day you crossed the threshold."

"It's de Burgh now, Dunstan," Geoffrey said softly. "Lady de Burgh." With his usual swift stealth, her husband had placed himself between her and his brother. No doubt he sought to protect his sibling from her sharp tongue and her sharper blade, she thought sourly.

"I'm sure that Elene intends to behave civilly," Geoffrey said, sending her an angry look of warning. Elene stared at him for a moment, surprised to feel an ache somewhere outside herself at his reprimand. It felt like the phantom pains of a leg that had been cut off—or a heart that had long ago ceased to function—and she scowled, glaring back at him, her fingers still clutching her dagger.

Only Marion seemed to have retained her composure.

"Come," the lady said, obviously trying to salvage the situation. "You must meet the newest member of our household! Would you like to see the baby?" She pinned great doe eyes on Elene, as if pleading with her for peace, and Elene was hard-pressed to ignore the entreaty. She was accustomed to fear and revulsion, but this gentle reproach she had seen only from her husband.

"I don't think—" the Wolf began, obviously disinclined to present his son to his enemy.

Amused, Elene opened her mouth to scorn his heir, but Geoffrey cut in before she could speak. "I would, but first I want to get Elene settled into her room."

"Perhaps you could see that your wife is disarmed, as well," the Wolf said, staring pointedly at her knife.

Elene glanced at Geoffrey in dismay. She had expected banishment, had sought it, in fact, but not the loss of her weapon. His dark gaze met hers, and for a moment, she could have sworn she saw regret. Or apology? Her surprise quickly turned to suspicion. Did he pretend to take her part against his brother and liege lord? Ha! Elene did not believe his furrowed brow for an instant, saint or no.

When the silence stretched out uncomfortably, the Wolf spoke again, taking Geoffrey to task. "Her father nearly killed me in this very hall. I would not have his daughter cause harm to any who reside here."

Pleased at the great warrior's wariness, Elene laughed loudly. "Do you fear me, a mere woman?" Hushed silence followed her challenge, and she hoped to push the Wolf's temper so far that he would rid himself of her presence, but again he was held back by a small hand on his arm. Elene blinked. How could this Marion hold such sway over a fierce knight more than twice her size? Angry at her interference, Elene opened her mouth to taunt the Wolf further, but Geoffrey turned on her abruptly, tying her tongue with the savage look upon his savage visage.

Elene nearly flinched. For once, he resembled his brother, and she berated herself for forgetting that he was a de Burgh. Here was no saint, but a man—a knight, a warrior who would stop at nothing to gain his ends. As if to prove her words, he spoke, his voice soft with a menace she had rarely heard from him. "Give me the knife, Elene."

She ducked her chin, letting her hair fall forward to hide the face she knew had drained of color. She could not give up her only means to protect herself. Not here, surrounded by strangers and enemies. Backing up a step, she thought to fend them all off: the brutish Wolf, his wife, their attendants, and the husband who had finally showed his true self. Although long expected, Geoffrey's betrayal caught her by surprise, and Elene felt that phantom pain again as she looked into his face. It was hard and determined.

Ignoring the strange ache, Elene straightened. She was the Fitzhugh, and she would never give in! She wanted to lash out at someone, especially at Geoffrey, for marrying her, for kissing her, for making her...see him as a man.

But even nearly blinded by anger, Elene could see that she was outnumbered. This was not her hall, and these people did not fear her as they should. Indeed, Marion's face held neither fright nor hatred, only a gentle compassion that made Elene wince. By faith, she would not be pitied! It was that expression that decided her. With a haughty snort that belied her inner turmoil, Elene tossed the blade at Geoffrey's feet, just to prove to them all that she needed it not. She could protect herself without it. She was the Fitzhugh.

Although the Wolf made a gruff sound as the dagger clattered on the tiles, Geoffrey said nothing. He only bent his tall body gracefully to retrieve it. When he straightened, his manner had gentled. "The other one," he said softly.

Elene blinked. How had he known of the small blade tucked into her boot? Loosing a stream of foul oaths, she reached down and threw it onto the tiles, too. He knelt again, his broad shoulders so wide, his dark hair falling like silk over his forehead, and Elene cursed herself for noticing. But then he stood and held out his hand again. "And the one strapped to your leg."

Damn him! Furious now, Elene balled her hands into fists and shrieked abuse at him. She railed and ranted so loudly that the servants backed away, but Geoffrey did not. Finally jerking up her skirts, she reached for the smallest of her daggers, intending to send it flying at his head, but when she glanced at him, the expression on his face halted her.

Geoffrey was staring at her legs.

Elene was so startled by the discovery that she stared back, for no one had ever looked at her that way. Her husband's eyes were dark and dazed, as if the brilliant scholar were bewildered. Elene stilled, her fingers poised upon the hilt for a long moment as heat seeped into her very bones, making them liquid. She rarely thought about her body, except to curse its gender, but now she was keenly aware of every inch of skin bared to her husband. She had the insane urge to lift her gown higher, to flex the muscles in her thigh, to watch him watch her. To display herself for Geoffrey's admiration. And more...

Her throat was dry, and Elene swallowed hard, jerking her attention away as she shook off the absurd notion. Suddenly cold, she fought back a shudder, pulled the knife from its berth and slammed it upon the floor. Geoffrey took a moment to retrieve it, as if he had to catch his breath first, and Elene felt a dizzying sense of satisfaction before he straightened.

"Come, I shall show you to your room," he said, his voice so rough and husky it sent tendrils of warmth through her. Belatedly she realized that her husband was taking her to a bedchamber. Uneasiness danced up her spine, along with something else she did not recognize, the same sort of strange obsession that had tempted her to bare herself to him.

"You will excuse us," Geoffrey said, and though the Wolf scowled, Marion nodded genially.

"It's where you stayed before, Geoffrey," she called as they moved away, and Elene glared at her. She did not like the sound of her husband's name on that woman's lips, or the sweet smile that came so easily.

For a moment, Elene was tempted to turn on the Wolf's wife and yank some of those dark curls from her head, but then reason returned. She had more important concerns right now, like being stuck at Wessex without her weapons. As the enormity of her situation set in, Elene's hands started shaking. She felt disoriented in this alien place, with strangers peeking out of the dark corners, whispering about her. Her hand drifted to her girdle but, finding no hilt there to give her strength, grasped at nothing. The dark stone walls seemed cold and threatening, and she felt naked and vulnerable without anything to protect herself.

Perhaps that was Geoffrey's intention. Over the past weeks, he had lulled her into complacency with that teasing grin and those warm, inviting eyes. But, as Elene had always suspected, they were a ruse, practiced, no doubt, on many a damsel, and now that she was defenseless, he could do what he would to her—even toss her into his brother's dungeon!

Elene twisted her trembling fingers into the rough fabric of her skirts as she tried not to panic. She could flee, but where would she go? And she would never give the de Burghs the satisfaction of driving her away. Nay, she needed to retrieve her knives, then attack, if she must.

Glancing about her, she saw nothing but bleak stone and a long, curving stair.

As they started up the steep steps, however, Elene's eyes lit upon the sheath of Geoffrey's sword, swaying with the movement of his long legs. Ducking her head, she let her hair hide her face while she eased closer and fell back, behind him a pace. Licking dry lips, Elene tore her attention away from the firm play of Geoffrey's muscles and focused on the hilt that bobbed just within her reach. Her husband was both clever and quick, but she, too, could move swiftly.

And surprise was a mighty weapon indeed.

Chapter Seven

Geoffrey stomped up the stairs, his heavy tread giving away his turmoil. He should never have come. Better yet, he should never have brought the she-devil! Obviously, over the past months, he had become inured to her foul behavior, but now he saw her for what she was, an ill-tempered, foulmouthed, ungrateful monster.

In short, his wife was everything he abhorred.

And yet, he had found himself staring at her bared leg like some randy youth! Geoffrey cringed in disgust. Was he going mad? He rubbed his eyes and trod along the narrow passage to his old room. For a moment, he recalled his stay at Wessex after the de Burghs had retaken Dunstan's castle. Although a time of struggle, those days seemed pleasurable and carefree, compared to his life since. Now he was burdened by everything, not least by his wife!

Angrily Geoffrey threw open the door to his old chamber, only to see Elene flit past him in a whirl of brown skirts. What was she up to now? Hurriedly he shut the door behind him to ensure their privacy, lest she start screaming at him. Her behavior in the hall had been bad enough, without her inciting new talk. Relieved to be locked inside with her, Geoffrey looked up, only to freeze.

She had his sword.

Poised a few feet away, her legs spread in the traditional fighter's stance, Elene swung the heavy weapon through the air with astonishing ease, to point it at his chest. Ducking her head, she glared at him fiercely. "Give me the daggers, de Burgh."

Geoffrey's heart pounded, though not from fear. Even as he tried to deny it, he found something exciting about her boldness, her strength, her speed, her indomitable spirit.... The madness was upon him again! Geoffrey cleared his throat. "You would run me through here in my brother's home? Have you a death wish, Elene?"

"Maybe," she answered. "Maybe I'd rather be dead than weaponless."

It wasn't her words, so much as the vulnerability Geoffrey thought he glimpsed in those amber eyes, that touched him. By faith, he had not wanted to take her precious knives, anyway, but had only acceded to the wishes of his brother. After all, it was Dunstan's home. And, at the time, he had been furious with her for embarrassing him in front of the entire hall. He should have expected it, he knew, but she had been comparatively quiet of late, and he had hoped... He should have known better. Elene would never change. She was a wild thing that no amount of gentleness could tame.

The last remnants of that rage left Geoffrey in a sudden rush, leaving only a cold disappointment in its wake. As his brothers often said, he rarely held a grudge against anyone for long, and his wife was no exception. As loud and obnoxious as she was, Elene had never really done him harm. Nor did he expect her to do anything more now than her usual blustering and threatening.

Geoffrey eyed her up and down, taking in the strain
that showed in her taut arms and face. He could wrest the
weapon from her, but someone, namely Elene, might get
hurt in the process. And something he could not quite
understand made him balk at overpowering her. What
would it prove but that he was stronger?

"Very well," Geoffrey said softly, and he saw her
shoulders sag slightly in relief. Apparently the heavy
sword was taking its toll on her. Digging into the pouch
at his waist, Geoffrey presented the weapons to her, hilt
first, and watched his sword clatter to the floor.

"But do not wear your favorite in your girdle while we
are here," Geoffrey cautioned as he bent to retrieve it.
"If Dunstan finds out you have them, there will be hell
to pay."

She nodded, furtively, behind the veil of hair, as she
clutched the knives to her breast, and suddenly Geoffrey
wanted to go to her. She seemed so alone and defenseless,
a strange, frightened creature who clung to the cold steel
for comfort. Abruptly he regretted bringing her to the site
of her father's death, into the home of a man who openly
showed his contempt for her. Without really thinking,
Geoffrey stepped forward, a hand outstretched, but as
soon as he did, she moved back, ducking her chin to glare
at him.

"I will hide them, but do not expect me to like it here.
I told you not to bring me here! I warned you, de Burgh!"

Geoffrey sighed as the beginnings of a headache
throbbed in his temples. Reaching for his sword, he slid
it back into its sheath and stared grimly at the creature
who was now ranting like a fishwife before him. Had he
ever thought her vulnerable? He shook his head.

It was the madness, he thought as he turned and left
her to her daggers and her hatred.

* * *

Elene spent the hours before supper pacing back and forth within the confines of the narrow room, her suspicions simmering like one of the manor cook's foul stews.

It had been too easy.

Her initial triumph at catching Geoffrey off guard had faded as soon as she held his own sword to his chest. It had been simple to steal it, confirming to Elene that he sorely needed someone to watch his back, the stupid fool. But then, as she swung the heavy weapon toward him, she had felt that strange phantom ache again, as if the stump of a missing tooth were suddenly rife with pain.

She had faltered, for despite all her fears, she did not want to hurt him. Indeed, she had nearly cried out, "Don't make me hurt you!" But there had been no need. Geoffrey had given in almost immediately, without even trying to disarm her or bargain with her or settle for half measures. He had returned all her daggers, with only a terse warning to hide them.

His response had startled Elene so that she almost fell to her knees in relief. Obviously, he had no intention of tossing her into the dungeon or letting the Wolf waylay her. The tension that had knotted her muscles left her in such a rush that she swayed, and only the recollection of her purpose brought her back to her senses.

She did not want to be here, and she set upon him at once with her objections, but Geoffrey only retreated, the sad look she had come to despise in his great dark eyes. Pushing aside the twinge of guilt that came with that memory, Elene tried to concentrate. He had given her back her weapons, but she was still stuck at Wessex, and she still did not trust him or his evil brother!

It had been too easy. Had Geoffrey another motive for returning her knives? Perhaps he simply enjoyed defying his brother, Elene mused, but she shook her head swiftly, certain that the saint would not engage in such pettiness.

And what of all the horrible schemes she had imagined him plotting? Thoughts of the dungeon seemed out of place in the small but comfortable space in which she found herself. Although the walls were plain, they were clean, and pegs were neatly hammered into the stone, so that she could hang her cloak near the hearth. The heavy chest brought with them from the manor had been put under the narrow window to serve as a makeshift seat.

And then there was the bed.

Elene swiftly looked away from the heavy piece of furniture that seemed to take up most of the room. The rather old and worn curtains had been pulled back to reveal an inviting pile of blankets, and the mattress beneath was soft. Elene knew, because she had sat upon the edge.

It was not a big bed, not nearly as wide as the one in the great chamber at the manor, yet it crowded the tiny chamber. How would Geoffrey find room to sleep upon the floor? Suspicion bubbled and popped in her head once more. Perhaps that was the plan—to ravish her here, where the thick stone walls would prevent any from hearing her screams. Far from home, she would find no allies in the Wolf's lair, where a Fitzhugh would always be the enemy.

Stilling, Elene considered the idea, and then shook her head. Even she could not believe in such a scheme, for Geoffrey had more than once voiced his disinterest in her...as a woman. Blowing out a harsh breath at that knowledge, Elene sank down on the side of the bed, her thoughts whirling in confusion until they came to rest on one tantalizing conjecture that refused to be dismissed.

Perhaps there was no plot.

Perhaps Geoffrey had simply come here to see his

brother's child and had brought her with him be-cause…because he didn't trust her at home alone. Elene tried to work up some outrage over that, but she couldn't. She felt tired, mentally and physically, and yet she knew she could not give in to the weariness. She had to be alert. There must be something she wasn't seeing, some plan they had for her that wasn't clear, here in the Wolf's lair.

Wearily Elene sank her head into her hands, but a knock on the door made her jerk upright. She had made it to her feet by the time the oak swung open to reveal Geoffrey, looking as fit as always, his broad shoulders filling out a deep green tunic that made him seem as dark and compelling as the forest itself.

The ends of his long hair were wet. Obviously, he had bathed and changed, and Elene knew a moment's pique that she could not. No one had offered such comforts to her, because she was not expected to want them. And that was just as well, she thought, smoothing out the rough brown wool of her skirts, for she had her reputation to uphold.

Elene glanced up again to find him waiting, his big brown eyes so warm and compelling that, for a moment, she nearly surrendered to the pull of them. But then she straightened her shoulders, took a deep breath and walked past him, reminding herself that he was a man and a de Burgh, and therefore not to be trusted.

She marched stiffly down the curving stair into the big hall, which was bustling with people, and felt more out of place than ever. Delightful smells wafted up to her as Geoffrey led her to a place at the lord's table. Servants hurried to set a hot trencher before them, and she felt doubly awkward. She had never shared food with him, although it was the custom. As he took his seat beside her, Elene was overwhelmed by his tall form, and inched farther along the bench.

Still, his muscular thigh seemed far too close, and his big shoulder hovered near her own. Hunching over, Elene let her hair fall into her face and peered out, searching for a distraction among the many inhabitants of Wessex. Watching silently, she noticed something strange about them all, and the mystery kept her thoughts occupied until she blinked in realization.

Everyone seemed happy.

The people at the lower tables were talking, smiling and laughing among themselves, while the servants did their jobs efficiently and without the sullen expressions Elene was accustomed to seeing at the manor. And all appeared to be pleased by the lord and lady.

That was the most astounding thing of all, for when her father meted out his orders, everyone had cringed, fearful of catching his attention. He had been a ruthless taskmaster, yet the Wolf, who was so much bigger and fiercer, seemed to inspire loyalty, not fear.

"Elene." Geoffrey's soft voice startled her, and she swung round, as if to fend him off, but he only pointed at the trencher he had cut in half, pushing her piece toward her. The meat looked savory and delicious, and she reached for her knife, forgetting its absence from her girdle.

Before she could open her mouth to complain, Geoffrey reached over and cut the large pieces for her. He worked silently, without comment, and Elene found herself watching the graceful movements of his large hands before jerking her attention away. It was easily caught by the lord and lady.

They were bent together over a single trencher, and while Elene watched in surprise, the Wolf sliced off a small piece of pigeon and fed it to his wife. By hand. And Marion did not flinch, but nibbled it daintily, even catching his wrist in order to lick at his finger with a dimpled smile.

Elene's breath caught and held. She had never seen such a thing. It was revolting, she told herself, and yet… Surreptitiously she glanced at Geoffrey's hand, big but gentle, his fingers long and strong. She wondered what he would taste like: savory juices, sweat and Geoffrey. Drawing in a strangled breath, Elene bent down. Practically dragging her hair in the food, she hid herself from the world—and the world from herself. And she ate, watching them all warily from behind her veil.

The Wolf's wife tried to include her in the conversation several times, but Elene responded only with grunts. She hated it here, where people were cheerful and strange and where the threat of everything unknown pressed down on her until it was hard to breathe. She wanted her dagger ready at her fingertips! And she made her displeasure known, muttering imprecations over her food.

But still Marion did not take offense. She only smiled in that gentle way that implied understanding, until Elene felt bewildered. How had this seemingly sweet creature become bound to the Wolf? Before arriving here, Elene had pictured his wife to be as brutish and frightening as this de Burgh. Someone like herself? Elene shook off the eerie thought as she considered the small and shapely Marion. Obviously, the woman was not as harmless as she looked. Else how had she restrained her husband's wrath with but a touch?

Odd, that. And, odder still, Marion looked happy with her lot. Indeed, she seemed warm and welcoming and contented. Elene shook her head. Perhaps the woman was touched, for Elene knew of no others who could claim happiness in their lives. A woman's existence was a hard one, from birth to death. Yet Marion chatted pleasantly, talking about the baby in glowing terms, her wide doe eyes alight with wonder and joy. Indeed, she acted as if the child were a blessing, not a burden she had nearly died trying to bring into the world.

Of course, it was a boy. Maybe that made the difference, for Elene's mother had failed to produce the desired son, each pregnancy weakening her, until she was so frail and sickly that her husband banished her from his chamber. She had shared the other small room with Elene, but still Fitzhugh had wanted a son, and every so often he would charge into the chamber, sending Elene away while he... Elene shuddered. One time she had waited outside the door, listening to her father's foul grunts and her mother's weak moans. She had cowered there, knowing that she should do something to protect her mother, that she should be braver and stronger and...

At the touch of something against her elbow, Elene reared back, reaching for the knife that wasn't there and cursing loudly. For a long moment, she felt as if she were facing her father, but when she tossed back her hair, it was only a small servant boy, fearful and puzzled, who met her fierce gaze.

"I just wanted your trencher, my lady," he said.

Geoffrey slid it over to the boy, with a low sigh of exasperation. Hearing the sound, Elene wanted to shove him from the bench, but, reaching down, she felt the comforting presence of her knife strapped beneath her skirts and looked away.

"I am sorry the boy startled you," Marion said, gently. "The leftover food is given to the hungry at the gate."

"My people have been beaten down by war and strife," the Wolf added, with a pointed look in her direction.

"But things are improving," Marion put in hastily. "Now, the Wolf is home for good and will do no more traveling." She smiled up at him, and his hard face softened. *How did she do that?* Elene wondered in amazement.

"Since you are safely delivered of our son, I might assent to a trip, if the need were pressing," the Wolf said.

Marion frowned, and Elene caught a hint of determination in her mouth. "But there will be other babies," she protested.

"No!" The Wolf's roar startled Elene, and she steeled herself against flinching. "'Twas too hard on you," he added gruffly. *Too hard on Marion?* Did the Wolf actually care about his wife's welfare? Elene stared in puzzlement.

"Nonsense!" Marion said firmly. "'Twas an easy birth—"

"An easy birth?" The Wolf pushed back his chair. "You call a day and a half of pain an easy birth?"

"The first one is always a little difficult, but the next will be—"

The Wolf surged to his feet. "I have told you there will be no more children!"

Elene bent forward, her fingers inching closer to the knife in her boot. Would the Wolf kill his wife, here in his own hall? Although Elene felt no love for Marion, neither could she stand by and watch the woman die. She dipped her hand lower, reaching for the hilt, just as Marion jumped to her feet.

"There will be more children!" she said. Then she advanced on the Wolf, sticking one small finger into his massive chest. "And if you think I can't change your mind, let's go up to our chamber and find out!"

The challenge hung in the air, a threat that would surely mean the death of her, but to Elene's surprise, hardly anyone at the lord's table was paying attention. Indeed, one fat old fellow was still eating, as if nothing untoward were occurring. Elene blinked at the sight, then glanced back at the Wolf, only to hear him growl something low and grab his wife off her feet.

Now he would kill her! Did no one care? As Elene looked on in horror, the Wolf did not harm his wife, but kissed her, right there in front of everyone. And, even more astounding, Marion did not fight him off, but snaked her arms around his massive shoulders, as if to pull him tighter. Elene stared in fascination as the Wolf seemed to devour his wife, his mouth covering hers with near violence. Elene had never imagined anything like it, and just as she wondered if his goal was to smother his wife, the two of them broke apart, grinning idiotically at each other.

"Perhaps we had better finish this conversation in private," the Wolf said gruffly. His wife nodded, and then they turned and gave their excuses to depart, and Marion, rather than looking terrified by the prospect, appeared flush-faced and eager. *Eager?*

Elene shook her head. They must both be mad to behave in such a fashion. And yet... Abruptly she recalled the one time Geoffrey had touched his lips to hers. Could the saint kiss like that? Moving restlessly on the bench, Elene told herself that her blood was racing because of the perilous situation she had witnessed. It had nothing to do with her husband or the carnal thoughts that Edred was constantly warning her about.

Her mind in a turmoil, Elene nearly jumped when she heard Geoffrey clear his throat beside her. "Well, 'tis late, and it has been a long day. I would find my rest, too. Elene?" He held out his hand to her, and for a long moment she stared at it contemptuously. If he thought that she would behave like that crazy woman, he was sadly mistaken.

"I am not tired."

Geoffrey sighed. "Nevertheless, I am, and I would have you join me, rather than terrorizing the servants." Elene frowned. She had not meant to scare the boy, and what if she had? She was the Fitzhugh and would frighten whomever she liked.

"Elene," Geoffrey said, prompting her. He wore that long-suffering expression that told her he would stand there all night if he had to, his hand outstretched, waiting.

"Oh, very well," she snapped. Ignoring his arm, she stepped past him to find the stairs. Her anger fed her steps until she reached the room and realized, once more, just how small it was. Then she backed up against the wall, fixing Geoffrey with a warning glare. "You will need extra blankets to make your pallet on the floor."

"Elene," he said, securing the door behind him, "there is not enough room on these tiles. I'm sleeping in the bed."

Panic edged up her spine, but Elene stilled it. Bending down slowly, she pulled the dagger from her boot and turned toward him, triumphant. "I don't think so."

Geoffrey stiffened as he saw the blade. "I'm sleeping in the bed," he repeated. "Where you sleep is up to you. If you want to try to lie with one foot in the fire, that's fine with me. Or perhaps you could open the chest and curl up inside? But *I'm too tall*," he added, without raising his voice. Then, ignoring her threatening stance, he stalked to the other side of the room and sat down. As Elene watched in dismay, he removed his boots and his sword and lay down upon the mattress, fully clothed, his arms tucked under his head in that arrogant pose that so annoyed her.

"Go ahead. Slit my throat," he murmured. "I'm so tired, I probably won't notice." And then, to her utter fury, he closed his eyes.

Elene stood staring at him for a long time, until finally she dropped her arm. She felt foolish brandishing a dagger against a sleeping man. And, from the sounds of his even breathing, her husband actually was slumbering, having forgotten her presence entirely.

Elene blinked. She was not accustomed to that. She glanced back at him, not sure what to do, but certain that she was *not* going to lie with him. Frowning, she assessed the tiles surrounding the bed and knew that she would have a hard night of it there. Then she walked around to where the chest sat in front of the window. Perhaps Geoffrey was right, and she could bed down inside.

Lifting the lid, Elene looked down at the clothes, taking petty pleasure out of wrinkling his finery. Dragging a blanket from the bed, she stepped inside, but there was very little space. And she felt too confined, as if the lid might come down upon her, trapping her. Elene shuddered. Perhaps that was Geoffrey's intention. As soon as she fell asleep, he would lock her in and carry her through the night to the grave the Wolf had prepared.... Elene sat up straight, suddenly seeing her cozy berth as a possible coffin.

Finally, she pulled a pillow from the bed and managed to prop herself upright, but, weary as she was, sleep escaped her. Resentfully she glared at Geoffrey in the glow of the fire, the slow rise and fall of his chest attesting to his own untroubled rest. Watching him, Elene had the distinct feeling that something had shifted between them irrevocably, a balance of power that she would not regain. Else why was he slumbering soundly in the bed, while she suffered in discomfort?

Somehow, when she wasn't looking, the saint had bested the Fitzhugh. Now what was she to do?

Elene shifted uncomfortably and knocked her head against something wooden. Sitting bolt upright, she found that her legs were twisted beneath her and one arm dangled over a hard rim. Faith, where was she? In a *chest?* Shaking her head to clear it, Elene immediately regretted her movement when her neck protested painfully. The edge of her makeshift bed had put a crick in it such as she had never known.

Groaning, Elene tried to lift herself out of her prison, only to collapse back down as her legs gave way. Taking a deep breath, she braced her hands on the sides and struggled out, even though every muscle in her body ached at the effort. With a gasp, she fell forward onto the bed, its giving softness mocking her sore limbs. For a moment, she simply lay there, like a fish on the shore, but then a slow, burning anger overtook her.

She ought to have slit his throat.

Images of Geoffrey sleeping peacefully while she sat up half the night fed her fury, until she found the strength to roll onto her back. Then she blinked as sunlight streamed in through the shutters over the chest, telling her it was well past morning. Faith, she had never risen so late! Sometime before dawn, she must have surrendered to the demands of her weary body, ignoring her uncomfortable position, her hard berth and the chill night wind blowing in through the window, to seek some rest. But, instead of feeling better, her battered flesh was in worse condition.

Although she longed for a good wash, Elene tossed her tangled hair over her shoulder, refusing to brush it or change her wrinkled garments. Now, more than ever, she

was determined to leave this place, and she would not get
her way by looking or acting agreeable. Scowling at the
flattened pile of Geoffrey's garments, she slammed the lid
of the chest and strode toward the door.

Her foul temper fueled her way down the stairs and
past the curious glances of Wessex's residents, although
her various aches and pains protested every step and turn.
Glancing around, Elene frowned more fiercely as she realized that she had missed the morning meal. Would she
have to starve now until supper? Opening her mouth to
swear loudly, she shut it abruptly when the sound of
laughter reached her ears. She stopped to listen, unwillingly entranced by the low, musical tones that were so
familiar and yet completely new and delightful.

It was Geoffrey's voice.

And his deep, gentle laughter acted upon her as a tonic,
a warm infusion of...something that traveled through her,
easing her anger and lightening her heart. The scowl faded
from her face as she realized just how rarely she had heard
it. Her goal momentarily forgotten, Elene sought out the
dark figure of her husband in the hall, leaning forward
over the table, his broad back toward her.

Stepping forward, Elene had nearly reached him when
she realized he was not alone. Of course he would hardly
be jesting with himself, she mused, but she halted, blinking in dismay, to see who shared his amusement. Close
beside Geoffrey sat Marion, gifting him with her dimpled
smile, while the Wolf was nowhere to be seen.

Elene felt that strange ache again, to see Marion cozy
and close to her husband, making him laugh and smile.
As she watched, they held a whispered exchange, and
Elene saw him lean back, his handsome face relaxed, as
she had never seen it before. Her throat tightened, making
it difficult to breathe. And to think she had wanted to save

this woman's life! Elene's eyes narrowed as the mystery of the Wolf's wife solved itself.

Marion was a harlot.

Elene knew of such women, for Edred railed about them constantly. They sold their favors to men or gave themselves willingly in a lust for power or attention, or from some misguided prompting of their bodies. Obviously, Marion had snared the Wolf with similar wiles, for men were always eager for those who feigned pleasure at their attentions. But why did she now dally with Geoffrey? Did she mean to cause strife between the brothers, or to feed her own twisted desires?

Well, it was no business of hers, Elene told herself, though she tasted a bitterness in her mouth that she could not so easily explain away. Geoffrey's vows to her were as nothing—and never had been—and she would never hold him to them. Yet, even as the thought flitted through her mind, Elene saw Marion reach out and place one of her small hands on Geoffrey's arm.

And suddenly, whether Elene willed it or no, the Fitzhugh roared to life.

"Whore! Get your hands off my husband!" she shrieked, and she charged forward, spouting her foulest curses, as Marion fell back, wide-eyed. But before she could reach the small woman, a large figure loomed in front of her as Geoffrey surged to his feet, coming between them. In one swift movement, he lifted Elene and slung her over his shoulder like a sack of grain. With the breath knocked from her, Elene could not speak as he swung around, bouncing her already aching body against his hard length.

"If you will excuse me, Marion, I have to speak to my wife. Privately," he said, his usually melodious voice rough with the force of an anger Elene had never heard before.

She blinked, her breath knocked out of her, as the tiles below swept dizzily through her vision. All thoughts of murdering Marion fled, and she decided to kill her hated husband instead. Resolutely Elene struggled upward, but her knives were in her boot and underneath her skirts, where Geoffrey had her with a muscular arm. When she wiggled, his hand came down on her behind, to steady her, and Elene fell back against him, her throat suddenly dry.

He did not even break stride as he took the stairs to their chamber, and Elene felt panic race up her spine at the reminder of his strength. Once again, the saint she had come to know had been replaced by a fierce warrior, a de Burgh. And, at last, she had pushed him too far.

Geoffrey had lost his temper.

Chapter Eight

Geoffrey strode up the stairs without a backward glance at the baggage over his shoulder. She had finally done it. For months he had been putting up with her wild behavior, foul mouth and senseless threats, but he would not stand for it any longer. Throwing open the door to their chamber with a loud bang, he kicked it shut with one foot, heedless of who would hear. Then he dumped the wiggling, kicking bundle in his arms onto the bed. She landed in a sprawling tangle of arms and legs and hair, spitting and hissing like a trapped feline.

Staring down at her, Geoffrey found that his usual eloquence had deserted him, for he could think of no words that would express his rage and disgust with the woman he had married. He opened his mouth, but all that came out was a strange gravelly noise that sounded suspiciously like one of Dunstan's growls.

Faith, he was not his brother! Clearing his throat, Geoffrey tried again, keeping his voice as low and even as he could. "I don't care how you treat me, Elene, but don't ever try to hurt Marion. She's an innocent, a warmhearted, caring and gentle woman." *Everything you're not*, Geoffrey thought as he watched his wife's mutinous expression. Obviously, his warning, like all else, was having little effect on the she-devil.

With an oath, he swung away. He was not sure what infuriated him more, that Elene had turned on Marion or that Marion had seen his wife at her worst. A slow heat burned his cheeks at Marion's knowledge of the painful truth of his life. It didn't matter what his brothers thought; they had never known of his secret yearnings, nor would they understand his wistful wish for love. But Marion saw things with a woman's insight, and he could not bear to face her pity for his lot. His fingers curled together into a tight knot. Faith, he longed to smash his fist into something—anything—to ease his frustration! And then, suddenly, he stilled, as he realized just what his wife had done to him.

He had lost his temper.

Geoffrey sucked in a sharp, angry breath. He had always prided himself on being different from his brothers. He was the one with the education, the son Campion claimed was most like himself. His conversation was not scattered with grunts or growls or drunken taunts, and he was not the kind of bloodthirsty warrior who took pleasure in battle. And yet now, he wanted nothing more than to grab his wife by that hair of hers and...

"I'll do whatever I please, and if I don't like your whore—"

At the sound of her voice, Geoffrey whirled around, effectively cutting off her defiant speech. Unfortunately, her rebellious manner remained in full force, for she was kneeling on the bed, her dagger drawn and pointing at him. Again. How many times had she threatened him with it? And each time he had let her, because she seemed to need the weapons, in some way he did not comprehend. But not this time. With one swift movement, Geoffrey knocked the knife from her hand and closed his fingers around her slim wrist.

"Marion is not my whore," he said, leaning over her with deliberate intent. "Marion is my *sister*. I know that you are so twisted inside that you have to make everything ugly, but don't try to turn Marion into something evil. She is well and truly good, and the best thing that ever happened to my family. And before this day is over, you will apologize to her for your execrable behavior."

Elene's amber eyes opened wide, as if in terror, and Geoffrey released her abruptly. Disgusted with himself, he sank down on the edge of the bed and rested his head in his hands. She was dragging him down to her level, and with the powerful imagination that came with his intellect, he could picture them quarreling like mongrel dogs for the rest of their days.

"Don't you ever lay a hand on me again, de Burgh."

At her words, Geoffrey lifted his head. He must be dreaming, he decided, for why else would he feel the prick of a blade between his shoulder blades? Why would any woman in her right mind threaten him again, when he had just bested her, when his temper was like a spark that could roar into flames at any moment? Geoffrey rose to his feet slowly, and turned, even more slowly, to face her. Incredibly, she was poised again on her knees, wobbly on the soft bed, her other dagger in hand.

"Don't come any closer," she warned.

With the swiftness born of skill and practice, Geoffrey knocked the second blade from her hand as easily as he had the first, rocking back on his heels as she howled in fury.

"Give me back my knife!" she screamed, launching herself at him with fists flying. She managed to scratch his face before he could subdue her, and the sharp pain made him shout at her in return.

"I'll give them all back to you when you start acting like an adult instead of a child, a bullying, willful brat! When are you going to take responsibility for your life? When are you going to take on some duties beyond scaring small children and giving me a headache? When are you going to serve as chatelaine, as you rightfully should? Oversee the kitchens? Make the manor into the kind of home it could be?"

For a long moment, she simply stared at him, her cat's eyes narrowed, her lips parted, as if in shock. Then her face twisted into a fierce grimace. "When you leave it!" she shouted, and she yanked her hands free to shove hard against his chest.

Geoffrey took a steadying step back and gaped at her, bewildered and infuriated because he could not make her see reason. Faith, the woman *had* no reason! With a low oath, he lifted a finger to his cheek. The she-devil had drawn blood.

"I should treat you like the child you are and turn you over my knee!" he said. Swiftly turning word into deed, Geoffrey grabbed her by the waist, sat down and hauled her down across his thighs. He was angry enough to do it, too, though his initial fury had settled into a cold, hard knot.

But, somehow, when confronted with the shrieking, kicking body on his lap, Geoffrey hesitated. His hand stilled upon her leg as his attention fixed on the gently rounded behind that the ugly wool of her gown could not disguise. The knot slowly dissolved under a growing heat while he stared at the bottom wiggling enticingly in front on him.

"Hold still," he said, but his voice was a rough whisper, barely heard over the pounding of his heart. Elene paid no heed, so he put his hand out to steady her, but when his palm met the warm softness of those curves, he drew in a sharp breath. His rage was gone, replaced by another dangerous, primitive force, and Geoffrey was dismayed to feel himself stiffen and jerk beneath her.

God's wounds, what had he become? Had he sunk so low as to be drawn to this wretched wench? Was he the kind of man who was excited by violence or the threat of it? Horrified, Geoffrey let his hands fall away, and Elene immediately twisted around to face him. Now, she was sitting on his lap, that soft bottom pressing into his hardness, and he stared at her, the thundering of his blood loosing something inside him.

As she opened her mouth to shout at him, Geoffrey took it with his own, his first, tentative touch turning hot and desperate. Suddenly, his wrath and disgust were forgotten in a rush of hunger such as he had never known. He wanted. He needed. The nearly feral desire consumed him, and he knew, with an instinct stronger than his intellect, that only this wild creature could assuage it.

His tongue breached her lips, seeking the taste of her, and he felt heady with triumph when it found her moist heat. Reaching behind her, he cupped the back of her head to hold her to him, but she gave no resistance. The fists that he thought would pummel him unfurled, and her palms slid up his chest to wind around his neck. Groaning low and deep in a voice unrecognizable as his own, Geoffrey turned and took her down upon the bed.

"Elene, yes, love, kiss me." He whispered encouragement against her mouth as he moved over her, his weight pressing them down into the mattress. "Yes," he breathed as she answered him with her lips. "Yes." All that stood between them was as nothing compared to the sweet meshing of their bodies. Geoffrey groaned again at the feel of her young breasts pushing against his chest. It was beyond his control now, the pounding in his blood, the heat in his groin. Never before had he grown so hard so fast, and he ground against her, driving his aching stiffness into the softness between her legs, decrying the clothes that stood between them.

It wasn't enough. Never in his life had his body demanded release so soon, so desperately. His liaisons were usually slow, flirtatious dalliances in which he took time to please the lady, as well as himself, never forgetting himself in the heat of the moment. But now reason and wit fled under the grinding force of his need, until he knew nothing but his desire. Reaching for the slender hand that was sliding down his arm, Geoffrey guided it downward, pressing the palm over his erection. "Touch me, Elene," he murmured, pushing himself into her fingers. "Yes. Oh, yes!"

Closing his eyes, Geoffrey sucked in a breath at the dizzying pleasure washing through him, unprecedented and beyond belief. But the momentary easement was followed by a sharp recoil. The warmth that enclosed him was snatched away, and the female body beneath his rolled from him, launching itself off the bed.

For a long moment, Geoffrey lay there, throbbing so violently that he could not gather his thoughts. He had been so close.... Blinking dazedly, he opened his eyes to the sight of a drab gown by the door, a tangle of long hair flying as the wood gave way, swinging open only to shut loudly, leaving him alone in the small chamber. Shuddering with stunned amazement, Geoffrey sat up and ran shaky hands over his eyes.

What had happened here...to him? He shook his head, shocked by his own behavior and by the knowledge that it had been Elene, the Fitzhugh wench of legend, who lay beneath him, furtively returning his kisses. And it had been her hand he placed upon himself with greedy abandon. Groaning, Geoffrey fell back against the mattress. He told himself that Elene was a shrew, a child in woman's clothing, a she-devil who represented everything he despised! Capable of God knew what manner of barbarities, she repulsed all who knew her, including himself.

Then why did it seem as if he had just awakened from a long sleep, his mind and body truly alive for the first time in memory?

For once in his life, Geoffrey ignored the question, instead of seeking an answer. Drawing in deep, fortifying breaths, he decided that his brief lapse of control with Elene was something that did not merit further study. It had been a momentary aberration, nothing more, brought on by the celibacy and stress of the past few months. An aberration, he termed it, even as he sensed the lie.

And although his knight's honor urged him to find Elene and apologize for his graceless groping, he balked at the task. He might have treated her more like a paid whore than like a wife, but she had threatened him, poked him with her knife and drawn his blood. Gingerly Geoffrey reached up to touch the long scratch. It would heal soon enough, but considering the cause of it made him frown.

She had acted like a child, as usual, until... Flushing, he recalled the taste of her on his tongue, the firm woman's body beneath him, and he swore softly as his heart began to pound once more. How could he, the calmest and most civilized of the de Burghs, have acted so impulsively? He groaned again, feeling oddly vulnerable. How would his wife treat him, now that he had all but attacked her? Would she stare at him with her cat's eyes vaguely accusing, or would she taunt him? Geoffrey stiffened, for he could well imagine the words she would use, the way she would mock his brief weakness.

Loosing an angry sigh, Geoffrey realized that he did not look forward to finding out. Nor did he relish facing Marion and her gentle pity. Rather, he would find Dunstan and pursue that relationship, which had soured somewhat since his marriage. The Wolf would take his mind off his wife.

Or, at the very least, remind him why he shouldn't want her.

Even a long day of riding Dunstan's lands could not drive Elene fully from Geoffrey's thoughts. He listened as Dunstan pointed out potential problems, and he made a list of repairs that should be completed on the demesne. But even as he hurriedly noted the Wolf's orders, he wondered about Elene.

Looking anxiously at the sky, Geoffrey tried to guess the hour and realized that he should not have left her to run free at the hall, wreaking havoc. What if she harmed Marion? All his efforts to subdue her had gotten him nothing but an unassuaged desire, he realized with sudden discomfort. What had made him think that her flight signified surrender?

By the time they finally returned for supper, Geoffrey feared what he would find, but nothing was amiss in the hall. Marion, smiling and untroubled as ever, was overseeing the servants, and Elene was not about. She did not come to the table to eat, either. The Wolf scowled at her absence, muttering about rudeness and questioning her motives, just as if he expected a lone female to disarm his entire army.

"Perhaps I should check on her," Marion suggested.

"No!" Geoffrey answered, a little too loudly. Either Elene was up to some mischief or she did not want to apologize to Marion, as required. Either way, Geoffrey did not want any further unpleasantness between his wife and his sister.

Although he would not offer up falsehoods to his brother, he explained away her behavior as best he could. "She was lying down earlier," he said. *With me on top of her,* he did not add. He had the fleeting notion that he had upset her sensibilities so much that she had killed herself, but quickly discarded that idea. More likely, she was planning to kill him, Geoffrey thought grimly. Gulping down his food, he made his excuses.

"I will make sure that she is all right," he said.

Dunstan snorted loudly. Obviously, he did not think it possible that anything could be wrong with the Fitzhugh, other than her disposition.

"I am weary, anyway, and would seek my rest early," Geoffrey added. He was not prepared for his brother's sharp glance of astonished assessment. Apparently, the Wolf could not imagine anyone sharing the same bed with Elene. Although his own thoughts in that direction were definitely not clear, the implied insult made Geoffrey stiffen, and he nodded curtly to Marion before taking his leave. Not for the first time, he rued his arrival here. Although he had been glad to see the babe, now he wondered just how soon he could leave without causing ill feelings.

His mood was not light when he swung open the door to the small upper chamber. It darkened considerably more when he saw that the room was empty. Where was she? Geoffrey felt a cold, hollow spot in the pit of his stomach, even though he had just eaten. Had she been gone all day? Had she left Wessex entirely? Although he knew Dunstan would be overjoyed at her disappearance, Geoffrey took no pleasure in it. She was his wife. And whether they willed it or no, they were bound together. He had lived up to his part of the bargain. Why couldn't she?

Because you attacked her.

"I didn't," Geoffrey whispered aloud. Although he had not exactly wooed her, he had not forced himself on her, either. He remembered her hands sliding around his neck and stroking his arm, and the tentative brush of her tongue against his. His heart pounded.

Yet she had fled as if the hounds of hell were after her. That image, a jarring departure from Elene's usual bold fighting stance, stuck in his mind like an out-of-tune note. Making him feel guilty for his sudden lust. Making him worry about her. About Elene? Geoffrey loosed a bitter sigh. And yet he sensed that she was not up to some mischief. He knew, without being aware how he knew, that she was licking her wounds somewhere. But where? Where would Elene go to seek comfort?

Nowhere. From no one. For she never had anyone to give it to her. The bleak answer came to Geoffrey abruptly, but he ignored it, telling himself that the Fitzhugh scorned solace. She was a termagant, a shrew! And yet he had seen her at times when she was asleep and vulnerable, when she was soft and yielding beneath him, when she was quiet and gentle with a pretty mare.... At the thought, Geoffrey drew in a sharp breath. Swiveling on his heel, he headed for the stables.

The groom who was drowsily watching over the horses for the evening knew nothing, but Geoffrey hardly marked the youth's replies. Elene was more than clever enough to sneak by the lad. Leaving the boy to nod off again,

Geoffrey strode through the building, halting before a ladder to a loft, where winter fodder was stored.

He found her there, curled up in a corner, looking so pathetic that he felt a brute for ever having raised his voice to her. Wrapped in an old blanket, she was sleeping soundly, and in the twilight gloom, he again saw the beauty that always surprised him. Yes, her hair was a tangle, but it was long and thick and spun with so many shades of spice that his hands itched to touch it. Her face was surprisingly small and smooth, her lips were firm and tempting. Faith, but when he looked at her now, he knew not to whom he was married. Sighing, Geoffrey leaned over and took her in his arms. Trying to ignore the sudden heat that swamped him, he kept a careful hold upon her, and she stirred only briefly as he carried her down the ladder, into the hall and up to their chamber.

Pulling back the covers, Geoffrey laid her on the linens and felt an odd sort of tenderness for his wild wife. She brandished no weapons now, nor did her mouth twist with a litany of foul curses. She seemed very young, clear-skinned and vital, and far more beautiful than any other woman he had ever known. Brushing back a lock of her hair, Geoffrey let his fingers sift through it, and his heart increased its pace. Dangerous business, this, he knew, for Elene could wake at any moment.

Stiffening, Geoffrey swiftly straightened and glanced around the room for a place to take his own rest. Unfortunately, as he had pointed out to Elene the night before, there was none. His gaze wandered back to the bed and lingered there.

She was his wife. That knowledge, along with the day's careening emotions, which had left him both tired and reckless, decided him. Walking around to the other side of the mattress, Geoffrey hesitated. And then, with a

rather uncharacteristic fierceness, he stripped off his
clothes and got into bed. At last, he would find his rest
as a man should, naked and comfortable.

Beside his wife.

Elene turned, burrowing closer to the body next to her
and the feelings it engendered. Warmth. Safety. Peace.
Things that had eluded her for years. Awareness hovered
out of her reach as she sank deeper into the dream of her
mother. If only it were real and she could lie again next
to someone who loved her. Comfort, security, and something else, a new sensation of delight, of pleasure, seeped
into her bones as Elene cuddled against the hard form,
her fingers resting upon heated skin. Bare, male, muscled
skin.

Elene opened her eyes abruptly to the dim light of early
morning. Staring at the unfamiliar bed hangings in confusion, she turned her head, only to blink in astonishment.
She had not been dreaming, nor was the figure beside her
that of her mother.

It was Geoffrey.

She stilled as panic soared through her. How had she
gotten here? Why was she with him? Why was he *naked*?
She drew a shaky hand to her throat and let loose a sigh
of relief when she found her own clothes intact. She
shifted slightly, but her body gave no signs of having been
abused. Weak with relief, she let her head sink back into
the softness of the pillow.

Her first inclination was to flee from the bed, the room,
the castle, but instead she stole a glance at Geoffrey. Since
he seemed to be still asleep, Elene took a moment to study
him. She rarely had the opportunity, and now, within the
confines of the bed, she could see just how beautiful was
the man she had married. His handsome features appeared

younger and more boyish, his thick lashes oddly appealing against his tanned cheek.

Elene drew in a harsh breath against the sudden urge to trace his straight nose down to the even curve of his lips, and she jerked her attention away from his mouth, to the strong jaw and throat, and... She swallowed at the sight of his muscled shoulders, so close. The one nearest her made her realize again just how strong he must be, yet the skin looked smooth to the touch.

Startled at the odd curl of heat growing in her belly, Elene returned her gaze to his head, where she noticed the thick, dark silk of his hair. It was getting long and a bit shaggy-looking, but even the need for a trim somehow made him all the more attractive, as if Saint Geoffrey were no more than mortal, after all.

The epithet Elene had given him made her frown, for it no longer seemed to fit the image of the man who had raged at her yesterday. Geoffrey had actually raised his voice and... Embarrassment flooded her as she thought of what had followed their argument, of what they had done together here, in this very bed. She blinked as the disturbing discovery returned.

He could kiss like his brother.

The memory of his hot, desperate mouth made Elene feel weak and giddy, but she had not feared that he would devour her, as the Wolf had seemed to his wife. Nay, it had been a sweet fire, a wondrous sensation that sent heat surging into limbs that had never felt the like, giving them life's blood, stirring something deep inside her.

Faith, she had never dreamed of such things! Of kisses that had made her dizzy and hot and hungry. And his whispers, broken, half-muttered pleas that had made her want to cede all to him, to do anything to ease him. Elene flexed her fingers, hardly able to believe that her hand had closed around him. The thought made her strangely rest-less.

And disgusted. No doubt his skills were well practiced upon many a maiden, Elene told herself. Was she mad, that she had let this de Burgh, however beguiling, work his wiles upon her? She had suspected some such scheme from the very beginning! Of all the brothers, they had chosen Geoffrey to wed her, because of his handsome face and soft speech. And now he would use them to steal her heritage.

Or would he? So far, Geoffrey had done nothing but try to improve conditions at the manor. Even as Elene tried to fit his actions into some grand scheme for revenge upon her, the accusations he had made rang in her head. *When are you going to take responsibility for your life?*

Elene frowned against the bitter memory of his words. She had taken responsibility for herself at an age when he was probably bouncing on his doting father's knee! If not, she would be long since dead or bartered off to the first passing knight with a handful of coins. Or beaten into nothingness by that bastard Walter Avery.

And she was still responsible for herself—not for her father's manor or for the people who fought over it. What did Geoffrey know of anything? The fool! She should have answered his taunts with her own, and she should have laughed at his attempts to seduce her, but he seemed to be able to strip away all her...

Elene scowled, refusing to finish the thought. So she had run away and hidden in the stables, when she should have been creating a scene, shrieking and throwing things and making herself unwelcome. But she had been so tired, weary from the long days of travel, the even longer night spent in the trunk, and the strain of her marriage. She had told herself she needed a moment to think, but her mind had closed down, giving in, finally, to exhaustion. So how had she gotten from a hay mound to this bed?

Geoffrey.

He must have found her and brought her back. The image of his hands on her when she was unaware struck her as both appalling and appealing. Who knew what indignities she had suffered in her sleep? But even as the suspicion appeared, she discarded it. Perhaps he thought to take her this morning, when she was sleepy and vulnerable. At the notion, Elene glanced over at him warily, but she could not work up the energy for the appropriate outrage. Despite his show of temper, she could not imagine Geoffrey forcing himself upon her.

But maybe he would not have to. Elene shivered as she remembered how easily he had moved atop her yesterday. It had been so sudden, so unexpected. That was how she excused her delayed reactions, she thought, flushing. One minute they had been fighting over Marion, and the next...

Marion. The memory brought her up short. Perhaps Geoffrey's sudden interest had been brought on by his brother's wife. Did he touch her because he could not touch his brother's wife? The idea struck Elene painfully where she had thought herself bereft of all sensation. Geoffrey had defended the dark-haired woman with a passion Elene had not known he possessed. Mayhap he loved her, but was too sainted or too afraid to betray the Wolf.

Elene frowned at the taste of blood, and she realized, absently, that she had bitten the inside of her cheek. Swallowing the sourness, she looked toward her husband through narrowed eyes. Suddenly, he seemed not so handsome and compelling, but only a man—a rogue and a brute. Sliding silently from his bed, Elene checked upon the knives she had carefully retrieved and hidden away.

Then she gazed once more upon Geoffrey as he slept so soundly. Oblivious to her scrutiny, he was vulnerable, and she rejoiced to see him so.

"Fair warning, de Burgh," she whispered, before turning to leave the room. She had no intention of playing the part of Marion for him, and should he try to cast her in the role again, she would kill him.

Chapter Nine

Elene wandered through the castle, surprised at the number of eager, bustling figures, although it was not much past dawn. In the great hall, a passing servant offered to fetch her an apple, and for a long moment, she simply stared in amazement. Didn't these people know who she was? She ought to show them, but somehow she didn't feel like shrieking and quarreling. And she *was* hungry. She had missed both meals yesterday and, having lost weight in the past months, she could hardly afford to grow any thinner. She needed her strength, and her voluminous gowns already were hanging on her frame.

Silently she nodded to the servant, who rushed off, to return not only with an apple, but with a hunk of cheese and a piece of bread, too. Elene eyed the offering suspiciously, for no one had eaten from her father's stores but at mealtimes. Except for her father. Resentment and hatred, long tempered, surged to the fore, and she snatched up the food.

"I hear that the weather is crisp and clear, if you care to take your meal atop the keep," the servant added. Then he hurried away, and Elene was left staring after him, wondering at that peculiar bit of advice. Did the Wolf wait above his lair, intending to push her off?

There was only one way to find out.

After a few twists and turns, Elene found the stairs up to the roof, but when she reached the top, no one awaited her there except a lone guard, who nodded as if he were accustomed to visitors. Elene blinked in surprise. Her father's soldiers had all been untrustworthy, and so she made a great show of slipping out her dagger and watching him warily while she ate.

But soon he turned his back and wandered away, walking along the battlements and surveying his lord's lands. Relaxing slightly, Elene looked out herself and drew in a sharp breath at the sight. Dawn was a glowing pageantry of colors on the horizon, casting light upon the hills and forests spread out before her as if God himself were moving his hand over the world.

Although she had been up early often enough before, Elene had never noticed, never having the opportunity or inclination for such a view. Nor had she been awed by anything for a long time. The rising sun hurt her eyes, and she blinked back moisture. It was beautiful, a beauty that was unlike anything she had seen, except perhaps…Geoffrey.

Choking on a bite of apple, Elene spat it onto the smooth stone. Such thoughts were dangerous, as was wasting her time admiring the landscape when she should be alert for possible threats. This was the Wolf's lair, and she had best remember it. For all its delightful scenery, Wessex was the source of all her woes, the lure that had driven her father to his destruction, stolen her heritage and left her a pawn in the games of men.

And yet, staring out over the busy, awakening demesne, Elene could not work up her usual sense of outrage. The calling of the birds and the brisk morning breeze, along with the vivid splashes of color above the hillsides, seemed to dispel her usual suspicions. She was weary of her constant alertness, of looking for plots and schemes in the behavior of others. Perhaps, just this once, she would sit here quietly and simply enjoy the morning as best she could, away from the turmoil that raged in the castle below—and within herself.

Elene's resolution engendered an odd sort of peace that teased her with a familiarity she knew was false. Her life had held no contentment, and yet it was as if she had felt this way before, and recently. Closing her eyes, she sought the memory, only to straighten abruptly when it came to her.

The only other time she was so at ease had been this very morning, when she awakened safe and warm in her husband's bed. Fool! Scowling at such wayward thoughts, Elene ignored the vague yearning that Geoffrey seemed to inspire, and turned her attention to her makeshift meal.

The small repast helped Elene to avoid dinner, and she kept to herself, for she was not eager to see the Wolf, his dimpled wife, or her husband. The thought of facing Geoffrey after he had carried her to their chamber and slept beside her was bad enough, and she also had yet to come to terms with the way he had kissed her yesterday. Her cheeks flaming at the memory, she determined to avoid him.

Rather than make herself unwelcome in the hall, she wandered through Wessex. She had seen drawings of other, larger castles, and had heard tales of those more luxurious. But no matter how often she told herself that Wessex was old and small and cramped and damp, Elene knew a treacherous admiration for the place. Obviously, Marion was doing her best to make it habitable, for Elene could hardly imagine the Wolf being responsible for the tapestries or the cozy pillows.

Hearing voices in a large upper chamber, Elene halted, stepping toward the open door stealthily. Inside, she saw Geoffrey, and for a moment she was arrested by the sight of him, so dark and handsome, but a glimpse of the Wolf's huge bulk sent her shrinking into the shadows. She lingered at the doorway, however, for she was accustomed to watching and listening. It was the best way to arm oneself against the treachery of others, and so she leaned forward to hear her foes.

She was rewarded with the Wolf's deep speech. "Why don't you come live here, Geoff? It would make Marion happy. You know how she misses all of you."

"She's got a baby now to think about. I'm sure she isn't pining away for a bunch of surly de Burghs," Geoffrey answered lightly.

The Wolf scowled. "Well, I wouldn't mind having you here myself."

Geoffrey smiled—a beautiful glimpse of white teeth that did something funny to Elene's insides. "Thank you, Dunstan. I'm flattered. Especially since there was a time when you couldn't get far enough away from your brothers." The Wolf grunted, as if he did not care for the reminder, but Geoffrey did not flinch. "No," he said, more seriously. "I thank you, but there is still much to be done at the manor."

The Wolf growled something unintelligible, then muttered, "Beginning with your wife." Elene tensed, moving deeper into the shadows as he continued. "Can't you at least get her to take a bath?"

Geoffrey turned, his mouth quirking, as if in amusement. "I'm afraid not. Elene has a mind of her own," he answered as he walked slowly around the room.

"That's just the problem, Geoff!" the Wolf replied. "Obviously, she needs a firmer hand. I knew that Simon would have been better suited to the task."

Geoffrey turned swiftly at the words, and Elene was startled by the fierce look he gave his brother. For once, he seemed just as dangerous as the Wolf, perhaps more so. "Nay," he said with a strange ferocity. "Elene is my wife, by God's will and my own."

Blinking, Elene swayed on her feet at his low declaration. It struck her like a hot iron, aching and burning parts of her that she had thought no longer existed, and she clung to the wall for support, while the Wolf, too, reeled in surprise. "God's wounds, Geoff, do you have to be so noble about it?" he demanded.

Geoffrey chuckled, the intensity on his features replaced by a rueful humor. "Aye. Elene calls me Saint Geoffrey. I expect the proper obeisance from you, brother."

The Wolf gaped at him, then shook his head, as if confused by the jest. "You could take a leman," he suggested.

Geoffrey stilled, and Elene sucked in a harsh breath. A leman! Although she had heard of lords who kept women other than their wives, her father had never done so. She doubted whether any female could have held his interest long enough to qualify for the title. But Geoffrey...

Elene imagined him turning the force of his concentration on one woman, and she shuddered. She told herself that if occupied elsewhere, Geoffrey would be less of a threat to her, yet somehow the idea was not comforting. Geoffrey's suspicious relationship with Marion made her anything but comfortable, but it could last only as long as a visit, while a leman would live with them at the manor. An errant draft tickled Elene's neck, sending a chill through her body, right down to her bones, as she waited to hear his answer.

"No," he said, coldly. "I would no more take a leman than would you." The words were a gentle scold, and Elene released a ragged sigh. Something akin to relief surged through her so strongly that she sagged against the wall once more, only to jerk upright at the sound of a soft rustling somewhere behind her. Intent upon her husband, she had forgotten all else, but she was swiftly reminded of her vulnerable position. Bending low, Elene ran a hand over the dagger hidden beneath her skirts and whirled to face the intruder.

It was Marion. To Elene's surprise, the lady of the castle did not flinch at her threatening scowl, but smiled. "Elene! How lucky to have found you," she said in a soft, conspiratorial tone that made Elene blink. "Come along to my chamber. 'Tis where I usually do my sewing in the afternoon."

Elene shot a quick glance at the solar, but Marion was already turning away, and she had to hurry to follow. The Wolf's wife led her into a spacious great chamber, twice as large as the one at the manor, and it was obvious she had made her mark here, too, with brightly colored pillows and a real chair turned to catch the sun from one of the long, narrow windows. Elene stifled the sharp bite of envy.

Restlessly walking around the room, Elene stopped to finger the edge of an unfinished tapestry. "Do you like it?" Marion asked. She held up the piece, and Elene had to bite back a gasp of astonishment. A wolf, stark and bold, was rendered on a field of green, while Wessex rose, partially completed, behind.

"No," Elene lied. Letting the material fall from her fingers, she moved past it, unaccountably annoyed by

Marion's talent. But the woman took no umbrage at the insult. She simply motioned for Elene to take the chair while she sat upon a low stool, and Elene did so, enjoying the petty pleasure of the better seat.

"Do you like to sew?" Marion asked.

"Not really," Elene answered, suddenly aware of her rudely fashioned garments. She made them because she had to, not for the joy of it, and she was not skilled. Nor did she have a host of attendants to do the work for her, she thought bitterly, like the rich, spoiled wife of the Wolf. Elene never had known anyone to help her, aid her, protect her....

"How long were you there?" Marion asked.

"Where?" Elene asked, confused by the sudden change in subject.

"At the door."

Elene blinked in surprise, then scowled. "Long enough."

Marion sighed. "I am sorry, then, for what you heard. I must apologize for my husband. He likes the world to be made up of black and white, the issues clear and defined, so sometimes the shades of gray elude him."

Elene stared at the woman, not bothering to hide her bewilderment, for she had no idea what the Wolf's wife was babbling about.

"He should never have suggested such a thing, to Geoffrey of all people," Marion explained, her mouth turning down into a frown.

Elene sat back and watched the woman from behind a tangle of hair. Obviously, the Wolf's wife did not approve of his talk of a leman for his brother. And no wonder, when she craved that position herself! "He doesn't want a leman because he wants you," Elene declared.

For a long moment, Marion just stared at her, agape,

and then she laughed—a lovely, fresh sound that filled the room. "Geoffrey and I? Oh, no! I love Geoffrey dearly, and I think he cares for me, but 'tis the affection of a brother toward his sister."

Elene's eyes narrowed suspiciously, for why should she believe the Wolf's wife?

Marion reigned in her amusement and took a deep breath. "Two summers ago, Geoffrey and Simon came upon me on the road. I was hurt, and they escorted me to Campion." She smiled wistfully. "Those rough warriors took me into the family like a sister. And a sister I was. If you do not believe me, you can question any of the de Burghs, for when it came time for me to leave, the earl asked each of his sons to marry me, and none would take me to wife!"

Although Marion related the story with a swift smile, Elene nearly flinched at the thought of such rejection. "Why not? Why would no one take you?" she asked, looking the short, shapely woman up and down, as if to find some hidden fault.

"They are all independent men, set in their ways and wary of change, especially of such an irrevocable kind!" Marion said, laughing. "'Tis amusing to see these big warriors shrink from something as simple as marriage, but they do. And they are all honorable men who would not take to wife even an heiress whom they did not love."

Her last words were spoken so seriously that Elene shot her a surly glance. "Not so Geoffrey."

Marion hesitated, as if unsure what to say. "No," she answered slowly. "I was there when the king's decree arrived, so all knew that someone would marry you." Pausing, she studied Elene with a surprising intensity. "You could do no better than Geoffrey. He is the wisest and most learned of them all. The gentlest and most kind.

I believe that things are often meant to be, my own fate included, whether 'tis the hand of God or some other force that moves us.''

Elene started at the mention of the hand of God, for she had fancied it moving the sun across the earth just this morning. Frowning, she glared warily at Marion.

''Although this marriage was forced upon you, perhaps it will work for your own good, if you let it. Geoffrey is a wonderful man who obviously has come to care for you—''

Elene shot to her feet with a snort. ''Geoffrey abides me sometimes. Nothing more!'' she snapped, unwilling to listen to such foolishness. Phantom pain assailed her again, and she had to choke back a cry at its sharpness. Faith, what was happening to her? Had she been struck by some malady?

''Very well,'' Marion said, gently. ''I shall speak of it no more. But come, I have something to give you!'' Walking over to a large chest, she pulled out a long length of fabric. Curious, Elene stepped closer, only to suck in a breath at the sight of the rich forest green cloth. She released the air in a rush when Marion took out a beautiful yellow silk and held it up to her.

''What are you doing?'' Elene snapped.

''Yes, I think these two will do,'' Marion said, blithely ignoring Elene's question. She dug deeper and Elene could see that the entire trunk was filled with material and furs. ''Ah, and this!'' she said, pulling out a heavily embroidered oyster white linen. ''Yes, it will look beautiful with your hair!''

''What?''

''We'll put my attendants to work upon making you some new gowns. I'll even help myself!'' Marion said.

Elene was stunned speechless by the suggestion, but

then suspicion returned, for she knew that nothing came without a price. Her eyes narrowed. "Why?"

Marion appeared surprised. "Why, because you have married into the de Burghs and should have some fine new things. I'm sure Geoffrey would have thought of it himself sooner or later, but his mind seems to be much occupied with the manor."

Elene stepped back, away from the tempting fabrics. Did Marion think to dress her up and make her a fit wife for one of the handsome and powerful de Burghs? Well, she cared nothing about her husband's family, or their heritage. Let them scorn her, for she had no wish to please those bastard brothers!

"I want them not," she said.

Marion's smile faltered. "But I have no use for all these lovely fabrics. Dunstan likes to give them to me, and, though he did not marry me for my wealth, I think sometimes it galls him to know what I brought to his coffers. So he would gift me often and well, perhaps to ease his mind."

Elene scowled at the lovely green material, which was far better than anything she had ever owned. Indeed, it seemed to surpass the finery her father had worn, and with that thought came a rebellious desire to have it, if only to spite his memory. She slanted a glance at Marion. "Why me?"

Marion grinned once more, revealing both of her dimples. "Because you are my sister now! You cannot know how I have longed for a family, all my life, really. And the de Burghs, they took me in, giving me not only a place to stay, but a place in their lives. Oh, they're warriors all, rough and gruff, and yet each one has a good heart, each one is special." Fixing Elene with those doe eyes bright with truth, she blinked away sudden moisture to speak more briskly. "And ever since I married Dunstan, I hoped that one of them would wed, so that I might have a friend, a lady with which to share."

Elene stared at her. A friend? She had never been one, or had one, either. A lady? No one had ever called her that. No one except Geoffrey.

That elusive ache was back, stronger and sharper than ever, making Elene wonder if she was wrong about the de Burghs. Perhaps they were not land-hungry scavengers, but a dynasty of decent men, knights who thought more of honor than of a full purse. Perhaps one, especially, among them was good and kind and learned.... A child's cry broke into her thoughts, and Elene jerked her hand away from the silk she had been absently stroking.

"Ah, the baby is awake," Marion said, unperturbed by the increasingly loud wail. "And he has the lungs of his father!" She walked over to where a cradle sat, in a corner not far from the hearth, and picked up the child as she made soothing sounds.

The Wolf's son, Elene thought, her bitterness returning. Although tiny and helpless now, the boy would grow up to be no different from his sire or his uncles, another great bully of a de Burgh. Or would he? Somehow, she could not work up any hatred for the babe, who was quieting in his mother's arms.

Elene eyed him warily. She rarely saw infants, for mothers kept their little ones away from the infamous Fitzhugh, as well they should! Having seen so few newborns, Elene gave in to her curiosity and stepped closer, to see his small face and his perfect little fists.

"He is a hungry one, just like his father," Marion said, and with a smile of apology, she took the chair that Elene had vacated. Watching Marion cuddle and coo to the babe, Elene felt funny inside, an eerie sense of both loss

and longing that made her turn away as the child began
to nurse.

It was not the first time she had seen a baby at breast.
Her mother's last child, the one she died bringing into the
world, had been fed by one of the village women, though
her father had begrudged the girl child even that. But it
had been sickly and had soon joined their mother. Elene
flinched at the memory, long buried. Although she had
resented the infant who had killed their mother, she had
cared for it, holding it, comforting it and drawing comfort
in return…until it left her. Like everyone else she had
ever cared about.

Elene sucked in a deep, shaky breath that sounded loud
in the sudden silence. She had to get away…from the
child, the Wolf's strange wife, and Wessex itself. Stum-
bling, she headed toward the door, but Marion's voice
stopped her.

"Come sit, and talk with me, while I feed him," she
urged. "I would know my sister better."

Sister! Marion choked back a bitter laugh. Child. Husband. All were naught but words, signifying nothing, for
in reality, there were no ties of blood. Not trusting herself
to speak, Elene turned on her heel and left Marion and
her perfect world of healthy babies, indulgent husbands,
besotted brothers, wealth and luxury. Pampered and pet-
ted, the Wolf's wife had no idea what life was really like.

And Elene hated her for it.

If Marion was upset about Elene's abrupt departure, she
said nothing, and at supper she was her usual mindlessly
happy self. Silently Elene watched her with disgust and
fascination, for she had never seen anyone who was so
relentlessly cheerful. And she was continually surprised
by the way the Wolf treated his wife.

Yes, he was gruff and growled a lot, like a big bear, but he also fed her the best morsels from his fingers, leaned close to whisper to her in a way that seemed shockingly intimate. Then he bragged about her and his son to all and sundry.

Elene studied him through narrowed eyes. Perhaps every new father behaved thus—when the child was a boy. If it was a girl, no doubt it would have been trundled off to the far corners of the castle and the negligent care of an unhappy servant. And if it died, all the better. After all, the de Burgh brothers boasted no female siblings. And yet, Elene could see no unhappy servants, and she could not really picture Marion giving up the baby easily. Somehow, the Wolf's wife seemed to be more substantial, as if her gentle warmth and good humor covered a core that was solid as a rock.

Elene scowled at the observation, for she liked not the woman, nor had she any intention of changing her opinion of Marion as spoiled and stupid. As if aware of her scrutiny, the Wolf's wife turned those large doe eyes toward her and laid a tiny hand on her husband's arm. "Oh, I think Elene's heard enough about our son," she chided him.

The Wolf blinked, obviously having forgotten Elene's existence, and, none too pleased by the reminder, he frowned at his wife. Marion, however, appeared oblivious to his grimace. "I would that you tell her more about the de Burghs, so that she can know one brother from another."

The convivial atmosphere at the table abruptly disappeared as several pairs of eyes focused on Elene. Lowering her chin, she glared at Marion menacingly. Why had the woman forced their attention upon her?

Geoffrey cleared his throat. "She's met them all, Marion. At the wedding," he said.

Elene opened her mouth to voice her opinion of the brutes, but something in Geoffrey's tone, an underlying weariness, made her stop. Instead of his six threatening brothers, she saw his face, dark and intent, over her as he put her hand to his.... Dropping her gaze to the remnants of her meal, Elene closed her lips and ferociously attacked a meaty bone with the small eating knife they let her use.

"Oh, but you know how fierce they can be at first!" Marion protested. "You would never know it to look at them, but they can be as playful as boys." Both brothers gaped at her as if she had gone mad, and Elene had to stifle a snort. "Of course, Robin is the most fun. He loves to play at jests, so be wary of him! Once, he filled my bed with chestnuts," Marion said, laughing at the memory.

"What was he doing near your bed?" the Wolf growled.

The deep, rich sound of Geoffrey's laughter surprised Elene, and she turned to stare at him, so handsome and carefree as his head tilted back, his long hair brushing his shoulders. "Did he torment you, too, Marion? I swear he put everything in mine over the years except for the Holy Grail—though once he had poor Nicholas convinced that Saint Gregory's shinbone had miraculously found its way under his pillow during the night!"

A low, rumbling sound erupted from the other side of the table, and Elene glanced in startlement toward the Wolf, who threw back his head and roared. "I remember that! He always had some false relic, like Saint Olaf's eyelash!"

"And the first coin owned by Matthew, patron saint of bankers!" Geoffrey said.

"Never mind that it was a smooth piece of rock!"

"Because Stephen told him the image had been worn off!"

"Stephen?" Marion prompted. She appeared totally enthralled by the ridiculous stories, of course, Elene thought with a frown.

"Aye, it was always Stephen who would hoodwink poor Robin and the younger boys into trading him their possessions or doing his work for him in exchange for such fakery," Geoffrey explained.

"And would those younger ones have included you?" the Wolf asked, a grin splitting his face that so transformed his features, Elene blinked in amazement.

Geoffrey chuckled ruefully. "All right, I admit it. When he showed me what he claimed was the toenail of John Chrysostom, patron saint of public speakers, I gave him my portion of the night's pudding, but only because I had to recite some of my studies the next day!"

Marion's laughter joined with the deeper voices of the men in such an infectious sound that Elene was hard-pressed not to smile herself. She frowned instead.

"Aye, that clever Stephen had quite a busy trade going," the Wolf said.

Geoffrey's grin slowly faded. "Until Father caught him trying to sell Reynold a tooth he claimed belonged to Gilbert of Sempringham."

"The patron saint of cripples?" Marion whispered, a stricken look on her face.

"Aye," Geoffrey said. The jovial mood of the three faltered, and Elene tried to remember Reynold. Had he been the bitter one with the limp? She had thought it some war wound, justifiably received in battle, but perhaps he had been born with a deformity. The notion disturbed her, for she did not care to think of the de Burghs as possess-

ing human frailties like a long-suffered injury. Or deep
pride in a new son. Or a fierce bodily need that made a
man beg his wife to…

"Nevertheless, Reynold can be just as playful as the
others. I remember once when he stole my sewing and
tossed my thread from one to the other so I could not
reach it," Marion said. "Why, even Simon, who is the
eldest after Dunstan, and the fiercest warrior of them
all—" she paused to grin at her husband, who appeared
to take umbrage at her declaration "—even Simon has a
sense of humor."

The two brothers eyed her with so much skepticism that
Elene felt her lips twitch. "He does!" Marion asserted.
And then the three burst out laughing once more. It was
such an odd experience, listening to them, that Elene felt
as though she were dreaming. Laughter was something
she had not often heard at the manor. Her father had
sought his amusement in the torment of others, yet these
de Burghs seemed to find humor in simple stories and
shared memories.

Elene tried to ignore them, but the insistent appeal of
Geoffrey's delight roused something deep within her, a
yearning so fierce she blinked in dismay. Although she
remained silent and unyielding behind her veil of hair,
some small, betraying part of her wanted to join them, to
become one of their…family, even if it was an illusion.

Even if it was all a scheme to ensnare her somehow.

With an effort, Elene forced herself to reject the de
Burghs and the inviting closeness they seemed to possess.
Lowering her chin, she glared out at them with a ferocity
that sprang only partially from enmity. Jealousy was new
to her, yet she embraced it, as a way to keep her husband
and his relatives at bay, for she dared not trust them.

Life was too hard, too full of dangers and threats that

Marion, with her pretty smiles and clever stories, knew nothing about. Elene was familiar with the perils that awaited the unwary, however, having vowed long ago not to be waylaid by anyone or anything. And she would not be tricked by deceit, charmed by a handsome face or lured by laughter.

She was a survivor, and she would survive the de Burghs.

Chapter Ten

Elene glowered at her sister-in-law, wondering if the woman's perpetual smile hid a vacant mind. She had heard of such people, although her father would allow none at the manor. Possessing of only a few wits, they were supposedly contented with their lot. Elene smiled evilly. Yes, Marion might well be an idiot and, as such, what a fitting wife for the Wolf! So amused was Elene by the idea that she choked back a snort of laughter. Marion, busily stretching a length of slender rope down to her feet, looked up in surprise.

"I'm sorry. Did I poke you?" she asked, concern so bright in those big eyes that Elene scowled. Shaking her head curtly, she nevertheless seized the opportunity to complain loudly about what was being done to her. Against all reason, she was standing still while Marion measured her for new gowns she had refused to accept.

"I would have you finish this foolishness, for, as I have told you, I want not your gifts," Elene snapped as Marion tugged on her arm. For a small woman, the Wolf's wife was surprisingly strong. And stubborn.

Still, Elene knew she was the superior fighter. She ought to just throw the dimpled creature to the floor and put a dagger to her throat. That might, at least, remove the ever-present smile from her face! Elene let out another short laugh, but this time Marion did not even glance at her. Obviously, the woman had no idea of the danger she was in. And it was that, perhaps, that stayed Elene's hand. That and…Geoffrey.

Elene flushed at the memory of her husband, and how she had, once more, awakened by his side. The night before, she had been too tired and out of sorts to sleep in a trunk. Defiantly taking her place in the bed, she had tried to sleep, but it had eluded her until Geoffrey joined her. She had held her breath in silence, her eyes firmly shut, as she heard him remove his clothes and slide in beside her.

It had been on the tip of her tongue to advise him to put his garments back on or face her blade, but somehow she had fallen asleep before she could make the threat. And she remembered nothing else until this morning, when she had stirred before dawn to find herself cuddled too close to his naked form. Faith, her knee had nearly brushed his groin, and her fingers had been curled in the hair upon his chest! Heat suffused her cheeks, and she lifted her fists to cool them.

She had fled to the battlements, where her first hot embarrassment gradually faded, leaving an odd sort of warmth deep inside her. Another spectacular sunrise had moved her, and she had no longer felt a bitter, driving need to leave Wessex. For the time being, she had decided she would watch and wait. For Geoffrey's sake.

And so, when Marion found her and urged her into a bath, she had complied—instead of slitting the woman's throat, which would not go over well with Geoffrey. And, in truth, she had been sorely in want of a good wash. The hot water had felt good, but now, standing here in her shift, her wet hair hanging down her back, she was rapidly tiring of Marion's prodding.

She opened her mouth to call a halt, this time for good, but a knock on the door diverted her attention. "Enter," Marion called cheerfully, while Elene started in protest. She was not used to wearing so little, even in front of female servants, and she snarled in dismay at the Wolf's wife as the door swung open.

To reveal Geoffrey.

It seemed to Elene that her husband grew more handsome every day. After his initial tension, he had settled in at Wessex with a casual familiarity. He seemed younger and more carefree, and she often heard the rich ring of his laughter in the hall. In fact, he was smiling now, as he held up a roll of parchment and strode into the room with an easy grace. "Marion, there's a message from Campion. Dunstan thought you would—" He stopped suddenly, the missive dangling from his lax fingers and his eyes widening in surprise at the sight of his wife in her shift.

For a moment, Elene simply stared back at him, her face flushing crimson at her state of undress. Since her marriage, she had always been fully clothed, even in sleep. She had never changed, or even removed her slippers, in his presence, and now, here she stood with nothing but thin linen, damp in some places, covering her, and her hair swept back behind her.

She had never felt more naked in her life.

The silence in the room was so palpable Elene could taste it, and yet, oddly, she could not seem to utter a sound to dispel it. Her chest rose and fell rapidly, her breath coming quick and shallow, as her eyes remained locked with Geoffrey's own—liquid, brown and inviting. Her whole body felt strange and warm, as if he had reached out to touch her with his overwhelming presence. Her legs were unsteady, and her nipples stiffened, to peak against the damp material. And when it seemed his gaze dropped to those hard points, something funny happened to her insides.

He cleared his throat, the rough noise jarring her from her eerie daze, and Elene frantically reached for her hair, dragging it over her face and breasts. She opened her mouth, but what came out sounded more like a weak moan than like the virulent oaths she had intended.

"I'll, uh, leave this for you," Geoffrey said in a strangled voice, and then he backed out of the room, looking pale and dismayed, before he disappeared into the passage.

"Thank you, Geoff!" Marion called after him.

Marion! Elene had forgotten all about the other woman's presence, and now she whirled upon her, ready to take her to task for this latest shameful episode. But when she turned, she was halted by Marion's peal of laughter.

"Did you see that?" she asked Elene, giggling delightedly. "I vow, I have never known Geoffrey to look so guilty—like a boy who has been caught up in some mischief!" She sat back on her heels and chuckled. "'Tis good to see him so smitten by your charms."

Elene stared at her, certain now that the woman was quite witless, but Marion simply rose to her feet and began laying out the rich, dark material she had chosen. "I can begin this myself. Why don't you go on to your chamber, and I'll send him to you?" Marion said, one dimple peeping out of her smooth cheek. But some of Elene's horror must have shown on her face, for Marion's smile swiftly faded. "What is it? Surely Geoffrey hasn't hurt you?" she asked.

"You fool! He doesn't want me, nor I him!" Elene shouted all the louder, in order to convince herself. She had never wanted anyone, least of all a de Burgh. Least of all her sainted husband, the man who had taken her own hand and put it to him. Shaking with reaction, she reached for the clean gown, old and drab and serviceable, that she had brought with her, and yanked it over her head.

"But I have seen Geoffrey with other women, and he has never been so discomposed. 'Tis obvious he desires you," Marion protested, with a look of bewilderment. "I don't understand. Surely your marriage—"

"You have no notion of my marriage or my life, you spoiled creature! An heiress living a life of luxury, what could you know of me?" Elene snarled as she thrust her arms into the sleeves, suddenly desperate to get away from this woman, with her probing questions and her feigned concern.

"No, I don't," Marion admitted softly. "Would you like to tell me?"

"*No!*" Elene cried, fumbling with the laces in her haste to escape. She had held her own against her father and his men, but this one small woman seemed to threaten her composure far more than they. They had been blissfully ignorant, but this woman, whether witless or no, seemed to see far too clearly.

"Well, perhaps you would like, then, to hear of my story," Marion said. "Though you might be disappointed to learn that yours has not been the only difficult life."

Elene froze, her fingers still tangled in the laces, and stared hard at the little woman who dared speak so to her.

Ignoring the harsh glare, Marion took her seat and drew in a deep breath. "Yes, I was an heiress. My father was lord of Baddersly, a prosperous demesne in the south, but

I lost my parents when I was young.'' Her matter-of-fact admission drew Elene's attention. She blinked, listening intently now.

''My life was then dominated by a cruel uncle who coveted my lands. Perhaps he was like your father. Perhaps not. I only know I was not as strong as you, for I became a shadow of myself, isolated from anyone who would befriend me, afraid of testing his wild moods. I learned not to speak or react, for fear that he would strike me.''

Elene flinched, for her father had never raised a hand to her. In truth, she suspected he had been too little interested to bother when she was young, and later, when she grew strong in her own right, he had let her be, professing amusement at his wild daughter.

''Finally, while he was away, I made my escape, but he must have known of it, for he sent his men disguised as common ruffians to murder me and my attendants. I live only because of the timely arrival of Geoffrey and Simon, who were running an errand for their father, but a blow to the head caused me to lose my memory. As I told you before, they took me to their home. However, my uncle soon demanded me back, and so Dunstan was chosen to drag me from the only family I had ever known into what I was too terrified to remember.''

She paused, as if struggling to go on. ''Our train was attacked, and all were killed. As I stood there, looking at the carnage, his men, the young squire, all dead...'' She drew in a deep breath and continued, more briskly. ''When I saw all the bodies, my memory returned. 'Twas both a blessing and a curse, for I knew what awaited, but could not convince Dunstan until it was nearly too late.''

She smiled, as if the Wolf's refusal to believe her had been nothing more than a slight annoyance. ''The rest of the trip was fraught with dangers, and when we returned to Wessex, Dunstan found his castle taken by your father. I was there when Avery captured him, but I hid myself away. Then I rode to Campion alone, guided by the sun and the stars, afraid that anyone I might meet would be an enemy—either my foe or Dunstan's. 'Twas not an easy trip.''

She sighed, her eyes luminous as they sought Elene's. "But I made it. The de Burghs came to our aid, winning back Wessex and my lands from the uncle who would have killed me, and now, at last, we live in peace. And I appreciate it all the more for the struggle.''

Elene blinked, stunned by the story, in which horrors were so swiftly related as to be forgotten. She knew they were not, and yet nothing in Marion's demeanor hinted at such a history. This woman had found her way across the countryside alone when Elene feared traveling beyond her own gates. The knowledge shocked her, shaking her to the very core of her being.

"So you can see why I enjoy my life to the fullest and celebrate our happiness," Marion said, waving an arm to encompass her luxurious surroundings. "We cannot always forget the past, but we can let go of it. Perhaps you should try doing that, too," she added gently.

Elene stared, too overwhelmed by Marion's simple declarations to even consider her advice. Suddenly, she realized the depth of her foolishness, and it cut her to the quick. She had thought herself brave and fierce and Marion a witless weakling, but now she knew the truth.

The Wolf's wife was much stronger than she would ever be.

Somehow Elene escaped. She wanted to rant and rave and scorn Marion's story, but nothing came out but a strangled sigh, so she fled the Wolf's wife, her chamber, the castle itself. Faith, she would have liked to run from her own skin, but that was not possible.

Elene didn't go to the stables, where she had so often found solace when she was younger. It was not comfort she sought, and, as Geoffrey had reminded her, she was no longer a child. She went to the walled garden, where the first buds were rising from Marion's well-tended earth, knowing that no one would think to look for her there. As everyone knew, the Fitzhugh despised all that was delicate and fresh and beautiful.

Didn't she?

Elene wasn't sure anymore. She was trembling. Shaken, inside and out. She had heard of great earthquakes and biblical reprisals, for Edred had spoken often of the punishments awaiting sinners, especially women who did not properly respect their masters. Elene had always laughed contemptuously at the time, but now she felt as if she were caught up in some great cataclysm, her world upside down, her outlook skewed. Her beliefs, her values, the very way she had chosen to live her life, were suddenly open to question, and she did not know the answer.

She had thought her way the only way to survive, but Marion had remained true to herself and had endured—triumphed, even—making Elene reassess all that she had ever done. And as her most basic beliefs threatened to crumble, so did others. Were the de Burghs murderous bastards or honorable knights? Was Geoffrey a land-grabbing brute or a quiet scholar, a gentle man who had treated her far better than anyone ever had? Was he acting and scheming, or was he simply good and kind? Elene shuddered like a fish out of water, flopping this way and that, uncertain.

Who was the spoiled child, Marion, with her luxuries

and her happiness, or Elene, with her shouts and threats? Had she fought for so long that now she tilted at shadows, automatically pushing away everything and everyone, when there was no need? She gasped and drew in a shaky breath as she realized she was certain of only one thing.

She no longer knew who she was.

Although Elene sat there for the rest of the afternoon, she discovered no answers, no great revelation that explained all. She simply acknowledged that there were other ways besides her own, other opinions, other truths, and she could no longer ignore them.

She was still sitting on the cold bench when Geoffrey found her, his speech rough with concern. "Elene! One of the servants told me you've been out here for hours without a cloak." She blinked, suddenly aware that the spring air had turned cold, the gentle breeze to a chill wind. But what cared she? She had already been through a storm, raging inside her.

"Are you all right?" Geoffrey asked. When she didn't respond he knelt before her. *Knelt*, without hesitation, as no man ever had before her. Was he even aware of his own beauty? His dark hair gleamed rich and clean, his eyes were warm and soft with anxiety. Feigned or real? Elene could no longer tell.

"Are you unwell?" She shook her head. "Faith, I would have you curse at me, so I know you are yourself," he said, giving her a crooked grin that made her want to weep. *But I am not myself. Do you know who I am?* she wanted to ask. Instead, she said nothing, and Geoffrey leaned closer. He took her hand, rubbing his callused fingers over hers, and she felt a surge of heat that was both alarming and comforting.

Instinct told her to jerk away, but Elene was too tired to protest, and she let Geoffrey wrap her in a cloak and put his hands on her without flinching. He spoke gently, softly, as was his wont, and she looked at him in wonder, as if seeing him for the first time. His face, poised over hers as they stood, was so handsome, and his brown eyes were soft and filled with knowledge. Elene marveled at that wisdom, at everything he had read and learned while she… His gaze suddenly dropped to her mouth, and Elene felt a new rush of heat that drove away the cold and the memories and all that threatened her. Then, as if to mock her thoughts, the wind swept a long tangle of her hair between them.

"Come," Geoffrey said hoarsely. "Before you catch a chill."

Elene went with him, but deep inside, there was a new warmth that had nothing to do with the heavy wool or the elements, a stinging awareness that the world just might be different from anything she had ever suspected.

For the first time in her life, Elene tried to make herself inconspicuous. Watching and listening had always been a way to know her enemies, but now she practiced it more, as if she were a visitor in a foreign land, studying the strangers with a sort of detached curiosity. Still suspicious, she remained on the periphery of the de Burgh family group, not participating, but looking and seeking her own kind of knowledge.

The relationship between the Wolf and his wife, especially, drew her attention, for she had known little of married couples beyond her father's cruel torment of her mother and her own brief, forced union. Certainly, she had seen village couples before, freemen and villeins, but their lives were harsh and distant, their wooing characterized by coarse humor and squealing—until the babies came.

Dunstan and Marion were as different from them as

night from day. They argued and raised their voices, yet
Dunstan never lifted a hand against his wife. And Marion
did not shrink or hide from him, but returned his shouts
with her own. And these bouts were usually followed by
passionate reconciliation, including public displays that
made Elene flush.

Indeed, whenever the two were together, they seemed
always to be touching, to brush against each other subtly
or brazenly, if only with their eyes. And Marion did not
giggle or shriek, but practically purred when the Wolf
caressed her gently, his great strength held in check. For
once, the big brute reminded her of Geoffrey. And, grudgingly, Elene decided that even the Wolf could not be all
bad.

Not only was he gruffly tender, but he waited upon his
wife, doing her bidding with ease, as she did his, and this
give-and-take astonished Elene. More amazing still was
how Marion *teased* the Wolf, coaxing from him a harsh
smile or rough laughter, just as Geoffrey sometimes tried
to tease her, Elene realized, swallowing an odd lump in
her throat. She could only shake her head in wonder when
she heard Marion bait her husband, or even scold him,
and the Wolf did nothing but grunt and grin while his
brother laughed.

What magic did the dark-haired woman possess, to
wield such power over her husband? Surely all this lar-
gesse did not come simply from eagerly embracing his
bed? To Elene, Marion's influence was awesome, and she
was determined to find out how the woman had obtained
it. And so she found herself letting the Wolf's wife fit her
with new clothes that she would never wear. Trying not
to notice how the soft material felt against her body, or
the richness of the fine colors and trimming, Elene studied

the other woman through narrowed eyes and ventured the query that haunted her.

"What is your hold upon the Wolf?" she asked abruptly.

Undaunted by the question, Marion slowly folded back the sleeve and smiled. "The only hold I have upon him is that of love—his for me and mine for him."

Elene snorted loudly. Did the woman think her stupid? Power was what moved people—the power of strength, wealth, soldiers or secrets—not some ethereal emotion. "Is it your money?"

"No, for Dunstan could have easily married me when he learned I was a heiress. He did not. He only wed me later, ostensibly to keep me safe, but he cared for me already. He just did not recognize his love for what it was. Sometimes people, particularly those of a stubborn nature," Marion said with a dimpled grin and a glance toward Elene, "refuse to admit the affection they feel."

Elene scoffed. Perhaps Marion was truly dim-witted. "What, then? Is it because you let him have his way with you whenever he would?"

Marion giggled gaily and stepped back to look at her, but Elene refused to meet the woman's gaze. Already she could feel a betraying blush steal up her cheeks, and she lowered her chin, letting her hair hide it.

"Having his way?" Marion said. "Is that how you view the delights of your marriage bed?"

Elene grew warm, both inside and out. Delights? The woman was mad. When Elene made no reply, Marion's great eyes filled with concern. "Surely Geoffrey has not hurt you?"

Elene laughed contemptuously. "As if he could, for I would carve out his liver should he touch me!" A brief look of shocked surprise crossed Marion's face before she knelt to adjust the hem of the gown. For a moment, she was silent as Elene watched the top of her dark head. Then she spoke gently.

"I suppose I was lucky in that I didn't have to fret about my wedding night. You may think ill of me for it, but I'm afraid that I had already given myself to Dunstan. I loved him, you see." Elene blinked in astonishment. She had done it willingly *before* she was wed?

"I admit I was quite shameless. Oh, at first I despised Dunstan. After all, he was taking me back to a bad situation and refused me a say in the matter." Marion paused, sighing dreamily. "But he grew on me, you see, and I came to realize that underneath all that arrogance was a very lonely man, who needed me as much as I needed him."

Elene made a choked sound of disagreement, but Marion ignored it, keeping busy with her task. "I yearned for his kiss and his touch, for the way his passion nearly consumed me with its heat. He is a big man, and forceful, but, if I wish it, he will lie back and let me ride him, or take him into my mouth until he is the one consumed."

Eyes widening in stunned astonishment, Elene simply stared when Marion glanced up at her. "You don't mind my plain speaking, do you?" Both titillated and alarmed, Elene could not even find her voice to respond, while Marion explained what she most liked the Wolf to do to her in their bed, and the finer points of the various positions they enjoyed.

The more explicit her speech, the more Elene felt like covering her ears. Visions danced before her eyes, visions of Geoffrey doing such things, and they intermingled with her memories of the day he had put her hand to his hardness, when he had whispered urgently to her, the great knight, the brilliant scholar, begging for her touch.... But woven in among the visions were others, more insidious, and they drove away thoughts of Geoffrey until all Elene saw was red, the vivid color of fury and fear and blood. *"No!"*

The shriek startled her, for it escaped from her throat in a long wail that sounded nothing like her usual harangues. Dimly she saw Marion look up in surprise, then heard the crying of the baby, protesting the disturbance.

"What is it, Elene?" Marion asked, her expression worried. "Have I offended you? I thought, since we are both married women—"

"See to your squalling brat and leave me be!" Elene shouted, glad for the interruption and eager for the chance to leave. She didn't want to think about what Marion had told her, didn't want to be plagued by strange, frightening yearnings, or anything else that marked her as vulnerable—because she was not.

She was the Fitzhugh.

Throwing off the nearly completed gown, she marched from the great chamber back to her own, leaving Marion alone in the great chamber with her son.

"There, there, sweet one," Marion whispered, as she picked up the boy and held him close. He quieted, as if puzzled by her unusual tone, and Marion sighed deeply, her heart filled with dismay.

"What have I done?" she asked the infant in her arms. "I thought to help her, but mayhap I have only made things worse."

Chapter Eleven

Geoffrey stirred in his seat in a corner of the hall, watching idly as his brother held court. He had often joined his father during such days of justice at Campion, but this was his first opportunity to watch Dunstan, and he was surprised at his brother's fairness. Too often he had thought of the Wolf as a warrior only, but age—or Marion, Geoffrey thought with a slight smile—was tempering his strength with wisdom.

He glanced up as Elene walked into the hall and blanched at the sight of him. For a moment, he thought she might turn tail and flee from him, and he stiffened in surprise. Surely not Elene? He rose to his feet and went to greet her. For the past few days, she had been looking at him strangely, or rather even more strangely than usual, and Geoffrey was at a loss to explain this new behavior. He had done nothing differently, yet he had caught her staring more than once, with such intense interest that his heart pounded warily. Then she would turn away, as if embarrassed. Elene, embarrassed? Geoffrey shook his head. She was ashamed of nothing.

And yet, he couldn't help remembering the other day, when he had come upon her in her shift, and she had blushed, a maiden's pink flush that suffused him with heat. Then she had seemed a different woman, lithe and lovely, with all that hair wet and gleaming, her breasts high and firm beneath a worn layer of linen, and that dark patch visible between her thighs. Geoffrey sucked in a breath as his body tightened at the memory of her, half-naked and tall and strong.

Was that why she avoided him, because he had seen her thus? Was it the lack of clothing that had distressed her, or that she had appeared more approachable, more human, more starkly female? Willing both his thoughts and body to his control, Geoffrey stepped forward to greet her civilly. Although she looked as if she would veer off into the kitchens, he moved swiftly, cutting off her exit. He had wanted to speak to her privately, but had had no chance, for she seemed to be avoiding him lately. And he dared not approach her in their chamber, for fear of what might happen...bloodshed or—

Abruptly he cleared his throat. "Good day, wife," he said, his voice coming out oddly hoarse. Elene ducked her head in the now familiar gesture, but Geoffrey thought he glimpsed a blush beneath her veil of hair. What had brought that on? Was she thinking of the other day, as he had been? His mind threatened to wander again down that path, and he forced it back to attention. "I would speak to you," he said.

"I am on an errand and have no time for idle chatter," Elene answered. She walked past him, but Geoffrey caught her wrist, halting her passage. He rarely touched her, certainly never to hold her prisoner, and yet he was piqued by her rejection of him, especially when she would so welcome his news. Too late, Geoffrey realized his error, for she would hardly tolerate his hold, and would surely turn into a raging termagant, disrupting Dunstan's court and bringing the Wolf's wrath down upon them both. Quickly he pulled her with him into a shadowed corner, thinking to somehow quiet her.

But she said nothing, only looked at him with amber eyes wide and confused, bewildering him in turn. Geoffrey opened his mouth to speak, but her skin felt smooth and warm beneath his fingers, and her pulse was racing in an unnatural rhythm that seemed to harry his heart into thudding loudly. He looked down at where they were joined and felt a pull, a compulsion to slide his hand up her arm and around her, to feel her supple curves. Then he heard the breath leave her body in a loud hiss as she jerked her wrist away. She rubbed at it, as if he had hurt her, though Geoffrey knew he had not.

"You can say nothing I wish to hear," she said, but her voice lacked its usual force, and her glare wavered. Her hair fell forward, thick and tangled, and Geoffrey felt an unreasoning urge to wrap his fists around it.

"Not even that you finally have your wish?" he asked, gruffly.

"What?" She lifted her head, and he could see the flush burning her cheeks. Was she unwell? Or had the hall turned oppressively hot? He felt warm, too. Too warm.

"To return home," he whispered, trying to focus his thoughts on the conversation, when they wanted to drift to her unruly locks and pink skin. She eyed him with such alarm that his concern grew. "Are you all right?"

Instead of raining him with abuse, Elene ducked her chin and looked away, mumbling, "I am fine. When do I go?"

Geoffrey stared after her, startled by her restraint. "We shall stay out the week, I think, and then, if the weather is clear, I would like to be gone, though I have yet to broach the subject with my brother." He glanced toward

Dunstan and frowned, for he suspected the Wolf would not greet his departure with enthusiasm. And as his liege lord, he could order Geoffrey to stay.

"We both go?" Elene said, her voice sounding oddly faint in his ears. Faint and low and husky.

He nodded. "Of course."

"Very well." She turned her back to him then, as if eager to escape his presence, and he followed her, annoyed by her hasty exit.

"Is that all you can say, after you've pestered me and threatened me for weeks? Elene!" He called after her, but she was already hurrying off, pretending not to hear him. Geoffrey didn't know what was more astonishing, that she didn't answer his charge with a hail of abuse or that she seemed less than thrilled by the news he had thought would so please her.

There was no pleasing her.

Sighing, Geoffrey pinched the bridge of his nose, where a headache was coming on, and cursed the cause of it. The woman was a lunatic, he decided, and more fool he for treating with her. Still, he was tempted to go after her. Where did she go in such a hurry? What errand could she possibly have? Geoffrey wondered. No doubt she was planning how to burn them all in their beds.

Beds. The thought of where he had been sleeping, and with whom, made Geoffrey draw in a sharp breath. He had been lying next to his wife, naked, nightly, and it was becoming increasingly difficult to sleep, especially since he had seen her damp from her bath. Groaning, Geoffrey rued the day he had defiantly taken his place beside her, for now he was stuck there, uncomfortable, his body waking up hard each morning, even though Elene was gone. Even though he knew better than to consider her anything more than a wife in name only.

She was a she-devil, who was probably plotting his demise right now, he thought sourly. He really ought to try to find her, just to be sure she was not up to mischief. Straightening, he looked toward the stairs, and moved with fresh purpose. Perhaps his wife was with Marion.

But Marion was alone with the baby, and Geoffrey felt an odd sting of disappointment that he attributed to his awkwardness around the newborn, certainly not disappointment at the absence of his wife. At least Marion was happy to see him. She was seated in a chair by the window, sewing something, while the infant slept in a cradle near her feet, and she smiled so brightly that he could not mistake his welcome.

"Geoff! Come, sit down beside me. You have been too busy with Dunstan of late to spare a moment for me," she gently chided.

Geoffrey grinned, a bit guiltily. In truth, he had not wanted to hear Marion's condolences for his bride or his loveless marriage, and so he had been keeping his brother company more often. But now that they were alone, he would take the opportunity to tell her of his plans.

"Forgive me, but I will do better the next visit," he assured her.

"You're leaving? So soon?" Marion protested. "Why, it seems as if you have but newly arrived. Surely you have not been here a month."

"No," Geoffrey admitted. "But 'tis time. I have much yet to do at the manor, if Dunstan will let me go."

"He will not force you to stay, though I know he would like you to remain. You are his favorite, Geoff."

Geoffrey shrugged away the compliment. "That is only because he sees me more than his other brothers. Now that the weather is good, you should invite them all to meet the heir.''

Marion dimpled. "I'm sure they can hardly wait to hold him!" she teased, and Geoffrey laughed at the vision of his rough warrior brothers delicately handling the baby.

"Perhaps not hold him, but they should pay their respects, and Campion must be eager to see his grandson,'' Geoffrey said, stepping toward the cradle.

"Yes,'' Marion said. "Now that 'tis not so cold, I will not worry about him traveling so.'' The two exchanged a significant glance, followed by an awkward silence. Although glad that someone else had noticed his father's needs, the reminder of the earl's age was not a pleasant one. He looked down at the baby, who slumbered so peacefully.

"Geoff.''

"Hmm…'' he murmured as he studied the sweet, if rather homely, infant.

"About Elene.''

Geoffrey nearly groaned aloud. It had been a bad idea to come here, he realized belatedly. He had no desire to discuss his wife with Marion. She wouldn't understand. No one did.

"Geoff? I wish you would not judge her too harshly.''

"Who?'' he said, looking up in surprise.

Marion smiled at him indulgently. "Your wife.''

"Oh.'' He stared at her dumbly. Surely Marion didn't like the she-devil?

"I think behind all that fierceness, there is a good person. In fact, sometimes she reminds me of Dunstan,'' Marion mused, and Geoffrey gaped at her in astonishment. His volatile, violent wife bore no resemblance to his honorable brother. Dunstan was a knight and baron, fair and just and beloved of his bride. He wanted to protest, but Marion continued. "She is much like Dunstan in that she sees only black and white. Sadly, in her case, 'tis mostly black. There has been little light in her life, Geoff."

"Still, you can hardly compare Dunstan to that wild creature!" Geoffrey sputtered.

"Oh, can't I?" Marion asked. She eyed him soberly. "When Dunstan was charged with taking me back to my uncle's home, he gave no thought to my pleas, no credence to my warning that he was taking me to certain death. He treated me as if I were a mindless fool, while he was all arrogant callousness. He never even asked me to marry him, just announced that it would be best to avoid my uncle's retribution."

Geoffrey was stunned by her frankness, but not by the story itself. Too well, he could recognize Dunstan's sometimes overbearing manner. And after their marriage he had often sensed the discord between them. Though it was apparent that they loved each other, Dunstan had seemed reluctant to admit to it.

As if reading his thoughts, Marion smiled. "Ofttimes, I thought of running away, but instead I fought for him, against his own stubbornness. As your father once said, I tamed the Wolf. It was not easy, but it was well worth the struggle. For whatever reasons, some people find it difficult to let themselves *feel*. In Elene's case, I hate to speculate, but I'm sure her upbringing had something to do with it. What kind of life could she have had with her father, no mother, no honor or gentleness in her life?"

"Yes," Geoffrey admitted slowly. "But you, too, struggled through a terrible childhood, and you are the sweetest person I know."

Marion laughed and dimpled. "Thank you, dear brother! But everyone is not the same, as you well know.

Each of us has our own strengths and must survive our own way. I do not think Elene is as fierce as she would have us believe, but, like a hedgehog, uses her prickly exterior to ward off her enemies. Have you ever seen her strike a person or an animal?''

Geoffrey lifted a hand to his healed face and frowned, but before he could answer, Marion continued. ''My uncle took delight in kicking his dogs and beating his servants. Yet I see none of his evil in her.''

''You forget that she murdered her first husband in cold blood,'' Geoffrey said dryly. Faith, sometimes he disregarded that little fact himself. He would do well to have a reminder.

Marion drew in a sharp breath, her serious expression turning bleak. ''I had forgotten,'' she admitted, almost to herself. ''Seeing her with you, watching the two of you together, I did not even think of Avery, that monster. Oh, dear, and just the other day I—'' She broke off, her eyes wide with dismay.

''What?'' Geoffrey asked, growing concerned at her manner.

''Oh, Geoff,'' she said, her voice breaking. ''I never saw him, but I heard him, heard him turn against his own lord, taunting and tormenting Dunstan for no reason but his own greed.''

''Avery?'' Geoffrey asked, shuddering at the reminder of the man who had betrayed and beaten his brother.

Marion nodded absently. ''So much was made of his murder, perhaps because Elene already had such a notorious reputation, or perhaps because his manner of death touches some deeply buried fears in all men. I won't presume to speculate. But I ask you to consider why a woman—any maid—would kill a man in her bed.''

Geoffrey's immediate response was to echo what all

the de Burghs had suspected: that Elene was a bloodthirsty wench who did not care to be married. He opened
his mouth to voice that opinion, but something in Marion's face stopped him.

"Why would she kill him and not you?" she asked
softly.

Geoffrey swallowed his reply, and for the first time
since taking his own vows, he wondered what exactly had
transpired that night. At first, he had not cared to dwell
upon his predecessor's fate, and later, for reasons he did
not want to study, he had preferred to ignore the thought
of Elene with another man.

But it had not been just any man who was knifed on
his wedding night. Walter Avery had been bereft of honor.
As Marion reminded him, the knave had betrayed and
brutalized his own friend and liege lord. If he could do
that, how would he treat a woman? Geoffrey felt a
strange, cold dread in the pit of his stomach. Had Avery
hurt Elene? Geoffrey flinched from the thought, but he
knew that the Fitzhugh would not suffer in silence. She
would strike back, as most women would not. Had she
been named a murderer for it?

Swamped with guilt, Geoffrey loosed a strangled sigh.
He knew more of Elene's past than anyone. Why had he
not considered this possibility before? Why hadn't he
made more allowances for her? Why hadn't he killed
Avery himself, in the chaos of battle? If only he could
have gotten his hands on the bastard! Geoffrey cleared his
throat roughly. "Did she say something to you?" he
asked, half afraid to hear the answer.

Marion shook her head sadly. "You know she would
not, but she also appears to know nothing of the ways of
men and women. And she became distressed when I spoke
freely of them."

Geoffrey felt himself flush hotly. Not only was he un-used to such conversation with a woman—even Mar-ion—but it was as if she were accusing him of some lack because he had not bedded his wife.

Just as the silence grew uncomfortable between them, the baby cried, and Marion rose to go to him. But before reaching for her son, she put a hand on Geoffrey's arm in gentle comfort. "I do not claim to know what has hap-pened in her hard life, nor would I push you to any action. All I would ask is this, for her sake and your own," Mar-ion said. "Don't give up on her."

It was time to go. As much as Geoffrey had enjoyed seeing Dunstan, Marion and their child, he was accom-plishing little at Wessex except dancing attendance upon his brother, while his new home required much. He told himself it was duty that called him back, but there were other reasons for leaving. Despite Marion's kindness, he felt under constraints, caught betwixt his wife and the Wolf. His marriage made it impossible to recapture his earlier, carefree days at his brother's castle, and he knew Elene was unhappy.

Or was she? She did not seemed thrilled with the news of their departure, but then, Elene never was happy, Geof-frey thought with a sigh. Then he paused, struck by his own blithe observation, while his talk with Marion made him reexamine his casual conclusion. Was Elene one of those who took delight in her own misery, or was her discontent real, and not of her own devising? When she cast aside his kindness and mocked him for it, Geoffrey had blamed her virulent nature, but now he wondered if the reasons behind Elene's behavior were darker and more complex. What, really, did he know of his wife?

Whatever the answers, Geoffrey knew that Elene was

not likely to give them to him. Rubbing his eyes, he leaned back against a soft pillow, enjoying his easy berth while he could. He would find no such comfort at the manor, which boasted no solar, or ease of any kind.

Nothing was easy anymore.

"When are you leaving?" The sound of his brother's voice made Geoffrey jerk in startlement. He had heard no one enter the chamber, and cursed himself for his inattention. Distractions were forever plaguing him of late. And he knew just what was the biggest one.

"I had thought two days hence," Geoffrey admitted. "But how did you know?"

"Marion told me, and made me swear not to growl at you, whatever the devil that means," Dunstan said. Although he appeared none too pleased by his own promise, he only looked Geoffrey in the eye, his expression sober. "I wish you would stay."

"I know."

"Humph." A grunting noise that could not quite be termed a growl escaped from his brother's massive chest. "Very well, but at least let me send some men on with you."

When Geoffrey would have protested, the Wolf halted him with a heavy hand. "I know you want to do it all yourself, Geoff. Day of God! I was the same way about Wessex, but I suffered for it, depriving myself of good advice, companionship, and your skill with my accounts." He smiled ruefully. "Don't make the same mistake. Take a couple of my trusted knights with you."

Although his first inclination was to refuse, Geoffrey pondered the offer. He did not want to introduce his own guards into the household, alienating his people further, but he remembered his confrontation with Montgomery and knew well that there was always the danger of further betrayals. As if reading his thoughts, Dunstan chided him gruffly.

"You are too trusting, Geoff. I like not the thought of you there all alone, among Fitzhugh's old army."

"They are sworn now to me," Geoffrey pointed out.

Dunstan made a low sound of disagreement. "We all know how swiftly allegiances may shift, especially when an heir lives on...." He trailed off, as if he knew better than bring up Elene, but he caught Geoffrey's gaze and held it. "You need someone to watch your back."

Geoffrey nearly laughed aloud, for had not his wife told him the very same thing? He was tempted to relate that piece of information to his brother, but somehow he did not think Dunstan would appreciate the irony.

"There's something else, Geoff." Dunstan's gaze slid away, and Geoffrey stiffened at his tone. Surely his brother would not harp upon Elene again? "I've been thinking about what you told me of the manor's empty coffers, and I just can't believe it."

Geoffrey relaxed, though he was puzzled by Dunstan's words.

"Fitzhugh had money, lots of it, from his wife, who was an heiress well above him. That's how he funded his war upon me, paying for extra soldiers and supplies. He always had the most expensive weapons and clothes and even jewels. Rumor had it that he took his wife's and had them made into rings and trinkets for himself."

Dunstan expressed his opinion of that practice with a low grunt before continuing. "The point is, Geoff, that I just don't think it was all lost in the war, even after his knights were ransomed. He knew the state of this castle, so he had to have something put by to keep it up, to maintain his comfort."

Geoffrey tented his fingers and studied his brother. Although Dunstan's arguments were reasonable, he was wary of the motive behind them. And he was not so sure he agreed with Dunstan's conclusion, for he could well imagine a greedy fool like Fitzhugh spending all in his quest for more land and power. Nor could he imagine the man coveting anything else. "I can't say that I've seen much in the way of luxury at the manor," he noted dryly.

"Oh, you know what I mean, Geoff!" Dunstan's voice was a low rumble that gave away his impatience.

"No, I don't," Geoffrey said, his own nerves becoming taut with tension as his suspicions grew. "Perhaps you had better make it clear."

Dunstan looked uncomfortable but determined as he spoke again. "I think she's got it hidden away somewhere."

Geoffrey laughed aloud, and the sound echoed bitterly in his own ears. "Yes, I see how she's wasting it upon fine gowns and jewels for herself," he said, his voice heavy with sarcasm.

Dunstan looked so fierce, Geoffrey feared that he might smite something. "Damn it, Geoff! She won't spend it on fripperies, but on buying men to turn against you or to bury a knife in your back. Don't let your misguided sense of honor blind you! This woman is dangerous! She needs to be locked up or sent away—a convent, perhaps, though few would take her in good faith. You'd have to find that fat purse of hers to bribe them."

Geoffrey tried to concentrate on Dunstan's words and ignore the hot, violent rage sweeping through him. It was out in the open at last, his brother's hatred for Elene, and he told himself that he should be glad of it, for he believed in truth and honesty and direct dealings. But for the first time in his life, Geoffrey wanted to leap for his brother's throat, to take him to the ground and beat some sense into his thick head, though Geoffrey was not sure he could succeed. Although older, Dunstan outweighed him—and with plenty of pure muscle. Still, Geoffrey was tempted....

This is your liege lord, he told himself as he wrestled the teeming red wrath to a manageable level. He was the one who supposedly possessed the cool head. The negotiator of the family, Campion called him! But now he struggled for control while trying to look at the problem logically.

He could understand why Dunstan despised Elene. The Wolf had gone through hell because of her father, and Dunstan obviously had transferred that hatred to the daughter. Although she had not pursued her father's war, she was not a woman who won hearts. She was the antithesis of sweet, gentle Marion, who mothered everyone with a welcoming warmth. And Dunstan, as Marion herself admitted, usually saw things in black and white, without the varying hues that made Geoffrey less decisive, less certain of his opinions.

Less certain of Elene. Despite his wife's behavior, Geoffrey could not hate her. Sometimes, he even found himself admiring her strength and her spirit and her other, less obvious attributes... Geoffrey sucked in a harsh breath. As Marion had reminded him, Elene had known none of the advantages that the de Burghs had taken for granted. Who knew what her life had been like, and who was he to judge her? Indeed, who was he to blame her, if she had taken her father's gold?

Yet Geoffrey found it hard to believe that Elene was hoarding money stolen from the manor's coffers. If he had not borrowed stores from Campion, her diet would have suffered along with that of the rest of them. And although she did not seem to care for anyone, he could not picture her robbing the very food from her people.

And then what? What would she do when she watched the manor falter and die around her—run off to London town with a fat purse? Geoffrey knew her distaste for travel, and he had the feeling that she gained strength from her birthplace. He sensed her connection to the manor with a gut instinct that all the reasoning in the world would not dismiss. And he could not imagine her betraying it.

Nor could he envision her buying soldiers to overthrow her husband. Mayhap he was thinking with other parts of his body, but Elene did not seem to share her father's lust for power. She professed contempt for all things men held dear. Often enough she had decried his presence and threatened to kill him, but with her bare hands, not by hiring another to do the deed. And, though given plenty of opportunities, she had done no more than scratch his face.

"'Tis not Elene," Geoffrey said softly. He heard the Wolf's impatience growl and ignored it. "But if, as you say, the money is gone, then someone else could be responsible." Deaf to his brother's arguments, Geoffrey suddenly wished he had not dismissed Montgomery so swiftly. The knight had been close to Elene's father. Perhaps he had availed himself of funds none except Fitzhugh knew about. Aye, Montgomery could be the culprit.

Or Serle. Abruptly the steward, with his beady eyes and unintelligible records, came to mind, and Geoffrey well recalled the hefty expenditures with no explanations noted in the accounts. Surely Serle, with access to the household's supplies, was the most likely suspect.

"All right," Geoffrey said. "I'll take the knights, and I will look among my people for a possible thief." He stood and fixed his attention upon his brother. "But I will take my wife, too."

"Geoff!" For a moment, he held Dunstan's gaze and the two wills clashed, Dunstan's stronger, but Geoffrey's tempered by patience, and finally the elder turned away, muttering a low oath. "I shall summon two of my best for you, Geoff."

"Thank you, brother," Geoffrey said softly, raising an arm to grasp his sibling in fellowship. For now, at least, all stood as well as it could with his elder, and Geoffrey was relieved at the knowledge. Yet, as he followed Dunstan from the solar, he realized that his eagerness to go home was now tainted with a dark unease. After the relative peace of Wessex, the manor loomed ahead, full of strife and suspicions. To return seemed like willfully stepping into a nest of vipers. And though Geoffrey had tried to shrug off Dunstan's warnings about Elene, they lingered in the air, clouding his thoughts, just when he most needed a clear head.

He realized full well that a den of enemies awaited him, but what of his wife? Could he count Elene as friend or foe?

Chapter Twelve

Elene's feelings upon leaving Wessex were far different from when she had arrived, far different, in fact, from any she ever could have imagined. Instead of being elated, she knew that now familiar tingling ache as they passed the outer walls, and cursed under her breath. Why was she so plagued? Was it some insidious illness, or was she truly possessed, as Edred so often claimed?

Whatever the sensation, it was not disappointment, Elene told herself fiercely. Had she not demanded to depart from the moment she entered the Wolf's lair? And to that end, she had made herself so unwelcome that only a fool like Marion would tolerate her. Despite herself, Elene flinched at the thought, especially the memory of how she had spat at the lady's feet. Filled with something that felt suspiciously like regret, suddenly she wasn't so certain about her past behavior. Or the return home. The manor didn't seem quite so inviting as it once had, while the Wolf's old castle, though drafty and cold, appeared warm somehow, as if Marion's dimpled smile and her husband's strength had infused it with heat, like sunshine through gloom.

Elene snorted aloud at such fancies, but there was no

denying that people acted differently toward her at Wessex. With the exception of the Wolf, they did not fear or revile her. Some were wary because of her outbursts, but most approached her in a friendly fashion and waited upon her with smiles. Because she was Geoffrey's wife.

Not the Fitzhugh.

Unaccustomed as she was to such treatment, Elene was not sure that she wanted it to end. And all tangled up with her confusion over her place in the world were images of Marion and the baby. The Wolf's wife had hugged and kissed her, practically growing teary at their departure, and although Elene still thought her dim-witted, she could not deny her kindness.

By contrast, the manor's residents—beady-eyed Serle, the surly servants, ranting Edred and the threatening remnants of her father's army—hardly seemed an improvement. Nor did the plain, cold walls of her old home bear comparison to Marion's, with its bright touches of color and comfort. Smaller and more crowded than the castle, the manor would nonetheless feel empty of life, as if death haunted every passage. And sometimes Elene thought it did. Swallowing a thick lump that had formed in her throat, she looked away from the disappearing castle and found that her gaze had wandered instead to a pair of wide shoulders in front of her.

She would still have Geoffrey.

The thought came to her from nowhere, stunning her with its appearance, and even more startling was the sense of peace that came with it. False security, she told herself with a mocking laugh, but it lingered, wrapping around her like a heavy cloak and driving away the demons. Frowning, Elene took a deep breath. Obviously, all this travel was taking its toll upon her. Why did Geoffrey have to drag her over the countryside, anyway? Once they were home, she wouldn't let him budge her from her own hall, her room, her bed....

The question of her future sleeping arrangements sneaked into Elene's thoughts, making her even more restless and unsettled. Would Geoffrey go back to his pallet, or would he insist upon sharing the bed? And, if he did, should she retreat to the floor herself? Elene felt both hot and cold when she considered the possibilities. Naturally, she didn't want Geoffrey, especially a big, naked Geoffrey, to lie next to her in her father's old chamber, but neither was she eager to take to the hard tiles. And, truth be told, she had grown used to the...warmth that emanated from his great body.

His great, naked body.

Elene shivered, though the breeze was gentle. Spring was turning into an early summer, and the hills around them exploded in green and heather. It was rather lovely, she thought idly, but not as appealing as the view ahead. As if possessing a will of its own, her attention drifted back to her husband, whose dark beauty taunted her more often than not these days.

If he wanted to share the covers, would she deny him? Nay, for she would only be denying herself that small, innocent pleasure of closeness, of another human being near her and that strange sense of safety that gave her the first restful sleep she had known in years.

Safe, with a man? Elene wanted to scoff, but the derisive laughter wouldn't come. Geoffrey de Burgh exuded warmth and security the way other men boasted cruelty and power, and it was time she admitted it to herself. She had a long ride ahead of her, and with it the opportunity to reassess her husband. Since first coming into her life, he had done nothing but give her undeserved courtesy and gentleness. Maybe she ought to begin giving some back to him.

Elene sucked in a ragged breath as doubts assailed her. Surely that way led to weakness, to a vulnerability that she had sought all her life to avoid. Or did it? She frowned fiercely as she stared at his broad back. Could she still be the Fitzhugh and give Geoffrey his due?

Elene wasn't sure. Not only must she struggle against her innate reluctance to follow such a course, but she was not certain she could act differently. She had been angry and hateful for so long, she didn't remember how to be good and kind. Another lump clogged her throat, and she swallowed, looking away from her husband's arresting figure to the tall ashes that marched into the distance. Strong but flexible, they swayed in the breeze, yet did not break.

Could she emulate them? Elene owed Geoffrey the effort, at least, for if she had been treated differently at Wessex, her husband had been feted like a king. Embraced by his loving family and people who obviously knew and liked him, Geoffrey was returning to a manor where all and sundry viewed him with dark suspicion. And Elene knew she had been the worst instigator of the lot, trading on their fears to turn them against their new master, calling him Saint Geoffrey and mocking his gentleness because she could not recognize it for what it was—the behavior of an honorable man, the kind of man she had not known existed.

Elene lifted her chin. She had never flinched from any task, and would set this one for herself, to ease his way as best she could. And while she was at it, she would keep a vigilant eye on her husband's back. For as each mile took them closer to home, Elene grew more convinced that her real enemies lay not behind her, but ahead.

And the manor itself seemed no longer a haven, but a dark spider, waiting to drag her into its web of treachery and hatred.

Geoffrey surveyed his holding with a mixture of emotions. Although mindful of Dunstan's warnings and the work that lay ahead of him, he also took some measure of pride in the place. This was his, and he would keep it, against all odds. Sliding a glance at his wife, Geoffrey felt that surge of possession again, more forcefully, and the thought made him smile, for surely none but the woman herself would contest his dominion over her. Unlike most husbands, he need have no fears that another man would steal his wife away!

Choking back a laugh, Geoffrey entered the hall, but his amusement vanished as a curious sense of unease washed over him. Either someone was watching him with ill intent, or Dunstan's suspicions were acting upon him all too well. Warily he gazed around the room, trying to judge which one of his people studied him with malevolence, but, in truth, no one looked happy to see him.

For a long moment, he stood in silence at the lack of welcome, his gaze sweeping his subjects for a hint of betrayal. Then Serle hurried forward to greet them, and his attention focused on one who might have cause to fear him. Although the steward's head was bowed submissively, his eyes darted over Geoffrey, Elene and their train, lingering on the two new knights with special interest. Following his gaze, Geoffrey nodded to them slowly, and noted when they slipped away from the group.

As he turned back to Serle, the strange feeling vanished, and Geoffrey wondered if he had imagined it. He had forgotten just how odd the manor and its people were, and though he considered himself above such nonsense, he was not impervious to the general atmosphere that pervaded Fitzhugh's walls.

"Excuse my tardiness, my lord, but I didn't think you'd be back," Serle said.

Geoffrey lifted his brows in question at the steward's excuse. "I told you we would return after a few weeks with my brother and liege lord," he said.

"Yes, but…" The little man shrugged expressively.

"But what?" Geoffrey asked, both curious and irritated. Had they thought he lied? That he would abandon his responsibilities toward them for the relative comfort of Wessex? Or… He nearly flinched at the more insidious suspicion. Had they thought he would die while away? And if so, at whose hands? Involuntarily his gaze once again shifted to Elene, who was eyeing Serle with ill-disguised contempt.

Geoffrey recognized the expression, for he had seen it often enough, but not recently, and he wondered if it meant anything. Although he did not concur with his brother's assessment of Elene, he could not outright dismiss all of Dunstan's warnings. Geoffrey swore silently at his quandary. If there truly was an enemy at the manor, he needed all his wits about him, and he would never be able to concentrate while constantly questioning his wife's motives. Elene was an unsolvable puzzle, and he would do better to reach for the stars than to try to understand her, he thought with some annoyance.

"Pardon me, my lord, but those knights," mumbled Serle. "Are they your men?"

Geoffrey fixed him with a certain stare. "Really, Serle, I'm surprised you've kept your head for so long, if you questioned your previous master in this manner."

He heard a muffled snort that sounded suspiciously like husky, feminine laughter. From Elene? She was distract-

ing him again, Geoffrey thought, for he would much
rather pursue that elusive bark of amusement than parry
with his steward.

"I ask only in the course of my duties, for I wonder if
they will billet below with the others, or will new quarters
have to be found for them?" Serle bowed his head as if
in apology, and Geoffrey found himself staring down at
a shiny bald pate.

"They will lodge in the cellar, as is the custom here,"
Geoffrey said, offering no explanation as to the identity
of the knights. "And they will protect the manor well,
adding new strength to the ranks depleted by Montgomery's departure," he added, in a voice loud enough to
carry to the others gathered around.

Then he made a brief speech proclaiming his pleasure
at his return and reassuring those present that he planned
to stay and redouble his efforts to restore prosperity to the
place. This eloquent oration was met with a host of blank
stares and wary expressions that were disheartening, to
say the least, but Geoffrey took it with good grace. He
had yet to prove himself to these people, who had been
worn down by a brutal master and a long war against their
neighbors.

A voice rang out. "You would do well to listen and
heed a man who would ease your lot." For a moment,
Geoffrey wondered who could possibly be commenting,
but he had only to follow Serle's startled gaze to realize
that it was his wife who spoke. His *wife?* "And any who
would work against my husband, know that I would find
no favor in it. Indeed, I can promise you will regret it
with your life," she said, with her usual fierceness.

Geoffrey felt the hairs rise on the back of his neck as
he gaped stupidly at Elene. The odd feeling was back,
though whether from the ill will of another or from his

wife's astonishing threat, he knew not. She looked slender and lethal as she challenged her own for him, and Geoffrey did not know whether to be insulted by the implication that he could not protect himself, or grateful for the support.

Gratitude won out and, shutting his open mouth firmly, he nodded toward her, but her glance slid past him, as if she were unable to meet his eyes directly. He sighed. Who knew what went on behind that veil of hair? Did she publicly champion him for a reason, or was she simply extending her misguided efforts to watch his back? Geoffrey grinned at the thought.

Suddenly, his homecoming didn't seem quite so chilly.

"My lord." Dismissing his wife's antics, Geoffrey swung around abruptly as one of Dunstan's knights called to him. The man, Talebot, carried an earthenware jar such as those kept with the stores, and the look on his face filled Geoffrey with both grim satisfaction and bitter disappointment.

As Talebot approached, the other knight circled around behind Serle, whose attention was firmly fixed upon the open container. The steward's normally small eyes were as round as saucers, and Geoffrey knew, without a doubt, the identity of his thief.

Serle made his bed in a tiny room off the buttery, meant for the preparations of potions and healing herbs. Since none at the manor were skilled in these arts, least of all the chatelaine, he had taken the space for himself and kept it locked at all times, presumably because of the unknown mixtures that were still stored there. But Geoffrey had obtained keys for every room in the manor, and having instructed Dunstan's men to search Serle's possessions, he could only assume they had found evidence of his misdeeds. "What is it, Talebot?" he asked.

"Coins, artfully concealed beneath beeswax," the knight answered soberly. "And jewels, hidden among dried nuts." He held out his hand, openly displaying a good-size ruby in his palm.

Geoffrey eyed it with disgust. "I can see why you hoped I would not return," he said, glancing toward his steward. "Did you think to continue stealing from me, as you had from Fitzhugh?"

For a moment, Serle trembled as if he would weep like a maiden. Then his gaze darted away, across the tiles, to another. "It was her!" he shouted, pointing at Elene with an outstretched finger. A collective gasp rose from the hall, followed by hushed silence so deep Geoffrey could hear the steward's labored breathing.

Although he caught only a brief glimpse of his wife's startled expression before it was replaced by her usual fierce grimace, the sight was enough to tell Geoffrey that she had had no knowledge of the thievery. No more than her father, secure in his greed and conceit, had guessed that his own man was robbing him year after year.

And Serle obviously thought Geoffrey would be as easily duped. "She made me do it, and bade me hide the money in my own room, on pain of death. She threatened me, my lord," he cried, falling to Geoffrey's feet in supplication. "You have heard her often enough. She is an evil creature, just as Edred has said! I feared for my life, else I would not have heeded her, my lord. Spare me, protect me from her, and I swear I will serve you well."

As Geoffrey stared down at the loathsome little man, he felt as though all the slights his wife had endured at Wessex, all his brother's harsh accusations and all the sullen taunts he had heard at the manor, had congealed, like so much rotten spittle, onto the steward's greasy pate. And it was all he could do not to smite it with one blow.

"How dare you!" Geoffrey asked, as rage, righteous and violent, surged through him. He drew his sword, tempted beyond logic to make an example of this man. The beady-eyed steward was the embodiment of everything he loathed: treachery, thievery and cowardice. Having stolen from his masters, to the detriment of his own people, he would now put the blame upon another. Elene! Outrage made Geoffrey lift his blade, but even as he stood there, ready to cleave the man's head from his body, reason stayed his hand. For killing Serle would not change people's mind about his wife.

With a shaky sigh, Geoffrey lowered his weapon, but not far. His anger, long denied, was too vast to be set aside, or reined in by scholarly temperament. Maybe he could not alter opinions, but he could prevent them from being given so freely. Whirling round, Geoffrey swung his sword in an arc, his gaze sweeping the sullen faces assembled before him like some bitter harvest. In his present mood, he cared not a whit for the lot of them.

"Does anyone else have any other comments about *my wife?*" he shouted, though the hall was hushed and silent. "Because I will hear them now, or never again! Speak up! You, Waltheof!" he called to a smirking servant. "What would you say?"

"Nothing, my lord, nothing," the man squeaked, backing away hurriedly. Geoffrey saw the manor's pathetic excuse for a priest sneak off, too, and the sight of the bobbing white head fleeing his wrath made Geoffrey pause. He dropped his arm, but continued his circle of the hall.

"Good, because I have had my fill of gossip, slander and falsehoods!" Even as he spoke, Geoffrey knew it was the truth. Although he was reacting far beyond the provocation now, his rage had been a long time coming. Indeed, it seemed to have begun the very day he drew the short straw back at Campion. And he had had enough—of sly insinuations, sympathy and suspicions—to last a lifetime.

"Elene is my wife, and I will hear no ill of her," he announced. Ignoring the stunned and bewildered expressions of his audience, Geoffrey silently dared them to dispute him, but no one moved or made a sound. Mollified, he glanced down at the quaking Serle. "As for you...I have no use for a man who cannot be trusted, or one who will use a woman to take his blame. Talebot, send him on his way, and make sure he takes nothing with him but the clothes on his back. You are banished from my lands and those of my liege lord."

"Nay, I would have my due! I am owed for my years of service. The Fitzhughs owe me!" Serle cried. He begged and babbled and threatened as he was dragged away, but Geoffrey heeded him not. Sheathing his sword, he looked toward Elene, feeling suddenly awkward and uncomfortable after his tempestuous defense of her.

Geoffrey was not sure what he expected to see in her face: shock, condemnation, or mockery, perhaps. One never knew with Elene. She might be insulted or angry, and he shifted uneasily, prepared for anything—even a tirade that would negate all he had sought to accomplish when he stood up for her.

But, as ever, she surprised him. From behind that veil of hair, her gaze locked and held with his own, unflinching. And for one moment, he felt a kinship with her that had nothing to do with the vows they had taken. It was a deeper union, of mutual respect and a bond that defied description even to himself. Seeing that stark, unguarded look of communion in her amber eyes, however briefly, Geoffrey could not regret his outburst.

After all, she was his wife.

* * *

Serle's expulsion came as a relief, and after his departure, Geoffrey hoped to forge a new beginning, aided by the gems and coins hoarded by the former steward. He immediately set about mending fences and clearing hedgerows, ordering the planting of additional acreage and encouraging the villeins to raise their own produce.

His suggestions were met with wary acquiescence, and sometimes even his vast patience was sorely tried by those who insisted on doing things the way they had been done for years, simply through force of habit. He had always held an interest in growing things, and he took the opportunity now to put his ideas into practice. He looked ahead, too, to moving the outer wall and strengthening it, in stages, and someday adding a solar to the rear of the manor. The future did not seem as grim as it once had, and with the absence of Montgomery and Serle, Geoffrey hoped that his enemies had been routed. He felt good, but for two niggling problems.

Unfortunately, his efforts to win over his people had met with little success. It was frustrating, this constant striving for acceptance, and Geoffrey sometimes overheard an odd whisper or caught a furtive glance that made him wonder what they were saying about him. Was someone actively turning them against him? Although Geoffrey welcomed the additional help of Dunstan's knights, he drew the line at spying on his own. He knew no other way to deal with their attitude than to prove himself, knowing that time would tell.

As to his other problem...it had been with him from the beginning, but now it was even more disturbing than ever—in a different way. No matter how hard he worked or concentrated, Geoffrey found his thoughts drifting more and more frequently to his wife. Something had changed between them on the day of their return, as if they had formed an uneasy alliance. An odd pairing, no doubt, but Geoffrey couldn't deny that Elene felt like an ally among the distrustful faces that surrounded him.

With a sigh, he shifted onto his side, suddenly restless, despite his weariness. He was lying before the empty hearth in the great chamber, a book propped before him, but he had not read a single word. It was getting late, and Elene had yet to take to her bed. They slept together now, but she always got in first, fully dressed, and he waited until she dozed before joining her. Otherwise, they would both be awake, aware, and...

Geoffrey slammed shut his volume, annoyed by the train of his thoughts. Whether he was deep in discussion or hard at labor, she intruded into his mind, and when she moved, his eyes followed her, as if they could not drink their fill. In the few days since their return, a new tension had leapt between them that spoke not of threats, but of a deeper, more primitive passion. It crackled in the air like sparks from ready tinder waiting to be brought to life. Leaning his head back, Geoffrey loosed a ragged sigh.

He was becoming obsessed with his wife.

Although she looked no different, as far as he could tell, Geoffrey saw her differently. No longer pretending interest in his book, he glanced over to where she was awkwardly mending some slippers. She should have new ones, he thought, and vowed to have them made for her on the morrow. His attention drifted to the long tangle of hair that fell over one breast, and he found himself staring at the thick mass, wondering what it would feel like beneath his fingers, running over his body like a river. It was a mess, he told himself, and yet he wanted... He wanted...

Releasing a long, low breath, Geoffrey rose to his feet, not at all sure what he wanted. If she was going to leave it so long, why couldn't she take care of it? She was not a helpless infant. If she would let no servant do it, why couldn't she groom it herself? Unaccountably annoyed, he stalked across the room to stand in front of her.

"Don't you ever brush it?" he snapped.

It was a measure of their shaky alliance that she did not flinch at his words or pull out her dagger. Instead, she simply stared at him. Then, when understanding dawned, her chin came down and that rebellious grimace appeared, marring her face. "No! I like it this way, de Burgh, and if you don't, all the better!"

"Well, then, let me brush it," Geoffrey said, over the sudden thudding of his heart.

She gaped at him in shock, and his words hung in the air between them for a long moment, pulsing with hidden meanings. As the silence dragged on, Geoffrey felt strange and restless. Irritated with himself, he longed to take back his request, but anticipation filled him, sharp and hungry.

"You want to brush my hair? Are you mad? You are mad!" When Elene finally spoke, it was in that shrill shriek Geoffrey loathed. Scooting from her position at the edge of the bed, she backed toward the door, as if he had gone brainsick before her very eyes.

Perhaps he had. He could not seem to stop staring at that thick fall of ginger and spice until, with a fierce oath, Elene stamped from the room, slamming the door loudly behind her.

His voice husky with frustration, Geoffrey swore, too, at his own folly. Elene represented everything he despised! She had not really changed; nor would she. Drawing in a deep breath, he told himself that it would be unwise to upset the wary truce between them, and doubly foolhardy to touch such a volatile creature. Yet, despite all logic, his hands still itched to grasp those tangled locks. And other parts of his body echoed their eager sentiments.

Sighing, Geoffrey turned toward the bed. At least now he could get some sleep, he realized. Stripping out of his clothes swiftly, he left a candle burning and slid under the covers, but the berth seemed cold and empty without Elene beside him. And for a long time, he lay awake, listening for her step and cursing himself for it.

Chapter Thirteen

In the fading light that signaled the end of the day, Elene silently slipped into her old room. She had left the high table early, after only picking at her supper, unease coiling like a knot in her belly. It had seized her ever since last night, driving her to the old chest that rested at the foot of the bed. With an angry grunt, Elene knelt in front of it, pushing aside the worn clothing she had long outgrown, digging deep until her fingers closed upon something smooth and flat. With shaking fingers, she dragged the object from its hiding place and cradled it in her hand. A small silver mirror, it had been one of her mother's most precious possessions, saved from her father's greedy hands by disuse. But now she took it out, compelled, for the first time in years, to look upon herself.

Holding it up to the graying light that slanted through the window, Elene frowned, a low noise of disgust escaping her throat. Feral yellow eyes stared back at her through a thick tangle of ugly drab locks, and she flinched at the sight. She despised her hair, its dull color and its rough, matted feel. It had served its purpose well, but now... Silently Elene wondered if she could abandon her former habits. They were so firmly engrained, so much a part of her, that she was unsure. She slammed down the mirror, hating it, hating the image that she saw in it, and hating her husband.

It was all Geoffrey's fault.

He was the source of every one of her problems, especially the disturbing aches and strange feelings coursing through a body and soul she had thought long inured to everything. He had made her view herself and, worst of all, long to see something else. He had made her want…things, mysterious, indefinable things.

And she hated him for it.

Scowling, Elene wished they had never left Wessex, for it had begun when they returned to the manor and the man she had called a saint turned into an avenging angel. Elene flushed, growing alternately hot and cold at the memory of Geoffrey challenging the entire hall for her. She laid her hands on her knees, as if to anchor herself somehow against visions of Geoffrey, dark and handsome, swinging his heavy sword in a graceful arc that promised swift retribution. The images assailed her. Tall. Strong. Powerful. And clever. Not only was Geoffrey possessed of scholarly wisdom, he was quick-witted beyond any she had ever known—as had been proved by his rapid discovery of Serle's treachery.

Ha! The steward's deception had come as no surprise to Elene. She had seen through his subservient pose for years. Although too cowardly for outright murder, he had always seemed capable of nearly any misdeed. Still, Elene did not begrudge him the stolen funds, for she enjoyed the irony of her greedy father taking a loss. Indeed, all she felt was a lingering resentment for the steward's position in the household. If only her father had let her serve as chatelaine, mayhap she could have prevented the thievery or discovered it herself, but then, her father would never have believed her.

Elene grimaced at the thought, for Serle's accusations against her had been another matter entirely. Were it not for Geoffrey... Automatically reaching for her dagger, Elene closed her fingers around the hilt, but it gave her no comfort. Although still well armed, she no longer found the strength she once had in her weapons, for she knew that something other than might had spared her.

Snorting, Elene tried to dismiss such notions, but she could not deny that she was alive and roaming free because of intangibles that she had always held in contempt. Faith. Trust. Respect. Impossible, unbelievable things that her husband held dear and that only fools like him and Marion believed in. Suddenly uncomfortable, Elene sank back on her heels, even as she knew that another man might not have taken her part so readily. Or at all. Ha! Any other man would have believed Serle and denounced her without delay, if only to be rid of her at last.

But not Geoffrey.

Elene swallowed a thick lump in her throat as she remembered her husband's impassioned defense of her. She knew him well enough by now to expect it, but habit had her preparing for a blow. Oddly enough, she had not drawn her blade in an effort to strike first, but had simply waited, like a doomed man, for his censure. Odder still, she had the feeling that Geoffrey's condemnation would have been more painful than death itself.

Although a protest rose automatically to her lips, Elene was forced to admit that such bizarre fancies were becoming more and more frequent. And some, she was even acting upon.... Her face grew heated at the memory of her earlier speech on his behalf. She was unsure whether her words had helped or hindered him, but she had found it impossible to remain silent. As she saw his cold reception and watched him promise so much only to receive so little in return, Elene had been filled with outrage.

The sight of him, strong, bold and proud, yet gentle and compassionate, too, had done funny things to her insides. Not an ache this time, it was more like a heat that had sparked her to action. Never impetuous, Elene nonetheless had heard herself take his part, threatening those who would work against her husband. She was not sure who had been more surprised by her actions—her audience or herself—for she had never before lifted a finger to help another. All her battles had been fought to protect herself.

And her own.

Elene choked back a sound at the memory of a time when there had been someone else to care for. Her fingers curled tighter around the hilt of her knife, and she wanted to scream out her denial. There was no comparison between those dark times and now, no connection between the woman and child she had tried to save and the grown man who needed not her help. And yet, insidiously, the thought crept into her mind. What was she doing when she watched her husband's back and spoke up for him? Wasn't she watching out for her own? The very idea was disturbing, for it took the simple notion of guarding her interests much farther than she wanted to go.

Shaking her head fiercely, Elene told herself that she looked out for Geoffrey only because he was the best of the lot. She could do far worse, and she did not care to be married again. They had developed a truce of sorts, which was working out well now that she was making an effort, but there was nothing more between them than a shared household. And a shared bed. And his offer to brush her hair...

Elene shuddered. She was alternately horrified and intrigued whenever she considered his offer of the night before. No one had ever tended to her except her mother, and she had long ago learned to fend for herself. Why should she let him touch her? And, more important, why would he want to do so?

Try as she might to plead ignorance, Elene had her suspicions concerning the answer. She had seen something in his eyes—that dark, dreamy look she had glimpsed the times when he kissed her. It spoke to her, as if he were traveling to some exotic, mysterious place and would take her with him.

Lies! Folly! Elene sucked in a deep breath as the familiar defenses fell into place. Her hand ached suddenly, and she realized that she grasped her dagger too hard. Slowly, she released her grip and spread her fingers wide. They appeared foreign to her, as if not a part of herself, but, then, nothing had seemed right since her return. She was changing, and although some of those changes were through her own efforts, some were not, and without her usual behavior to fall back upon, she felt vulnerable and confused.

As she had last night.

Elene frowned, for instead of taking her blade to her husband's throat, she had fled from him like a frightened child. Certainly, she had vowed to try to be nicer to the man and to keep her knife firmly sheathed, but her flight had sprung from more than that, and the knowledge had been pressing upon her ever since, threatening her far more than arms or brute strength could. Although the evening was warm, Elene shivered suddenly. Little though she cared for the truth of it, she had run from Geoffrey, rather than face those compelling eyes of his that called to some hidden place within herself.

But she was no coward, and she had learned long ago

that it was better to face danger with weapon drawn than to cower in a corner, waiting for it to sneak up on you. And so, finally, she had returned to the chamber that had become so unsettling, to the bed she had never thought to sleep in and to the man whose broad shoulders gleamed in the light of the gutted candle. His hair, richer than the finest sable, had fallen over his neck in a dark wave that made her weak. Forcing herself to look upon him unflinchingly, Elene had removed her slippers and blown out the candle, then slid in beside him. The unseen menace he had presented was past, or so she had believed, but he had stirred, turning over in the darkness.

"Elene?" he had mumbled in a voice so husky that she shivered in response. Then, she had felt his arm close around her, pulling her against him, so that even through her gown her back burned with the heat of his chest, her legs with the hard muscles of his thighs, and she felt dizzy and breathless. She had waited, uncertain what to do, until she felt his big hand go slack against her belly, his breath sound low and even in her tangled locks. Never had she thought to allow a man's fingers there, on her stomach, but he had been asleep and could do her no harm.

At least that was what she had told herself in the still quiet of the night as she relaxed herself, closing her eyes against the wicked pleasure of his body and the delight of his embrace. All thoughts of threats forgotten, she had let Geoffrey surround her like a soothing blanket. Safe. Warm. Comforting beyond imagining.

Elene blinked as lethargy crept over her along with the memory. Her bones felt liquid, and she shifted, shaking off the heaviness, for she knew that the danger her husband presented her had not been vanquished. Nor had her own qualms. Oh, she had managed to overcome her terror of closeness, but it was his offer she had run from, and all day the thought of her cowardice had been goading her, driving her to meet his challenge. She had fled from Geoffrey once too often.

Unwillingly, Elene's gaze strayed to the discarded mirror, and the distorted image it tossed back at her. With a hesitant touch, she lifted her hand to finger a clump of hair. Uncombed and too long unwashed, it repelled her, and she released it with a foul oath, while the means to change it—and so much else—dangled before her.

The unease that had coiled in her belly all day twisted and rose like bile in her throat, for it was not just Geoffrey who frightened her, but herself. Unnatural feelings and strange longings that she dared not act upon had plagued her ever since their return, and Elene was afraid of what would happen should she give in to them. If she let herself truly...be...how would she survive? Who would protect her?

The answer came out of the darkness, a single name that whispered strength and safety, and Elene blinked, realizing that the twilight had turned to night while she lay alone in the silence. Angrily she stood up and drew in a deep breath. She would not cower here in her room ever again.

It was time to face her demons.

Geoffrey shifted onto his side and stared down at the book Marion had given him. Normally, he would have absorbed every page in loving detail; tonight, he had yet to fully comprehend one sentence. He should have stayed below, instead of coming to the chamber so early, but he could not find Elene, and he was worried about her. She had seemed tense and strained during the meal, keeping well away from him, while scowling ferociously.

Of course, Geoffrey realized he had gone beyond the

pale the night before, and he had been half expecting a sword in his gullet ever since. He frowned guiltily, knowing he had shattered their uneasy truce with his absurd urge to groom that tangled mane of hers. Running a hand through his own, Geoffrey swore softly. He should know by now that Elene hated to be touched, and lashed out at any hint of intimacy. And he should accept those terms of their marriage eagerly. And yet...

At the sound of the door, Geoffrey looked up and sighed in relief. There she was. He told himself that he kept his eye on her to prevent any mischief, even as he knew it was not the truth. He liked looking at her, messy hair, fierce expression and all. There was something about her that stirred him as no well-groomed, mannered lady ever had, and he sighed at the perversity of the human heart.

Heart?

Geoffrey shifted uneasily. Mind. He meant mind. Pressing his fingers to the bridge of his nose, he pinched, trying to clear his head. His usual concentration was failing him lately. Perhaps it was his eyesight. Mayhap he needed lenses to help him see better. That would explain why he viewed his wife so favorably, he thought with a wry smile.

He nearly started when he lifted his lashes to see her new slippers in front of him. She had accepted them without comment, the old wariness appearing in her narrowed gaze, but Geoffrey was heartened that she was wearing them. Squashing an errant query about the shape of her calves under that gown, he let his attention wander up her body to find her hand outstretched toward him.

What now? Geoffrey wondered idly. Would she brandish an eating knife, or a bit of hemlock, or did she plan to simply grab him by the throat? With a sigh, he sat up and glanced at her open palm, only to stare in amazement, his heart slamming in his chest, for it was no weapon she held, but a brush. A hairbrush.

For a long moment, Geoffrey sat there, dumbfounded. His eloquence having deserted him, he lifted his brows in a mute question as she stretched out her arm, presenting her offering to him. Still, she said nothing, and her face, hidden behind the thick mass, revealed little enough to his curious gaze. She simply stood before him, silently giving him the brush and, he assumed, permission to use it.

Geoffrey rose to his feet slowly, careful not to make any sudden moves. He felt as if a doe in the forest had come forward to feed from his palm, and although filled with a sharp-edged anticipation, he struggled to control it. He did not want to send his wife scurrying away like the wild creature that she was.

He wanted to tame her to his hand.

The notion sent his heart kicking even more frantically against his ribs, but Geoffrey forced himself to breathe evenly as he took the brush. Elene was allowing him to groom her messy locks. That was all, he told himself, yet the thought of actually touching her hair made him hot and breathless. To hide his eagerness, he motioned toward the fur lying on the floor, and after a moment's hesitation, Elene sat down on it awkwardly. Moving a low stool behind her, Geoffrey paused, struck by her pose, head bent before him. He swallowed, oddly affected by the sight, for he knew how much trust it took for her to turn her back to him, and he swore she would not find it misplaced.

Lowering himself to the seat, Geoffrey forgot his vow as swiftly as he made it, for he found himself facing his obsession at last. Her hair, in all its disarray, fell before him—thick and alive and full of so many colors that his head swam with thoughts that had nothing to do with grooming it. He wanted to bury his face in it, wrap it around his fists and lift it away from her shoulders, so that he could kiss the hidden spot at the back of her neck....

Drawing in a deep breath, Geoffrey struggled for restraint. Keeping his attention firmly fixed on the length right in front of his eyes, he lifted the brush and tried to use it without touching Elene. It was impossible. Her tresses were in a terrible tangle, and he had not finished one stroke ere he came upon a great knot, all twisted together. Raising the section with one hand, he tried to undo the mess, carefully, with his fingers, but it was slow work, and even holding the strands away from her head, he could feel the tug on her scalp.

"'Twould be best, perhaps, if I cut out these clumps," he said, but she jerked away.

"Nay! Take scissors to it, and I'll carve you up!" she warned, rising from her seat. Gently pressing her shoulder, Geoffrey urged her back down. Now that he had the chance to groom her, he was not going to let her go until he had well and truly done his job.

"Very well, but 'twould be better done wet," he said. Although loath to let her go, Geoffrey dropped his hands and strode to the door, calling for a servant to bring hot water and a small tub. To his surprise, Elene did not argue, but he still did not waste any time, lest she change her mind. Resuming his seat, he began working on the knot again, first with his fingers and then with the brush, freeing the strands as best he could. When he finally completed the stroke, he breathed a sigh of relief, cut off abruptly when the long ends pooled in his lap. His member stiffened, and he stared at the strands of spicy color falling over his thighs like something from his darkest desires.

He might have remained there in a dazed state forever, tempted beyond reason, had the door not opened. At the sight of the servant, he shifted uncomfortably, calling for the tub to be placed beside him. When the servant left, he put the wooden container on the stool and dropped the heavy mass of hair into it. Although the interruption had given him an opportunity to regain control of himself, his hands shook as he ran his fingers through it. Thick. Wet. Smooth. His heart hammered so loudly, he wondered why Elene was not taunting him, but she remained silent and passive for once.

"Lean your head back," Geoffrey ordered gruffly.

Even the stark command did not garner the expected response from Elene. Indeed, she seemed to be in a dreamy, sleeplike state, and did as he bade without comment. The sight of her pale face, eyes closed, as she heeded him stirred Geoffrey in ways he never would have thought possible, and he moved restlessly around her as he soaked the thick bounty.

Trying to concentrate on his task, Geoffrey worked the scented soap Marion had given them through the wet tangle, but no matter how he tried to distance his mind from his hands, he could not. Her hair felt smooth and alive, and he felt himself grow and harden. The weight of it, flowing over his knuckles, was incredibly erotic, as was the texture of it, cleansed in the warm water. A sweet, flowery fragrance arose from the soap, mixing with Elene's own spicy scent until he felt dizzy.

As he wound his fingers through the thick, wet coil, Geoffrey realized that he had never been so intimate with any other woman, even those he bedded. Never would he have thought it, but the simple act of washing his wife's hair was more erotic and arousing than anything he had ever done to another.

Maybe she was right, and he was going mad. Grabbing a length of cloth, Geoffrey lifted the sodden weight from the tub and wrapped the linen around a large portion of it. He could see why Elene did not want to take care of her hair; obviously, it would take a very long time to dry. He should have begun his task in the morning, not at night, he thought, his heart pounding at the images that swam, unbidden, before him. *Elene going to bed, her hair slick and wet against his naked body, his hands, his mouth...*

With a low oath, Geoffrey squeezed tightly on a long coil and grabbed another cloth, wringing the sodden mass until it no longer dripped freely. In the process, his clothes became soaked, and although the night was warm, he shuddered. He was not chilled, but too hot, and he stifled a sudden urge to remove his tunic. Irritation with his own lack of control made him throw the linen cloths to the floor. He had asked for this, and now must suffer through it without complaint. The irony of it was not lost on him, for this torment was surely more hideous than anything Elene could have planned for him.

And she knew it not.

Glancing down at her, Geoffrey sucked in a deep breath. Her eyes were still closed, her pale face more relaxed than he had ever seen it beyond sleep, and he feasted his eyes on her features, no longer hidden from him. He didn't care what anyone else saw or didn't see. She was beautiful. His hand reached out as if of its own accord, for he wanted nothing more than to lift her up and take her to his bed. But he couldn't. He stood there, bound by his own sense of honor and by the lashes that lay so innocently against her flawless skin.

She trusted him. Guilt gnawing at his insides, Geoffrey mercilessly reined in his baser urges. He was not a creature of impulse. If his mind could not control his body, then he was no better than an animal, his fine education for naught. Gritting his teeth, Geoffrey took his seat once more, stifling a pained groan as his groin protested.

Ignoring it, he picked up the brush and began again, concentrating on undoing the knots and tangles. Unable to speak coherently, he went about his work in silence as the night stretched on, until at last he could sweep the brush from the top of her head through the longest strand in one long stroke. A smooth, easy glide, it reminded him of other, more primitive rhythms, but Geoffrey forced his attention back to her hair, heavy and luxurious and drying with a sheen he had never seen before.

And then he stood. He wanted to abandon the brush, to toss it into the far corners of the room and bury his hands in the heavy locks, but he dropped his arms and stepped back. He gazed upon his handiwork with no little awe, for Elene's hair fell straight and smooth down her back for the first time in his memory, so lovely that surely even his brothers could not deny it.

The candlelight gleamed on the long strands, a vivid mixture of cinnamon and spice that would be the envy of any woman, Geoffrey decided as he gently nudged Elene to her feet. She rose, blinking in surprise, as if awakened from a dream, and it was a moment before her eyes narrowed with their usual wariness.

Geoffrey sighed, looking away from what he did not want to see. He could take pride in his efforts, but that would have to be enough. To wish for anything else would surely be to court disaster.

Chapter Fourteen

Geoffrey strode to the high table, a small parcel tucked under his arm. He had yet to see Elene up and about this morning, and he looked forward to sharing his meal with her. Placing his bundle under his seat, he flushed, oddly embarrassed by the gift he had chosen so carefully for her. But something had changed between them last night. Elene had trusted him enough to let him close to her, and Geoffrey did not take her faith lightly. In return, he wanted to celebrate the new accord between them.

For hours, as he went about his duties, Geoffrey had considered and dismissed flowers and trinkets and sweets as inappropriate for his wife. Elene was…unusual, and he needed a gift that would both appeal to her and mark the seriousness of the moment. He had nearly given up when, just before the call to dinner, the answer struck him forcefully. At the time, he had been certain he had found the perfect item to express his feelings. Now, however, he shifted restlessly in his seat, like a besotted boy. He told himself he had no cause for unease, but he never knew how Elene would react. Would she treasure his prize, or toss it back in his face with a sneer?

Clearing his throat, Geoffrey reached for his cup of ale,

then put it down without even taking a sip when he saw his wife enter the hall. How different she looked! It was more than the hair that flowed long and loose past her shoulders, instead of over her features. She moved gracefully, no longer in a perpetual crouch, ready to pounce, her eyes darting around the room as if to gauge each enemy.

Now she strode across the tiles with her head held high, more serene than he had ever seen her. And he was not the only one who noticed the change in her, for the room fell silent as the diners stared, some furtively, some openly, at their mistress. Watching her regal manner, Geoffrey felt a constriction in his chest that was not the rapid pounding of his heart. It wasn't lust he felt, but something else entirely. Geoffrey took a deep drink then swallowing swiftly, so as to greet his wife with a smile. Friendship. That was what he sought between them, and his gift would cement such a relationship, he decided.

The meal was simple but good, the food tasting better to him each day, and Geoffrey partook of it heartily. Only the sense that someone was studying him too intently dimmed his pleasure. He looked around, but Montgomery and Serle were gone, and he could find no eyes upon him. With a shrug, Geoffrey shook off the feeling and chose a few of the first cherries of the season. They were so tangy they made his mouth water, and he grinned, enjoying the sharpness. Leaning over, he presented a plump one to Elene.

To his surprise, she reared back, blinking at the proffered fruit and then at Geoffrey with a startled expression. "What? Don't you want it?" he asked.

Staring at the cherry, she shook her head slowly. "No. I...I don't know..." she finished lamely, then she reached forward and snatched it from his fingers as if he might burn her.

As usual, Geoffrey didn't know what to make of her odd behavior, but when she popped the fruit into her mouth, she made a face, glaring at him in a way that was all too familiar. "Aren't they a little sour?" she asked.

It was plain she thought his offering no treat, so Geoffrey bit back a laugh and ate his remaining berries with relish. "No," he said, between swallows. "Just the way I like them," he noted, with a grin. She was eyeing him strangely again, and he didn't know what to make of it. "When we were young, Stephen and I were always the first to get the early ones. Invariably, he ended up with a bellyache, while my other brothers would have no part of them until later. But I..." Geoffrey paused to consider his wife with a wry smile. "I always preferred the tangy ones."

Was she blushing? Geoffrey felt his own cheeks heat at the admission that had suddenly acquired new meaning, but he held her gaze. She was the first to glance away and, mumbling an excuse, began to rise from her seat. "No, wait. I've something for you," Geoffrey said, stopping her with a hand on her wrist. Feeling peculiarly vulnerable, he brought out his gift.

At first, Elene hesitated, but when he placed the slim volume in her hands, she sat down slowly. She stared at it silently, and Geoffrey couldn't gauge her feelings. A lock of her hair fell forward, and he wanted to slide his fingers into it, tucking the thick strands behind her, but he did not. He waited, watching her with far more trepidation than he cared to admit. It was a book of psalms, certainly appropriate for a woman, with beautiful illuminations that anyone would appreciate. Finally, Elene stroked the leather binding with one finger, as if in wonder, and the tightness in Geoffrey's chest eased. He shared that awe, of all his precious volumes, and knowing that they had something in common made him feel a kinship with his wife that he had never known before.

"Open it," Geoffrey urged, impatient now. She was slow to respond, but by the time she let her hand fall onto a brightly colored page, tracing the detailed edging, he was grinning like a fool. Still, she said nothing, and he wondered if the notoriously loud Elene had been struck dumb. Then she lifted her head and peered out at him through the shining strands of hair.

"It's beautiful." For once, she spoke so softly only he could hear it.

Emboldened, Geoffrey turned back the first page. "Read the inscription," he said, no longer embarrassed by the words he had written there. In a hurry to reach the table earlier, he had scribbled down the first thoughts that came to mind, knowing he might regret them later. Now he had no such regrets.

"I can't," she whispered.

"Go ahead," Geoffrey urged, strangely touched by her reluctance. Did she suspect how much this present meant? How much the night before had affected him? He smiled ruefully, for how could she know the depth of feelings that confused even himself?

"No, I can't," Elene repeated, louder. Ducking her chin so that the clean sweep of her hair fell forward, she rose to her feet.

Again, he stopped her by closing his fingers around one slender wrist. "Then later?" he asked, vaguely ashamed of begging his wife for a boon.

She shook her head, backing away from him, into herself. When he did not release her, she spoke, her voice fierce but low enough for only him to hear. "I can't read," she muttered.

Geoffrey gaped at her, unable to believe her words, but the face that looked back at him was stony and set through its veil of hair. Too stunned to speak, he loosed his grip on her wrist, and she slipped through his fingers. Letting his hand fall, he stared after her in numbed surprise as she turned and walked away without a backward glance.

Elene could not read.

Geoffrey released a ragged sigh. It was not so astounding, really. Not many people did, for few had much use for such a skill. Faith, his own brothers probably never would have learned, without Campion's unswerving example. And of all his siblings, Geoffrey was the only one who had studied for the sheer joy of it.

Even some of the nobles and landowners didn't see the need, and Geoffrey abruptly realized that Fitzhugh had undoubtedly been among them. How else would Serle have fleeced his master so easily? Geoffrey bit back a groan as he wondered if that was why Elene was not chatelaine. Perhaps she could neither read nor keep accounts.

The knowledge struck him low in the gut, like foul meat, and his stomach churned sickeningly. There was certainly no shame in her lack, and yet he had never dreamed that his wife would not be able to do sums or read the simplest inscription. Geoffrey shook his head, astounded, yet again, by how different Elene was from the woman he had envisioned for himself. Lately, he had forgotten just how odd was their pairing, but now the reminder weighed down upon him with a deadening pressure. No matter how he might try to manipulate or disguise the truth, there was no use in hiding from it.

Elene was the antithesis of everything he admired and respected.

Around him, Geoffrey was dimly aware that the world went on. He could hear the low mutters of those still seated and the rustle of movement when diners rose to leave. Their words rose in volume, yet they were meaningless, and suddenly, the manor and all that it stood for threatened to choke the very life from him. He needed fresh air and a quiet spot away from it in which to think.

Striding past Edred, who was standing near the wall, watching him avidly, Geoffrey hurried toward the doors. He had no patience for the priest, not when the hard-won peace he had claimed here seemed empty and false and dissatisfaction, long unacknowledged, gnawed at his insides. Ignoring the startled whispers of those around him, Geoffrey headed for the outside and escape.

But even as he strode swiftly through the bailey, he knew it held no real freedom—from his responsibilities, his life, or the woman who was his wife.

Elene spent the afternoon sharpening her daggers, honing each one to the finest, deadliest point, and envisioning all of them planted firmly in Geoffrey's gullet. Spinning the small wheel as she had so often in the past, she tried to muster the appropriate blood lust, but her usual glee was missing. In truth, she could not summon up the proper anger.

Although loath to make the admission, it was pain she felt, an ache no longer vague or dim, but as real and pointed as one of her weapons, and she despised it. Worse yet was the possibility that others might have seen it! Cursing, she wished she had never gone down to dinner. Better that her humiliation be suffered in private! Unfortunately, she had been taking more and more meals in the hall, because when she tried to eat alone, Geoffrey soon joined her. Although she still disliked the crowded high table, being closeted in the great chamber with Geoffrey had become awkward and uncomfortable, as if there weren't enough air in the room for both of them to breathe properly.

Ha! Fool! That she should have let a handsome face affect her so! That she had tried to change for him! Elene choked back a foreign sound. All her good feelings from the night before were gone, slain in a bloody purge by Geoffrey's hand—the same hand that had taken her hair and washed it with infinite gentleness, brushed and stroked and groomed it until she felt as though she were drifting in some long-forgotten dream.... Slamming down her longest blade, Elene picked up another and viciously put it to the stone.

For the first time since her mother's death, she had let someone touch her—not only her hair, but deeper, the part of her buried away, and look what had happened. She tried to laugh, but all that came out was a bitter gurgle. More fool she! Trust brought only grief. Weakness made you weaker, and not only did she know it, but the whole hall had witnessed it. If others suspected her vulnerability, then how could she protect herself?

The name that had come to her the night before echoed in her mind like a taunt, and Elene sat back, pausing in her task. Faith, but he had looked so well, so boyishly handsome, at table that she wanted to reach out to make sure he was real. She hadn't seen him appear so carefree since Wessex, and when he had offered her the cherry... Even now, Elene flushed, remembering how he had held it out to her, relaxed and smiling, as if it were the most natural thing in the world to give her the choicest morsels. *Just as the Wolf did his wife.*

At that moment, Elene had felt as if her heart were swelling within her and all that she dared not acknowledge might burst forth, free at last. But she had realized her error as soon as he gave her the book. She hadn't wanted to take it, for her delight in the treasure was tempered by dread at what must surely follow.

And follow it had, as the night did the day. Geoffrey could not hide his expression, of course, and even prepared as she was, Elene had flinched from it. Although she had seen that look many times on many other faces, she could not bear to see it upon his. The de Burghs had all viewed her with revulsion from the beginning, but never Geoffrey—until now. His shock and contempt had knifed through her more painfully than the mightiest sword, and Elene shook with the memory of it.

Although she had turned away, pretending she didn't care, she was hurt as surely as if he had driven the point into her heart. She wished for the first time that she had married one of his brothers—cold, hard Simon, or the bitter one with the limp. Such a marriage would have been easy, mutual hatred being far preferable to this return of feeling to her limbs, her mind, her heart. Then she would still be strong, and Geoffrey's contempt would have no power over her.

Choking back a strangled sound, Elene glanced toward the window, where the lengthening shadows told her that supper would soon be served. She ought to take her meal in the hall. With a scowl, she told herself that the Fitzhugh would go below and snarl at anyone who dared smirk at her, but Elene had grown weary of the pretense. Now that she had let herself *be* again, her old armor was a poor fit.

This is what he had done to her.

When Elene heard the door open, she jerked and put her blade to stone again, though it was already honed to perfection. She did not glance up, but she knew who had entered. She could sense him. The room vibrated with his strength, and she caught the clean smell of him, luring her even now.

The wheel spun with undue force as she glared at her weapon. How dare he come in here! Surely he did not plan to eat with her? Although Elene knew she ought to rise and shriek and toss him out, she could not. Weakened and hurting, she could not even look at him, for she was afraid of what she might see in his face. Coward! Appalled by her own vulnerability, Elene almost cringed, but she kept at her work until he moved in front of her. When he crouched low, she had no choice except to meet his gaze, so she ducked her head, letting her hair fall over her face.

He was as handsome as ever, his even features a perfect foil for the thick, dark hair, his great brown eyes soft, and different, somehow, as they sought her own. Regretful. Elene nearly flinched at the realization. Did he plan to taunt her more? Or would he leave now that he had discovered just how unworthy she was to be his wife? Even immersed in her misery, Elene felt a flush of panic at the thought of never seeing him again, of being alone once more, more truly alone than ever before.

"I'm sorry," he said, and Elene blinked, unsure of what he was saying. "There is no shame in not being able to read," he added, his warm gaze holding her own. "I was surprised, but that's all. You know how I am about books," he said with a rueful smile. For a moment, Elene could only stare at him. No one in her life had ever taken the blame for anything, yet this strong, powerful man was kneeling before her, tendering his regrets.

"I brought you the book," he said, lifting the volume in one hand. "'Tis my gift to you, no matter what you

do with it. But I would have you know the inscription."
To her astonishment, his deep voice was rough and unsteady as he opened the book and read aloud. "'To Elene, wife by chance, companion by choice.'"

Silently, his dark head bent, as if he dared not look at her, Geoffrey closed the volume, and Elene felt a strange pressure behind her eyes. She was seized by an altogether foreign urge to slip from her seat to join him, to put her arms around him and feel his arms around her....

Oblivious to her bizarre thoughts, Geoffrey put down the book and took her hands in his. "I swear I never meant to offend you in any way, Elene, and if you will forgive me, I would be happy to teach you how to read myself. If you are interested," he added quickly. There was no longer any judgment in his face, only the sincerity that was Geoffrey, and Elene felt something shatter inside her. He would teach her to read—a gift far greater than any other, an act more selfless than any kindness! And no other tutor would be as good or as gentle.

"Geoffrey," she whispered, and then, giving in to her desire, she stretched out her arms and leaned forward. He took her in his embrace, an embrace full of warmth and comfort and safety, and Elene pressed the side of her face against his chest.

"Shh," he crooned softly, though she had made no sound. "'Twas all my fault. I was so full of myself, so righteous." Absurdly, Elene found herself smiling at his description, though she could not agree. In her mind, her husband had assumed a godlike grace, and she wondered that she might forgive him anything.

For a long time, Elene rested against him, nestled close and comfortable, and then, gradually, she sensed a change in him that well bespoke his mortality. His chest rose more swiftly below her cheek, his heart beat more loudly beneath her ear, and Elene froze, uncertain, in his arms. His palm, resting on her back, moved slowly in a stroking motion that suddenly seemed less like succor and more like something else. She held her breath.

Would he kiss her? Although heat rushed through her at the thought, Elene shivered, for she realized that for the first time in her life, she wanted a man—Geoffrey— to put his mouth on hers. And that was not all. In truth, she wanted him to take her down to the floor and beg her to touch him as he had once before. Without waiting for her defenses to fall into place, Elene lifted her head in breathless anticipation, but Geoffrey only smoothed back her hair with a light caress.

"There, now. Will you take some supper with me, or throw it at me?" he said, a wry smile on his face. He was teasing her, and she had only a brief glimpse of that dreamy look in his eyes before it was replaced with good humor.

"Actually, I was planning to test my sharpened blades upon your gullet," Elene said, moving out his arms. Tamping down her disappointment as he released her, she stood and frowned as best she could. She caught his grin, but refused to smile herself. The moment was gone, and Elene knew she ought to be glad of it.

But she wasn't.

All through the meal that followed, she eyed her husband surreptitiously. Her breath coming quickly, she trembled as images assailed her of those instances when Geoffrey had held her, past and present. The courage that had filled her last night surged through her again, urging her to act upon it, to take one more step. As the evening wore on, Elene felt apart from herself, and yet in tune with her body for the first time ever. And when her husband turned to her and offered her the choicest bit of lamb, Elene knew what she must do.

It was time she gave something back to Geoffrey.

Geoffrey lay awake for a long time. Although Elene seemed to drop off to sleep immediately, he could not, for today he had almost destroyed what little they had between them with his own callous arrogance. It was not her fault that she could not read! Her father had been an uncaring bastard, and with advisors like that treacherous thief Serle... Geoffrey shuddered to think what her life had been like or what his own might have been in the same situation.

It was only after he had a chance alone to contemplate his actions that he had rued his hasty reaction and the idea to teach her himself had come to him. He had felt rather generous and contrite at the time, but when he tried to talk to her, he had been swamped with guilt. Obviously, Elene was not so hard as she claimed, for as soon as he entered the great chamber he had seen that he had hurt her deeply with this careless contempt.

Elene, whom everyone claimed had no feelings, had been in pain, and when he offered to teach her... Faith, for a moment Geoffrey had thought she would weep with joy and gratitude, and he had felt no better than the lowliest dog. For him, the suggestion had been no more than a whim, but for her it meant far more. It was knowledge, and he, better than anyone else, should know that power and freedom and wisdom flowed from it.

All through supper, she had been suffused with the glow of hope, the promise of learning, and Geoffrey had been ashamed for not thinking of her education sooner. He had been too busy feeling proud of himself—for marrying her, for his forbearance and his duties—to discover one blessed thing about his wife.

Sighing softly, Geoffrey leaned his head back into the pillow, only to abruptly still as he felt the soft brush of fingers against his chest. Apparently, Elene was stirring in her sleep, but he could not remember her touching him willingly. Ever. With another sigh, Geoffrey closed his hand over hers, halting its wanderings. Draping his other arm around her shoulders, he pulled her nearer to him, idly stroking the smooth skin of her shoulder as he contemplated his sins.

He would make it up to her somehow. Tomorrow he had no pressing responsibilities, so they could begin her lessons immediately. If he was kind and patient, perhaps he could atone for his earlier boorish behavior and his total lack of consideration for the woman he had married.

Skin? Geoffrey nearly jerked upright at the realization. He must be dreaming, for Elene always slept fully clothed, and yet... Slowly Geoffrey dragged a thumb down her arm, and met only supple flesh. Then, more hurriedly, he slid his hand back up to her throat, startled to discover that she was wearing only her shift. She must have taken off her gown before she got into bed, but why? Was she hot? Although the night was warm, a linen sheet covered them both.

Letting his head sink back into the pillow, Geoffrey swallowed. How was he to sleep now? It was bad enough that he was naked; now the only thing between them was a length of worn linen, made soft from the wearing. At the thought, his entire body stiffened, especially his tarse, but he dared not move, dreading an outburst—or worse—should Elene awaken to find herself curled up against him.

Lying prone, Geoffrey tried to think clearly, but it was

difficult when Elene's knee slid innocently across his thigh. He bit back a groan, determined to ease himself away, but then he felt something else, even more astonishing—the trembling of her hand beneath his own.

Instantly Geoffrey's eyes shot open, but he could see nothing except vague shapes. The chamber was sunk deep in darkness, with only the faint glow of moonlight through the window for illumination. He waited for his eyes to adjust to the dimness and then slowly turned his head toward Elene. Despite evidence to the contrary, he was certain she must be dreaming—or else he was—and he half expected her to thrash about, mumbling in her sleep, at any moment.

She did not. Indeed, she made no sound, except for the low exhalation of her breath, so close that he could feel it upon his cheek. Geoffrey's heart began pounding loudly, for although her expression was shadowed, he could see an unmistakable tension, and when his gaze traveled upward, he met her eyes, wide open and watching him.

Sucking in a startled breath, Geoffrey nearly pushed her away. How often had she threatened him with violence should he touch her? Yet here he was, holding her to his naked body, and she was simply staring back at him solemnly. "Elene?" Her name came out hoarse as he wound his fingers in her own, entwining them upon his chest.

She gave him no answer, but rubbed her knuckles against the hairs there, as if in wonder. "Elene…" Geoffrey whispered, unable to voice the questions that lodged in his throat. Turning onto his side, he leaned over her cautiously, but she buried no knife in his back; nor did she kick him. She only gazed up at him, as if in silent assent, and Geoffrey waited no longer. Lowering his head to hers, he sought her lips.

It had been too long.

That was Geoffrey's first thought as her mouth opened beneath his own. And the few kisses he had stolen since their wedding paled in comparison to this heady meeting. She had never welcomed him before, but now she did, and Geoffrey reveled in the greeting, in the taste of her, spicy and hot, as his tongue found its way inside.

And then she kissed him back.

Gripping his fingers in a tight grasp, she pressed her lips to his, and the touch of her tongue sent his senses reeling. Gentle at first, she soon became bolder, more insistent, mating her tongue with his own, running it over his teeth and exploring his mouth in a way that well reflected her passionate spirit, until hunger for her raged through him. He felt it driving him, but he leashed it violently, all too aware of the times he had frightened her away with his need.

Slowly, Geoffrey eased himself down over her. Careful to keep his weight on his arms, he let his lower body rest upon hers and groaned when his hard tarse settled against the soft linen that covered her thighs. As if startled by the weight of him, she released his fingers, and he wound them in her hair. At last. "Elene," he whispered as he lifted a fistful to his face, inhaling her perfume.

"Your hair," he muttered. "I've wanted…" His eloquence deserted him as he threw it over his shoulders, shuddering as it slid down his back. Elene made a shaky sound, as if she could no more understand him now than she ever did. "Mock me not," he muttered, attempting a smile. Sensing her uncertainty, he longed to reassure her, but the words would not come. He was too hard, too hot, and her hair… Filling his hand with the heavy locks, he leaned down to her lips again.

Her wariness vanished when his mouth met hers, and

Geoffrey relished her capitulation. Elene kissed as though she had just discovered pleasure—and perhaps she had. Struck by a sudden qualm, Geoffrey firmly squashed it. No matter what her history, she was his wife, and he had wanted her for too long. Giving way to her questing tongue, Geoffrey sucked on it until she thrust and parried again, and then she jolted him by mimicking his actions.

Tasting her desire, Geoffrey fed off it eagerly, relishing each hot, wet union, as if he had never kissed a woman before. Indeed, he had never kissed anyone like Elene, never known anyone like her, and his body clamored to make her his. Now. Pausing only to gasp for breath, Geoffrey moved his mouth across her cheek to her ear, then lifted her locks with unsteady hands to caress the length of her throat. When he found a spot that made her shiver, he suckled there until she jerked in his arms. His body rocked forward in response, and he sucked in a harsh breath, taut with the force of his need.

Now! Surely, he would die if he didn't bury himself deep inside her, but he could not. Not yet. Maybe not ever. Loosing a ragged sigh, Geoffrey lifted a trembling hand to her hair, dragging the long smooth strands through his fingers and inhaling the sweet fragrance like a man possessed. "So beautiful," he whispered. "I have dreamed of it draped over me, our only covering." Gazing down at her questioningly, he saw no denial, and she did not protest when he reached for the hem of her shift, gliding it slowly along her thigh to her waist. Raising her up, Geoffrey lifted it gently over her head and stared down at her, his heartbeat a deafening noise in his ears.

The moonlight gilded the curve of her breasts, neither small nor large, but perfectly formed. *Mine,* Geoffrey thought, then shied from such a primitive notion. He was an educated man, a scholar, who gently wooed, and yet he was consumed with ardor for his wife. *Elene*. Whispering her name, Geoffrey took a thick lock of smooth strands and spread it over her throat, her shoulders and her chest, until she shivered and threw her head back. Then he bent down and touched his tongue to her nipple. She started, staring up at him wide-eyed.

"Easy…" Geoffrey said, trying to slow his pounding blood. He would die if she fled his bed now, when her breasts were bared to him, when his sex nudged against her silky thigh. Instead of suckling, he rubbed his cheek against the supple mounds, gently, softly. He wanted to taste all of her, to lave and nibble on every bit of her skin, but he sensed her reluctance, and so he kissed her mouth.

When she wound her arms around his neck, Geoffrey moaned, pressing his ready member to the juncture of her thighs. The entire length of her lithe body touched his, and her nipples rubbed against his chest. She was beneath him at last, naked in his arms, and he could no longer deny the raging hunger that consumed him.

"Touch me, Elene," he urged in a raw voice. He had to have her hands on him, willingly this time. Holding his breath, Geoffrey waited, then expelled a harsh groan when he felt her fingers, hesitant at first and then more sure, close around him. And then, to his astonishment, she began to stroke him.

"Elene!" he gasped. "Yes. Don't stop. Faith, I…" Coherent speech escaped him as she tightened her grip. "I'm not making sense, am I?" He ground out the words, barely able to string together a sentence. *Nothing made sense*, he realized, for this was his wife, a woman who stood for everything he was against, and yet he wanted her more than he had wanted anything in his life. He would die if he didn't have her. Now.

"Elene. I can't… I must…" Taking her hand from him,

he entwined their fingers again. He paused to gasp for breath, his tarse throbbing painfully, and gazed down at her in question, afraid to see the answer, uncertain he could stop himself should she deny him. But she did not. She blinked, her eyes so dazed and dreamy that he shuddered, and opened her thighs to him.

Now. Geoffrey groaned as his fierce control slipped away, as his body claimed dominance over his mind, and he positioned his hips, mounting her at last. He found her opening easily, shuddering when he met moistness there. She was ready for him, but he was a big man; he didn't want to hurt her. And she was skittish, her thighs trembling.

"Elene. I…" Geoffrey gasped, searching her face, but he could not divine her feelings in the darkness, and the need was driving him on, pushing the head of him into her heat. Taking her other hand, he entwined those fingers too, so that he held both her hands and their palms pressed together in an intimate embrace that mimicked their bodies. And then, he could wait no longer. With his own hoarse cry ringing in his ears, Geoffrey thrust deep inside her.

Elene's fingers gripped his convulsively as he drove into her body, but she made no sound, and Geoffrey groaned when her tightness gave way, welcoming him to her womb as if he belonged there. She was unhurt, and he was glad of it, but along with the knowledge came a feeling so powerful that it shook him to the core, and he jerked spasmodically within her in reaction.

Looking down at her, Geoffrey wanted to speak, to express, somehow, his tangled emotions, but the words would not come. Thus he reined in his own fevered needs once more, for if he could not tell her, he would do his best to show her the depth of his feelings. He waited, keeping a stranglehold on himself, until he felt her relax beneath him, and when she let out a soft sigh, he smiled.

"Tell me what you want," he urged. "Tell me what feels good."

"I can't," she whispered, turning her face away.

"Yes, you can. This?" Geoffrey asked hoarsely as he pressed his open mouth against her throat. She moved restlessly under his touch. "This?" Lightly he kissed the swell of her breast. Freeing his fingers, he slid them through her hair, only to groan and crush them in his fist. He couldn't wait, for the need drove him, robbing him of the power of speech, making him rear back and thrust into her again. He cupped her bottom, forcing himself deeper, and then he stilled in surprise when he heard her soft sound of pleasure.

"Ah," she said again, the small noise making his heart leap.

"This?" he muttered as he eased himself out of her and back again. Sweat beaded on his forehead as he tried to keep to a slow pace and entwined their fingers once more.

"Yes...every...thing," she said, and Geoffrey groaned in relief, giving himself up at last to the passion that consumed him. Mindless now, he thrust again and again, so deep that he could go no farther. And Elene kept pace with him, her fingers gripping his as their hips met in perfect rhythm.

His fierce wife, known far and wide for her shrieking, made the tiniest sounds, as if they were wrung from her against her will. The gentle sighs and low pants were nearly Geoffrey's undoing, until finally she dug her nails into his palms, breathless and taut, and he plunged on to his own release, his heart pounding out a frantic rhythm.

At last, Elene was his.

Chapter Fifteen

Afterward, Geoffrey pulled her close, wrapping his arms around her, and Elene nestled against him, drawing the warmth and comfort of his embrace around her like a cloak. She had thought that would be all for her, a bit of closeness, and she choked back a laugh at her own naiveté.

In her first unselfish act in years beyond counting, she had planned to give herself to Geoffrey for his sake, never expecting to feel anything but a pleasant stirring at his kisses before the deadening weight of him and the pain that followed. But there had been no pain, only joy and pleasure such as Elene had never imagined. Closing her eyes, she clung to the memory as he laid his cheek atop her hair. She felt spent, but sweetly so, as if Geoffrey had taken her with him into his dream.

"He raped you, didn't he?"

The question, although softly spoken, made Elene flinch. She tried to pull away, but Geoffrey held her tightly, and she could not muster the strength for a struggle. Obviously, he had no intention of letting her go until he heard the truth, and the knowledge robbed her of her brief contentment.

Now it would come, Elene thought, blinking at a sudden pressure behind her eyes. At last, he had roused the thing that lay between them, the history that he had chosen to ignore. She had ignored it, too, at first in careless disregard and later in thoughtless complacency. Faith, she had never thought it could matter so much! After a lifetime of courting low opinion, she wanted more from this man. Coward that she was, Elene could not look at him, for she was not sure she could bear to see his horror and revulsion. And if he knew this much, then he must suspect the rest.

She had done murder, and she did not regret it.

Swallowing a lump that had lodged in her throat, Elene steeled herself as best she could. Better a swift end to what had developed between them than a long-drawn-out death. "Yes," she admitted without equivocation. "Cowardly bastard that he was, Avery ran from the Wolf. All his grand plans had gone awry, but he thought to get himself the manor, if nothing else. He came straight from the battle, still reeking with blood, and made Edred marry us, though I would have him not. Then, afraid it might be laid aside, he tried to consummate it. Filthy bastard!"

Elene felt herself start to shake, as she had that night, after it happened, but she forced herself to stillness, unwilling to let Geoffrey see her agitation. "I warned him not to touch me, but he heeded me not. And so I killed him." She spat out the words, just as she had spat on Avery's body, for no matter what came now, she did not rue his death. He had taunted her, put his dirty hands on her and borne down on her with his dreadful weight, heaving and sweaty....

Scowling, Elene put the images from her mind, turning her thoughts instead to her new husband. He would be outraged, surely, and quick to condemn her, for he had not only married a murderess but lain with her. Now he would regret it, pushing her away as if she befouled him, as Edred said she befouled all who came near to her.

But Geoffrey only drew her closer, rubbing his cheek against her hair in a soothing gesture that was lost on Elene. What was he doing? Why wasn't he calling for his soldiers to drag her to the dungeon? She wanted to ask, but could not find her voice. And then, at last, Geoffrey spoke. "I would slay him myself, if I could," he whispered. He sounded so fierce, so unlike himself, that Elene lifted her head to look at him.

Even in the darkness, she could see the brightness in his eyes, the taut angle of his jaw. She recognized anger, but it did not seem to be directed toward her. "Would that I had been here to protect you. Or that I could have found him at Wessex and killed him then, before he could hurt you," Geoffrey swore savagely.

Elene blinked in astonishment at his vehemence, uncertain how to react to a response so different from what she had expected. As if he sensed her dismay, his tone softened. "I would take away all memories of his touch, if I could." And though she could still discern the strength of his emotion, his fingers were gentle as they brushed back her hair from her face.

"I would have you know only my touch," he whispered, staring down at her so intently that Elene shivered. She felt as though all Geoffrey's great intellect, strength and compassion were focused solely upon her, the concentration she had observed so often before firmly fixed. And she could do naught but surrender to his compelling gaze. Bemused, she gaped, wide-eyed, while he kissed her cheek, her hairline, her throat, and then he moved lower, his lips moist and warm, his breath soft against her skin.

Her arms, her belly, the tips of her fingers, all received

his tender caress, and Elene lay back, dazed, while he continued his ministrations. She shuddered, still unable to believe that a man had taken *her* side, speaking no word of blame or judgment. But that was Geoffrey, and as she blinked back a hot pressure behind her eyes, Elene knew he was one like no other.

She shuddered again when he parted her legs, his touch tender as always, his breath teasing her, his kisses taking away whatever darkness lingered and branding her with his warmth. Then she drew in a sharp breath, dizzy and hot, as he brushed his mouth against the juncture of her thighs. Unable to stop herself, Elene sighed, a low, keening sound that made him deepen the contact, and slipping into a waking dream once more, she gave herself up to her husband.

Elene woke to find the sun high in the sky, and she rolled over in surprise. She never slept late, for fear her enemies would gain some advantage while she lay senseless. Disoriented, she blinked and groaned as her body protested movement, and then her eyes flew open wide.

Geoffrey.

A sound escaped her, soft and hazy with memory, and she turned back to gaze about the chamber. To her surprise, she saw that cheese and bread and ale waited for her on the stool, and a small tub of water stood nearby.

Geoffrey.

Elene had no doubt that he had done it himself, bringing in the bath and the food, as no other lord would do. Although her father and his ilk would never lift a finger for themselves, let alone another, she knew that Geoffrey had brought these things here. For her. Suddenly ravenous, she threw back the sheet and grabbed a hunk of bread before going to the tub. It was not large enough to sit in, but she stood, washing the stiffness from muscles never used before. And then, wrapping herself in a strip of linen, she waited in sudden indecision.

Frowning, Elene stepped to the chest that had gone with them to Wessex and back. There she hesitated once more before falling to her knees and lifting the lid. Digging beneath her husband's finery, she reached for the gowns Marion had made for her, put away but not forgotten. Although she had scoffed at the time, now Elene stroked the beautiful material in wonder. Could she?

Why not? she thought giddily as she donned the new linen shift and the yellow silk gown. Wide-eyed, she turned around, smoothing the fabric with her palms, delighted by the feel of it. Stopping abruptly, she sobered and found the hairbrush Geoffrey had left lying out the other night. Sitting on the low stool, she swept it through her hair, trying to restore it to order as Geoffrey had done, but she was not as gentle as her husband and had not the patience. The thought made her halt in her task, and she flushed, remembering well Geoffrey's gentleness and patience during the long hours of the night.

Setting aside the brush, Elene put her fists to her warm cheeks, suddenly uncertain. Perhaps she should not show herself below so...changed. What if the manor's residents scoffed at her attempts to look the lady? What if Geoffrey joined them? Coward that she was, Elene feared facing him in the light of day, with the memories of what they had done fresh in her mind.

As if chafing at her indecision and delay, the object of her thoughts appeared in the doorway, and Elene bit back a cry of dismay. Glaring fiercely at his wide chest, she refused to meet his gaze, for she was unsure of what it would hold this morning. Elene knew she could not bear to see censure or indifference after their union, and she cursed this new weakness. She opened her mouth to attack him instead, to mock him before he could hurt her, but his low voice, sober and full of awe, stopped her words.

"You are so beautiful that it hurts my eyes to look upon you," Geoffrey said, and Elene felt her mouth drop open in surprise. Her cheeks burned as she recognized the undertone of warmth and familiarity in his words. Glancing up at him, finally, she was suffused with heat, for his eyes had taken on that dreamy aspect that told her he desired her. No one had ever desired her. Except Geoffrey.

All Elene's concerns melted away with his gentle reassurance. In the bright blaze of late morning, he still wanted her, and Elene could not help the answering smile that came to her lips.

"Elene," he whispered, stepping closer. Shivering with anticipation, she hoped he would lean over and kiss her mouth, but he simply held out his hand. "Come, before I change my plans and take you back to bed."

Elene flushed anew, at both his blatant speech and the disappointment that pulsed through her. Would it be so bad to return to the nest where they had found so much pleasure, or was she wicked to think such things during daylight hours? Hiding her chagrin, Elene ducked her head. Perhaps Geoffrey would touch her only under the cover of darkness. Vexed by the notion, Elene frowned, but she let him take her hand and pull her toward the door.

"Come. 'Tis a beautiful day, and I would go riding with my wife." His low whisper seemed to hold some hidden meaning, but he said no more as he entwined his fingers with hers.

Feeling awkward, but greedy for the press of his palm against her own, Elene let him lead her down through the hall, past the gawking servants and out to the stables, where horses had been readied. Obviously, Geoffrey had been busy this morn, while she lay sleeping, she thought with a scowl.

But her frown soon eased as they headed through the bailey and past the gates into the hills. Geoffrey halted his mount in a meadow rife with tall grass, fresh and sweet-smelling. Along a nearby slope Jacob's ladders nodded their bright blue heads, and Elene breathed deeply. Never had she felt so alive and yet so at peace. Silently she glanced at her husband. Gracefully sliding from his horse, he stepped forward to assist her, and she felt like laughing aloud, for no man had ever helped her.

Except Geoffrey.

Elene's amusement vanished when she felt his warm hands resting on her waist and the brush of his firm body against her own. He lowered her slowly, and by the time her feet were on the ground, she was as breathless and dizzy as if she had fallen. With a secretive smile that made her flush with heat, he turned away, reaching for a blanket he had brought along. Then, to her surprise, he spread it on the grass and sat down upon it, calmly removing his boots and sword and laying them aside.

Elene's cheeks grew crimson at the suspicion that was forming, but, ducking her chin, she took a seat beside him. Pretending to admire the view of the distant peaks, she turned away, only to feel his fingers in her hair, combing through the thick strands, and her head fell back in helpless delight. Never before had she thought of her hair as something special, or that any part of her was…beautiful. It was absurd, and yet she had the strange notion that Geoffrey could convince her of anything.

He must have moved closer, for Elene recognized his warmth at her back, and then her locks were lifted aside so that he could kiss a place on her neck that made her shiver. "Geoffrey!" she muttered, struggling against the lassitude that crept over her.

"Elene," he answered, a thread of amusement in his husky tone. Then she felt the slow glide of his hands as they moved around her to cup her breasts.

"Here, like this?" she asked in a shaky voice. "Are you mad?"

"No, just hungry for you," he answered in a rough whisper.

Elene blinked. Although heat was overwhelming her, she turned to face him. He could have had her in their bed; why go to all the trouble to bring her here? She looked up at him, the question in her eyes, and found the answer in his own. With sudden, heart-wrenching certainty, Elene knew that Geoffrey deliberately had taken her away from the great chamber and the manor that held so many bad memories. He wanted her to know pleasure here, unsullied by darkness, in the bright beauty of the meadow, and his kindness made her tremble. Swallowing a sudden lump in her throat, Elene placed her palms on either side of her husband's face, more dear to her than any other, and shook her head at the depth of his goodness.

"Oh, Geoffrey." He kissed her then, in a tender meeting so fraught with emotion that Elene felt as if she might burst with the strain of it. The phantom aches that had assailed her turned into tiny pricks of joy and wonder that were no less painful in their own way. They bore down on her, creating pressure behind her eyes and driving her to action.

She deepened the kiss, expressing in the only way she knew the feelings that coursed through her. Geoffrey groaned, and it pleased her, heightening her already intense sensations. She wanted... She *needed* to do *some-*

thing, and so she ran her hands down his chest over the smooth linen of his tunic.

"Touch me, Elene," Geoffrey urged and, breaking the kiss, he lifted the edges of his tunic and tossed it over his head. Catching her breath, Elene found herself facing his chest, massive and muscular and covered with dark, springy hair. In the bright light of day, he was astonishing, so broad, so strong, but, strangely enough, no longer intimidating. She knew this body and the gentle man who inhabited it, and as if to prove her thoughts, he waited, sitting back on his heels while she stared in wonder. *She* was the restless one, struck suddenly by nameless longings and heat that forced her to act.

Slowly, hesitantly, Elene lifted a hand and pressed her palm over her husband's heart. It was thudding wildly against his ribs, and she glanced up at his face in surprise. Her cheeks flushed at the look he gave her. More than dreamy, it was intent, and it connected with some place deep in her belly.

It emboldened her, and Elene ran her fingers through the thick mat of hair, glorying in the feel of it and the hard planes beneath. Then, more daring, she slid both hands up his arms to caress the solid muscles that marked him as a knight, strong and brave, and she tasted not bitterness, but a comforting warmth along with the heady thrill of excitement.

This was Geoffrey, and he was the most beautiful thing she had ever seen. Leaning close, she put her cheek to his chest, as he had once done to her, and inhaled the masculine scent of him, but it was not enough. She turned, pressing her mouth to his skin, spreading kisses across the wide expanse. And driven by a dizzy thrumming in her blood, she found a hard nub and put her tongue to it.

When Geoffrey groaned, she took it in her mouth,

prompted by her long-forgotten conversation with Marion. Now the married woman's advice came back in vivid detail, reminding her of this and so much else, things that she had thought wicked and strange, but that now seemed compelling and...necessary.

Geoffrey was tugging at her gown, and, seized by a reckless feeling, Elene lifted it over her head, tossing it with his tunic. She followed it with her shift, and when she looped her arms around his neck and pressed her breasts into his hard chest, she knew no shame or fear, only hot pleasure. Feeling the gentle glide of his hands down her back, pulling her to him, Elene made a sound low in her throat, part delight and part need. Did he have any idea how wonderful he was?

"Help me with these," he whispered, and Elene saw that he wanted her to strip off the rest of his garments. His erection strained at the thin material, and with only a slight hesitation, Elene reached for his hips, sliding the braies low to release him. His tarse was large and thick, but she felt no panic or revulsion, only a hot yearning that compelled her to reach out a finger to touch the very tip. Geoffrey shuddered in response, falling back upon the blanket and taking her with him. She sprawled atop him, her body so restless that she rubbed against him helplessly. Her lower body pulsed with need, yet he made no move to alter their positions, and, impatient, she bit his shoulder.

Geoffrey jerked upward in response. Whispering her name hoarsely, he dragged her knees forward so that she straddled him, and once again she was reminded of Marion's words. Flushing at the memory, she sat up so that she was pressed against his hardness. Was this what he wanted? Closing her eyes, Elene let her head fall back and moved dreamily against him, enjoying the friction she created with each motion.

And then she realized just what her husband was about. Straightening suddenly, Elene blinked and looked down. Geoffrey was eyeing her intently, his mouth quirked at the corner, as if he would smile but had not the strength, and she knew, without a doubt, that he had done this for her. Somehow, he sensed that his weight—any weight— bothered her, and so he arranged it so that she felt none. This knight, tall and bold, a rich and powerful de Burgh, lay beneath her, his hands resting lightly on her thighs, prone and ready to let her work her will upon him.

Blinking against the sudden pressure behind her eyes, Elene felt bright stabs of wonder so sharp they would pierce her heart. She gazed at Geoffrey, so beautiful and giving, and she wanted to gift him with something in return—everything. Drawing a deep breath, she shook out her hair and let it fall all over him.

Letting out a harsh sigh, he took handfuls of it, rubbing them over himself, over her, and capturing her mouth for deep, wet, driving kisses. Elene shifted impatiently, rotating her hips in increasing abandon, until he broke away, gasping. "Take me inside you," he whispered roughly.

His urgent plea startled her, and yet Elene felt a hot, answering need in her belly. Lifting her hips, she ground against him, but desire raged, unabated. A sound, dazed and helpless, escaped her throat as she lifted herself again and looked down between their bodies. The sight that met her was so raw and compelling that she gasped.

Then she touched him.

"Yes, do it, Elene," Geoffrey groaned, his fingers tightening upon her thighs. "Now." His blunt words seemed to heat her very blood, and Elene's hand shook and fumbled in her haste to do his bidding. At last she felt the silky glide of his entrance and sank down upon him. Shuddering in relief, she leaned forward, gasping at the dizzying stab of pleasure she had given herself. Settling back once more, she began to move in a slow, sensual rhythm. Geoffrey rose to meet her, his hands gently guiding their meeting until she threw back her head, her hair brushing his skin, then flying over her shoulder as she stiffened and moaned in fulfillment.

Geoffrey's harsh groan soon joined with her tiny cries, rising above the rustling of the breeze and the calls of the twites, and Elene thought that nothing ever could mar the perfection of this moment, the two of them joined together in a shared dream, while the harsh reality that had always been her life existed a world apart.

But she could not so easily escape, for not far away, hidden in the tall grasses, someone lodged and watched and, decrying their union, plotted its demise.

Elene refused to go inside. Even after they returned to the manor, she did not want to go back to the great chamber or her old room, where she had spent so much time a virtual prisoner of her own devising. The wonderful feelings Geoffrey roused in her lingered, and she wanted to catch them close all the rest of the day. Someday he hoped to build a solar, a room for gathering with family, he told her, but for now she chose the garden after he left her, stolen away by one of his men to attend to the business of her father's holdings.

Pausing, Elene frowned, surprised at the change in her own attitude. No longer did she covet the manor, but would gift it freely. It had never really mattered to her; she had clung to it out of necessity for her own protection. Now she had other...needs. With a strangled laugh at her wayward thoughts, Elene settled upon the low wall and looked over the area with a jaundiced eye. New rows of herbs were growing at Geoffrey's behest, but she remembered a time when the place had bloomed with both flavorings and beauty. And hadn't there been a bench here? She should find one for enjoying days such as these.

For once, Elene did not scowl at memories of her youth. Their strength had been dimmed, their darkness banished to mere shadows by Geoffrey's light. And instead of giving them power over her, she denied them, reaching for the bright and the good that surrounded her today. Risky, it was, but with rewards well worth the price.

And although the ground had lain fallow since before her mother's death, it was not too late to revive it. Idly, Elene wondered at the names of the flowers she recalled, and then smiled. She would describe them to Geoffrey. He would know; he knew everything.

And soon she would join him in his love for knowledge... Drawing in a deep breath, Elene glanced down at the book in her hands. Geoffrey had left it with her, along with apologies for not beginning her reading lessons at once. Other, more physical interests had taken precedence, but Elene did not mind, for she had enjoyed this day as she had no other. Flushing, she opened the volume of letters he had given her to study and found the first page.

A lightness of being flooded her as Elene stared at the first symbol that would take her into a whole new world—and perhaps make her worthy of her husband.

The hall was already filling when Geoffrey went in to supper. The new steward he had appointed had kept him long, and he found himself unusually impatient, not just for food, but for a sight of his bride, now his wife in every way. This morning he had made her his—not last night in the chamber that had been her father's, but today in the bright sunshine with no darkness to mar their union. It was a new beginning for them both, and for the first time since his wedding day, Geoffrey felt rife with hope for his future.

It died when he pulled back his chair.

Catching a whiff of something putrid, Geoffrey stiffened and stepped back as the candlelight lent form to a dark shape upon his seat. Automatically his hand drifted to the hilt of his sword, only to fall when it became apparent that what awaited him was already dead. Dunstan's knights, alerted by his hesitation, hurried forward, crowding around him, gasping in shock at the filthy offering.

An arrow such as he had never seen before pinned something to the worn wood. Smaller than usual, it was black as if it were crusted with old blood or had been dipped in pitch, and it was buried into a pulpy mass that looked like a piece of meat gone bad. Sucking in a deep breath, Geoffrey leaned closer and bit back an oath when he saw that it was a heart—too small to be human, thankfully, but belonging to some animal. Offal from the butcher? Although it was not the time of year for slaughtering, wild game was always sought for the manor's table. Yet who would leave this mess, like a token of ill will, for him?

Anyone. The reminder of his continual unwelcome in his new home filled Geoffrey with rage, and he reached out to yank the offending weapon from his chair, only to be stopped by one of Dunstan's knights.

"Nay. Look at it, my lord," said Malcolm. "'Tis black and sticky with some foul substance, poison perhaps!"

"Aye, 'tis evil," Talebot agreed.

"An omen?" suggested Malcolm in hushed tones.

"Or a warning," Talebot said, and Geoffrey stared down at the hideous mess angrily. Did it have some meaning known only to the local people, or was it simply an unpleasant business meant to annoy him? His first thoughts were of Montgomery and Serle, but they were both gone, banished from his lands. Who else here was his enemy?

Lifting his head, Geoffrey looked around the hall grimly. It seemed as if he had fought against efforts to drive him away ever since his arrival, first from his wife, then the rogue knight, then the thieving steward. Would there be no end to the struggle? Did every stunned expression hide a treacherous heart? Those closest to the high table looked properly appalled by the grisly gift left him, and some, farther away, were pale and frightened.

As Geoffrey scanned the hushed group of assembled diners and servants, searching for a guilty glance or surly stare, he noticed all eyes gradually turn toward the entrance from the kitchens. Dropping his hand to his hilt once more, he swiveled to face the figure pausing under the archway and drew in a sharp breath of surprise. 'Twas no errant knight or threatening peasant who stepped forward.

It was Elene.

Geoffrey frowned, his dismay growing as the silence around him became filled with whispers and muttering. Although too low for him to decipher much of it, he recognized the word *witch* and stiffened. He had heard his wife called many things, before and after their marriage, but never a witch. The Fitzhugh had a reputation as a threatening presence by dint of her strength and her fierce temper, not through the use of potions and spells. This new appellation made Geoffrey uneasy, for much of the uneducated populace thrived on superstition, and they were often all too eager to accuse one of their own.

And Elene had never been one of them.

Keeping his hand on his sword, lest any dare speak more openly, Geoffrey glanced at his wife. She must have heard the epithet, too, for she ducked her head, letting her hair fall forward while she glared at them all, her ferocious hatred her only defense.

In response, Geoffrey felt his own righteous rage surge to life, for this creature bore little resemblance to the woman he had held in his arms this afternoon, full of passion and wonder. Her gown was the same, but she was not, and his angry gaze swept the room once more. Had they made her what she was? Why could no one see how vulnerable his fierce wife truly was, despite all her strengths? When he saw that Elene refused to come any closer, while the whispers grew louder around her, Geoffrey took matters into his own hands.

"Quiet!" he roared, in a voice not unlike his elder brother's. "Speak not of nonsense in my presence," he warned. Pivoting slowly, he again let his gaze sweep the hall, noting with interest the bowed heads and the eyes that would not meet his own. Faith, were they all guilty? He sighed. Only Dunstan's knights stood apart, untainted. "Serve the meal," he ordered.

Frowning, he turned toward Dunstan's men. "Talebot, take the chair out in the bailey and wash it off. Bury the offal away from prying eyes." The knight nodded grimly, while Malcolm appeared relieved to have escaped the foul task.

Motioning the other diners to move closer, Geoffrey had them make a place on the bench for himself, then called to his wife. For a moment, he thought she might refuse to join him, for she hesitated and he could almost see her weighting her options, but finally she came forward, seating herself beside him sullenly. Geoffrey felt a slow surge of anger at the foul deed that had ruined their reunion, but quelled it, knowing it would be best to eat as usual, as if nothing had happened.

For now. But the matter was not yet laid to rest, by any means, Geoffrey vowed. Tonight he would question everyone privately. Whoever left the bundle on his chair must have done it sometime after dinner, and since the hall was a busy place most of the day, Geoffrey was certain that someone must have seen something. He had only to discover what and where and when, and then maybe he would know *who.*

Chapter Sixteen

No one had seen anything.

Heaving a sigh of impatience, Geoffrey ran a hand through his hair. If he didn't know better, he would have thought every resident of his lands, from the last of Fitzhugh's knights down to the lowliest villein, was conspiring against him. But that made no sense. Everyone had enough to eat, and Geoffrey was overseeing the repair of fences and cots. With work, the manor might even prosper. And who here would not want that? He shook his head, baffled. To a sensible person, the whole business was frustrating beyond belief.

Leaning against the wall in Serle's old chamber, where he had met with each diner and witness, Geoffrey tried to attack the problem logically. If not dissatisfaction, then what else would make the people revolt? Allegiance to someone else? Geoffrey shook his head. He had long since discovered that Fitzhugh had been universally despised, and his daughter, unhappily, was liked little better.

Montgomery? Serle? Geoffrey could find no obvious supporters of either the bullying knight or the ill-favored thief. Yet the manor residents still were guarded and closemouthed, as if afraid to speak. Sighing once more,

Geoffrey pinched the bridge of his nose, unable to find a reason for their wariness. He was not a hard man, and he had done no violence since his arrival here. Faith, he had even let Serle go, when another lord might well have slain him for his treachery.

Perhaps it was the de Burgh name that made them uneasy. Although Geoffrey rarely thought about it, he knew that his father was well-known throughout the kingdom. The Campion name stood for power and wealth, and fear and resentment were often a reaction to both among the ignorant.

Pushing away from the wall, Geoffrey snuffed the last candle, weary of his questioning efforts. Perhaps Dunstan's knights could discover what the lord of the manor could not, he thought with disgust. It was late, he was tired, and he did not want to make too much of what might only have been a childish prank. It was time to get himself to bed.

The thought gave Geoffrey his first smile in many an hour. Elene awaited him above, and well he recalled her supple skin, her musk scent, and the soft, breathy cries she made when he pleasured her. Suddenly, he could not move fast enough, up through the hall and up the narrow stairs to the great chamber. Although anticipation seized him, he purposely slowed his step, entering the room quietly, in case she slept.

A lone candle lit his progress as he moved toward her, and he stopped beside the bed, looking down at her with a surprisingly fierce proprietorship. Her hair spilled upon the pillow and across her face, and the remembered feel of it made his heart beat loudly in response. Leaning forward, he lifted a long strand and crushed it between his fingers. Smooth. Springy. Alive.

Just like Elene.

Geoffrey glanced down at her again, only to frown when he saw a hint of linen peeping out from beneath the locks that rested upon her breast. She was wearing her shift, and he felt strangely disappointed. After their naked union in the grass, he thought clothing no longer necessary between them, yet a lot had happened since this morning.

Geoffrey's frown deepened. Witch, they had called her, and she had not taken it well, disappearing into herself like a turtle behind its shell. Only Geoffrey suspected that his wife's armor was not so rigid. Abruptly he felt the smarting of guilt. Elene appeared so ferocious that it was easy to assume she was, but he knew better. And he should have done better by her.

All through the meal, she had been stony and silent, and instead of taking the time to reassure her, Geoffrey had been contemplating the upcoming interviews, his thoughts fixed upon finding the culprit. Since all his questioning had served him naught, he would have done better to have treated with his wife.

Sighing softly, Geoffrey realized that he was not accustomed to this role of husband he had recently assumed. But he would improve himself, he vowed. With a wry smile, he decided practice was what he needed—and plenty of it.

Leaving the candle burning, Geoffrey stripped off his clothes and slid in beside his wife.

Elene blinked in the dimness, awake and intensely aware of Geoffrey. After what had happened in the hall, she was not sure how he would behave here, alone with her, and so she had taken the coward's way and pretended to sleep, thinking to put off the inevitable confrontation.

Oh, she had seen it at once, how everyone thought she

had left the warning for him. And how could she blame them? It was a nasty trick, and one she might well have tried in those early days of her marriage, if she had thought of it. Then she had wanted only to drive him away, but now... Oh, not now, she thought to herself, biting back the moan of distress that threatened to escape. It had been building within her ever since he walked into the room and stood by the bed, regarding her in silence.

Was he looking upon her with dread? Disgust? Would he leave her now, or make her leave him? Elene did not think she could bear to be parted from him, and that weakness frightened her. She was becoming too vulnerable, too dependent upon her husband's good faith. Faith, ha! Elene choked on her bitter laugh, for who would believe her? And she could surely go mad if Geoffrey questioned her about what had happened below, not in anger or accusation, but in that gentle way of his that told her he was trying vainly to understand her.

"Oh!" The tiny cry broke from Elene abruptly as she felt Geoffrey's heat against her back. His strong arm closed around her, pulling her tight against him, and she heard herself sigh again, in sweet surprise, when she felt his hard desire. He wanted her still, and he asked her nothing. In fact, he spoke not at all, but nuzzled her hair, groaning with pleasure, as if they were back in the meadow where they had lain this morning, and Elene blinked, overcome by sudden, fierce emotion.

Turning, she pushed him onto his back and covered him with her hair, just the way he liked it. He groaned again, gripping her tightly, and Elene knew there would be no questions. This was Geoffrey, after all, and, giddy with relief and gratitude and her tumultuous feelings for him, Elene pressed kisses to his chest. Her nimble fingers caressed smooth muscles that on any other man would have filled her with revulsion, but upon Geoffrey were as sleek and wonderful as the man himself.

She slid lower, dipping her tongue in his navel and smiling at his start of surprise. Since this morning, she had reflected well on all that Marion had told her—shocking things that she had pretended not to hear. But she had listened, enthralled and repelled by what the Wolf's wife claimed were common doings between man and wife. And now, she found herself wanting those same things.

And so she moved lower again, touching her tongue to him, and reveling in his swift jolt of response. Braver now, Elene took him into her mouth and heard his harsh, guttural cry. Her name. It compelled her, along with her own hot, quivering excitement and the delicious taste and scent of him. Elene felt dizzy and powerful, for her magnificent husband lay prone beneath her, his fingers fisted in her hair, his body jerking and sweating because of her.

And she delighted in it, not only in the sense of being in control, of overcoming his strength to make him tremble and groan, but in giving him pleasure. Everything that had been locked away inside her for so long seemed to spill forth, and Elene wanted to gift it all to him, body, heart and soul.

And afterward, when he fell back against the pillow, exhausted, she smiled and curled against him. There, secure in the warmth of his embrace, she forgot the one foul incident that had marred her day as other, more vivid, memories overtook her, and, closing her eyes, Elene drifted from one dream into another.

Geoffrey rose early, restless for some kind of resolution to yesterday's incident and the continuing hostility of his people. With a last, lingering look at his peacefully sleeping wife, he stepped outside, only to find Dunstan's knights already waiting, their faces grim.

"What is it? Have you discovered something?" The two men exchanged wary looks, as if reluctant to speak, and the scene, so reminiscent of his futile questioning of the night before, made Geoffrey even more frustrated.

"Let us go to the old steward's room, then. Perhaps a bit of privacy will loosen your tongues." Striding through the hall, Geoffrey called for bread and ale to be brought to the small chamber. Seating himself on a small cask, he waited until the food and drink were delivered, then leaned back against the wall and lifted his brows. "Well? What have you for me?"

Again, the two exchanged glances. Finally, Talebot spoke. "We have heard little except wild conjecture and rumors."

"There is much talk," Malcolm said, busily tearing off a hunk of bread, as if refusing to meet Geoffrey's gaze.

"Then you have done better than I, for I could persuade no one to say a word," Geoffrey admitted.

Talebot, who ignored the food, cleared his throat. "Perhaps they fear your reaction."

Geoffrey ran a hand through his hair. It had seemed that way to him, as well, but he was at a loss to explain such apprehension. "Why? I have ever been just. Indeed, I can find no motive even for this prank."

Again, Malcolm appeared uncomfortable. "'Tis deemed no prank, but a warning to you to leave the manor," he said. Geoffrey sighed, for he still could see no reason why anyone would desire his departure.

"Perhaps you should go, for a while at least," Talebot broke in. "'Tis well-known that your brother would welcome you at Wessex."

Shaken from his thoughts by the suggestion, Geoffrey

laughed. "I should run from a bit of undone meat skewered on a fancy arrow? Surely you jest!" He would heed no threats, especially none so ridiculous as this.

Talebot did not share his amusement, but eyed him grimly. "You claim you know of no motive, but there is one here who would gain from your departure, aye, even your death."

"Who?" Geoffrey asked. He would gladly learn of such a one. Indeed, he would rejoice to know his enemy at last and have done with this continual mystery.

Although Malcolm hung back, Talebot met his gaze, unflinching, as he spoke. "Your wife."

Halfway to his feet before he regained control of his temper, Geoffrey swore viciously when he took his seat once more. Pushing aside his personal feelings, he forced himself to use logic in Elene's defense. "And just what would she win? Her manor, her inheritance?" He snorted, contemptuous of their faulty reasoning. "The king would not let a lone female hold this property, but would simply wed her to another." The notion left a sour taste in Geoffrey's mouth, and he vowed that none would take Elene to wife.

"Would he? Mayhap after burying enough husbands, the widow would have her freedom," Talebot suggested. "There are some things more powerful than even the will of kings."

Geoffrey laughed—a derisive sound that resembled his wife's efforts at humor. "You speak nonsense!"

"Do I?" Talebot asked. "The arrow itself was smaller than usual, a size more befitting a woman. And your wife is well-known for her skill with weapons."

Geoffrey stiffened in disbelief, but Dunstan's man continued. "And when we looked at it closely, it appeared to be covered in some foul substance, belladonna or monks-hood, perhaps.''

"The mere touch of which have been known to fell a man,'' Malcolm whispered, and Geoffrey felt unease curl through him. He did not care for the direction in which this conversation was going.

Ignoring the other knight, Talebot went on. ''And when we examined the workmanship, we discovered the arrow had no ordinary fletch, but was made with owl feathers. Owl feathers,'' he repeated, as if awed by the significance of this discovery.

"Aye,'' Malcolm agreed in hushed tones. "'Tis common knowledge that they are used in the practice of the dark arts. The owl feathers, the black coloring, the poison, the sacrifice...'' He leaned forward, as if hesitant to speak loudly. "'Tis obviously a piece of witchcraft.''

Geoffrey surged to his feet so swiftly that Malcolm backed up a step and stumbled over a barrel. "Are you calling my wife a witch?'' he asked, his voice deceptively even. Although his ways were different from the Wolf's, the knights obviously noted the resemblance, for both of them paled in the face of his displeasure.

"Nay, my lord,'' Malcolm sputtered. "'Tis just that these things are women's wiles, not the practices of men.''

Geoffrey started forward, only the great strength of his will keeping him from striking. His fist shook with the force of his struggle, for he would as soon bloody these two as not. Aye, he would gladly take on any man who spoke ill of his wife, and if that meant laying low every resident of these lands, then so be it, he thought with righteous wrath.

"I would not insult you, my lord, but the Wolf bade me watch out for his brother, and I would rest easier if your wife were given fewer privileges,'' Talebot said.

Geoffrey stared at the man, astonished by both his insolence and his request. He was a knight, tall and lean, but hardened and scarred by battles, a man capable of taking on a horde of foot soldiers, and yet... "You fear my wife?" Geoffrey asked, incredulous.

Talebot's lips twitched, as if he cared little for Geoffrey's amusement, but he did not deny it. "Considering her past threats against you, I think it would be wise to imprison her, at least for now."

Geoffrey knew the hot rush of anger once more, and reached for his sword, but the very violence of his feelings made him pause. He, the most patient and calm of the de Burghs, wanted to bring this man to his knees. Now. And make him crawl to Elene in abject apology. And the only thing that stopped him was the suspicion that Elene would not laud his efforts. She had nurtured fear of herself for some purpose he could not fathom, hiding the real woman from all eyes but his own. And so it must continue until she should choose otherwise.

Slowly, with some reluctance, Geoffrey withdrew his hand from his sword hilt and stepped back. Visibly relieved, Dunstan's knights bowed their heads, and Geoffrey knew he could not fault them for their vigilance. In their efforts on his behalf, they were hampered by their own ignorance and suspicion, as were so many others.

"Nay. I will not imprison my wife on the basis of a few feathers and blood," Geoffrey said. "Nor will I run from this so-called warning, so I suggest you look to another to find our culprit. Unless you are too sorely afraid," he added, lifting his brows in a deliberate taunt. "In that case, I release you to return to my brother."

Shaking their heads in fierce denial, the knights swore their allegiance, and Geoffrey dismissed them impatiently. Once they were gone, he sank down on a cask and leaned against the wall, again turning his concentration to the mess that had been left upon his seat. If a prank, it had escalated far beyond that now, thanks to the fertile imaginations of the uneducated. And, if not...he needed to have done with it as soon as possible, before it grew greater than his power to contain it.

With a sigh, Geoffrey wracked his brain for a clue once more. He thought of Montgomery and Serle, and was not as quick to dismiss them as before. Indeed, he suddenly found them most appealing suspects.

As for the other possibility... It was unthinkable.

Ignoring the threat against him, Geoffrey spent the next few days following his usual routine, despite the misgivings of Dunstan's men. They trailed behind him like wearisome shadows, advising him not to eat in the hall or go among his people. Indeed, they seemed now to want *him* imprisoned, but he would not give such satisfaction to whoever wished him ill.

Nor would he punish Elene for someone else's perfidy. And so he spent the nights making love to his wife, while during the days he made sure he was seen with her often. And here and there, he managed to snatch a few hours alone with her in which to teach her to read.

She was quick and clever beyond his expectations, and Geoffrey found himself as proud of her as he had ever been of his younger brothers. She was an apt pupil, and so eager to learn that he sometimes found himself staring at her breathlessly, totally captivated by this bright, beautiful girl who was so unlike the woman he had married. And yet, the closer they became, the more he felt the differences between them, as if they were a chasm he was unable—or unwilling—to cross.

That tension was exacerbated by the darkness that

seemed to hang over the manor like a funeral pall. The residents, ever wary, were furtive and frightened, as if expecting retribution any minute for their lord's presence. A bout of wet weather did not improve the situation, but made tempers short and fields soggy.

Seated at the table awaiting his supper, Geoffrey could feel them glaring at him, blaming him for bringing the rain. After all, he had ignored the pointed warning to depart, and woe betide the witch's wrath! Snorting, Geoffrey pushed in his chair impatiently. He was sick unto death of such nonsense. Anyone who saw a toad fancied himself targeted by some evil spirit, when it was obvious the animals simply thrived in the newly prevalent puddles.

With a sigh, Geoffrey turned to eye his two guards askance. Little better than the peasants, they would not even take their meals when he did, but stood behind him like sentries, as if he were a palsied old man who could not protect himself! The situation grated, making his mood even more foul.

He felt helpless, as if his very hands were tied, and angry for it. Sometimes he wanted to lift his sword and slay every last resident within a mile of the manor. That would eliminate his problem—or would it? Despite all his cleverness, Geoffrey still had no idea where his enemy might be hiding or who he might be, and it sorely galled him.

What kind of coward would strike and slink away? The answer that came to him made his head throb, for he well remembered the tactics Elene's father had used against the Wolf. Refusing to follow that train of thought, Geoffrey wondered if perhaps Montgomery or Serle was implementing what he had learned from Fitzhugh. Had they truly left his lands, or was one of them lurking just beyond his reach?

Longingly Geoffrey thought of Wessex or even Campion, but he would not run away from some ruffian, no matter how miserable his life was swiftly becoming. Nor did he care to admit to his brothers that he could not catch one single miscreant. Pinching the bridge of his nose, Geoffrey sighed again. It was summer, and he wanted to spend more idyllic days with his wife, alone in the meadow, but that brief interlude seemed a lifetime ago.

Where was Elene? As he nodded at the servant who placed his trencher before him, Geoffrey could not see her anywhere nearby. He had asked her to always eat in the hall, hoping to avoid further speculation, but she was late. Again. Geoffrey bit back an oath of annoyance, but his food was here, and he had no intention of trotting upstairs to search her out with his two protectors in tow.

Deliberately Geoffrey decided not to wait, and he picked up his knife, sawing off a juicy piece, only to be halted by Talebot's low voice. "Let me taste it, first, my lord, for it might well be poisoned."

Geoffrey stiffened and turned to stare at the man in stunned surprise. His initial response was to laugh aloud, but in this simple knight's eyes he saw both fear and self-sacrifice. Obviously, the man was willing to eat something he thought might well kill him, and Geoffrey had to respect that, even if he gave no credence to such a suspicion.

Uncertain how to handle the request, Geoffrey hesitated, then leaned over abruptly, tossing the small piece of meat to one of the dogs that roamed the hall. And just at that moment, when he was bent low toward the tiles, Geoffrey felt a strange rush of air above his hair, followed by a loud *thwack*.

"My lord! Up there, Talebot!" he heard Malcolm shout, and then he was thrown to the floor under the knight's heavy weight. With an angry grunt, Geoffrey rolled free, only to stare up at his chair in astonishment. A familiar-looking black arrow protruded from the wood of his chair, right where his chest had been.

"Touch it not!" Malcolm shouted to the crowd, though everyone close by shrank away from the weapon in horror. "The tip is wet with poison."

The word, along with the accusation of witchcraft, echoed around the hall so swiftly that Geoffrey could almost feel the panic spreading like a contagion. He opened his mouth to halt its advance, but even he felt a shiver of unease as he stared at the wicked barb buried in the wood, where he had been. Plainly, it was no simple weapon, but the tool of someone wicked and foul.

Who? Geoffrey followed the arrow's path back to the spy hole near the arched ceiling. Elene claimed her father had used it to watch his own guests, but now he wondered who else knew of the space at the end of the upper passage. One of Fitzhugh's former knights, perhaps? It would take some skill to hit a target from that distance, Geoffrey mused.

A series of loud gasps made Geoffrey swivel toward the stairs. Talebot, who had raced off in the direction of the archer, was returning, and he was not alone. Apparently, Dunstan's knight had reached the passage in time to capture the culprit. At last! Geoffrey straightened, eager to finally face his enemy.

But just as swiftly as his mood had risen, it plummeted, sending his heart to his knees, when a flash of yellow told him just who Talebot dragged behind him. Geoffrey heard a strangled sound that seemed to come from his own throat as he watched their descent, then the mutterings of the crowd as they, too, recognized Talebot's prisoner.

It was Elene.

Chapter Seventeen

She could have killed him. Although he had rushed toward her with his sword drawn as she hurried toward the stairs, Elene could have thrust her favorite dagger into his belly before he had time to blink. She was quicker than most big, slow-moving knights, and she had had the advantage going down the steps. But she had recognized him as one of Geoffrey's, called Talebot, and so she had done nothing when he grabbed her by the arm and pulled her with him toward the hall.

As she willed herself not to struggle within his harsh grasp, Elene suspected his actions stemmed from more than her tardiness to supper. But it wasn't until she viewed the scene below that she felt the sharp bite of panic. At first Elene could see only Geoffrey's chair, with a black arrow embedded in it, and she choked back a cry of sheer terror until she saw him standing to one side, unharmed. She stumbled then, weak with a relief so great that her legs threatened to give way.

Geoffrey was all right.

Elene told herself that was all that mattered, but she could hardly ignore the whispers that rose about her. "Witch!" they called, and they hid their faces from her.

Elene would have laughed to see their fear, but she realized, all too well, why Geoffrey's man gripped her arms so tightly. And she felt a pain so deep that death seemed preferable.

Talebot pushed her forward roughly, as if she might foul his very fingers, and Elene knew she ought to trip him, or prick him with her blade, but her heart hurt so that she could barely breathe. A hush fell over the hall when they reached Geoffrey, and the man behind her was forgotten. It was the man in front of her who consumed her thoughts, and Elene was afraid to look at him.

"Release her," Geoffrey said. Blinking, Elene glimpsed his jaw, hard and set, and she felt sick. Bile rose in her throat, choked back by force of will. Surely she would not vomit here, in front of all her enemies, all her past victories for naught in the final humiliation? Eager to let go of her, Talebot thrust her away, and Elene did not even reach for her knife. It was all she could do to retain her footing.

"She was in the passage," Talebot said.

"And she is well-known for her skills with weapons," said the other knight from Wessex, called Malcolm. He eyed her with little-disguised fright, but Elene could not even muster the energy to glare at him. It didn't matter anymore.

Nothing did.

"Aye," she heard that old bastard Kenelm mutter. "I've seen her hit a target no man could match, with her own bow, specially made." He grinned, and Elene stared at him, unblinking, until he glanced away uneasily. He gave her something to look at, for she could not meet Geoffrey's gaze. Not yet. Maybe not ever.

She was still armed, but she gripped her hands in front of her until the knuckles were white with the might of her grasp. Those already at table were joined by servants from the kitchens and latecomers, all milling around, drawn to the horror like flies to butter. And, like flies, they buzzed, eager to see her downfall, until soon the very air seemed to vibrate with tension. Finally, Elene knew she could wait no longer. If she saw that same accusatory look on Geoffrey's face, she would die, but better that she do so now, quickly, than that she draw out this torment.

Taking a deep breath, Elene lifted her head, but her husband's attention was on Kenelm. Laying his hands on the table, he leaned toward the knight, and others who had fought with her father. "Who else could make such a shot?" he asked.

Elene blinked as much sputtering met his question. Straightening once more to his full, glorious height, Geoffrey turned to Malcolm. He was thinking, Elene realized, and so caught up in his fierce concentration that he noticed not the gaping mouths of the crowd. "Do you remember who among these men were here at table when it happened?"

Several loud protests were drowned out by the whispers of surprise that grew and filled the hall as everyone began to realize that Geoffrey was still searching for the archer. And Elene, her benumbed brain one step behind them, let out the breath she had been holding, her relief so great that she felt faint.

A strange, keening noise escaped her throat, and she swayed on her feet. She would have fallen if Geoffrey had not stepped forward with an anxious glance. He held a hand to her waist in gentle aid, but still Elene wanted to fall, to drop to the floor at his feet. A pressure was building behind her eyes and in her chest, and she reached for her husband—wise, wonderful Geoffrey, who had ignored the charges against her, just as if he had not heard them.

A loud choking sound burst upon her, and suddenly Geoffrey's face blurred, as hot, wet drops coursed down her cheeks. Elene lifted a hand to them, stunned to feel the moisture and momentarily at a loss to explain its source.

"My wife is upset," she heard Geoffrey say. The tiles swam and careened below her as she felt him swing her up into his arms. He was so strong and warm, and she felt so cold, as if wracked with chills, that she buried her face against his shoulder. His men protested, but Geoffrey swept them aside, striding toward the stairs with sudden urgency.

"Later," he called over his shoulder as he took the steps two at a time, her weight seeming as nothing to him.

Once inside the great chamber, he shut the door and set her on her feet, letting her slowly slide down his body. "Are you all right? Can you stand?" he asked. Elene nodded, but another loud sound burst from her throat, uncontrollable.

Geoffrey swore softly in a fierce voice she rarely heard him use. "I'm sorry! I should never have let Talebot touch you, but I was thinking about the arrow, and..."

Elene tried to smile, but the wetness was dripping down her face, and Geoffrey swore again, his hands moving aimlessly over her arms as if he knew not where to touch her. "Did you think I was hurt? Faith, I didn't even consider what you might see! I'm a thoughtless bastard, not fit to be your husband!"

His words, so absurd, made Elene want to laugh, for it was she who was not worthy of him, and how well she knew it. Opening her mouth, Elene meant to protest, but all that came out were great, gasping sobs, and, overcome by the force of them, she fell to her knees before him and threw her arms around his legs.

She didn't deserve this man, this great, powerful man who, in the face of overwhelming evidence, had never even imagined that she might be guilty of witchcraft or some other effort to harm him. Such faith was something she did not understand, but she welcomed it, embracing it, embracing him, as she had nothing else in her cold, hard life.

Dimly Elene felt his hands on her as he crouched low in front of her, and vaguely she heard his soft, troubled questions, but she was making so much noise that she could make no sense of them. She could not remember ever crying before in her life, but it felt good to release everything at last, as if her very soul were being cleansed with each tear.

Geoffrey shook her gently, alarm clearly visible on his handsome features, and she knew she must answer him, if only to alleviate his fears. "I'm crying!" she managed to say, touching her cheek as if to demonstrate.

"Yes, but why?" Geoffrey asked, grasping her shoulders. "What is it?"

Finally, gulping and sniffling, Elene found her voice. "You didn't suspect me," she whispered. He looked so baffled that Elene choked back a laugh.

"Of course I didn't suspect you," he said. His dark brows lifted. "Should I?"

Elene blinked. He was so brave and handsome and clever and so certain of her that she was overwhelmed with the force of her feelings for him. They welled up in her, taking the place of her tears, filling her with joy and wonder and passion, until she could contain them no longer.

"I love you, Geoffrey," she said.

* * *

At the sound of Elene's even breathing, Geoffrey relaxed. He had never seen her like this, so vulnerable and...human. It worried him, and he swore silently that he would uncover his enemy as soon as possible, for he could not have Elene upset in this manner. After all, she loved him.

She loved him.

Geoffrey felt a surge of masculine pride at the thought, for wasn't that what he had always desired, to love and be loved? And yet he also knew a niggling sense of guilt, for he was not as certain of his own feelings as Elene. Of course, she was the more volatile of the two of them, he told himself, and, as such, more given to deep emotions. Faith, even he had never imagined the passions Elene had kept locked inside her! Just the thought made his body stir, and, ruefully, Geoffrey slid away from her supple form. He had other matters to attend to this night, he thought grimly.

Silently slipping from the bed, Geoffrey dressed hurriedly and left the room. As he suspected, Talebot was keeping watch at the top of the steps, and he motioned to the knight to join him. A torch still burned in the passage, and he headed for Elene's former chamber, now unoccupied. He did not want to go too far from his wife, yet there they would be able to talk privately.

Both Talebot and Malcolm soon followed, and Geoffrey shut the door before turning to face them. They met his gaze warily when he leaned back against the worn wood to study them as a tutor would his worst pupils. "I hope you have thought long and hard on your work this day," he said evenly. When they would have spoken, he stopped them with a sharp glance. "Because while you were accosting my wife, the real culprit undoubtedly escaped. Easily."

"But, my lord—" Talebot began.

"No," Geoffrey said, cutting him off. "Don't tender your excuses. You have shown yourselves no better than the lowliest peasant who covets a piece of coral as a ward against witchcraft!" Pausing to take a deep breath and tame his burgeoning temper, Geoffrey fixed the two knights with a steady gaze. "Let's look at this logically," he said wearily. "You found Elene in the spy hole?" He turned toward Talebot as he asked the question.

"No, I—"

"In the passage, then."

"Not exactly," Talebot said, appearing chagrined.

"Then where? Exactly," Geoffrey said dryly.

"She was rushing toward the stairs, as if fleeing."

"Or hurrying down to supper," Geoffrey noted, with a sigh. "And where was her bow?"

Talebot had the grace to look uncomfortable. "I searched the area after you left the hall and found nothing," he admitted. "But perhaps it is in here, or in the great chamber, for I did not take leave to enter as you were...uh...there yourself."

Ignoring the knight's awkward explanation, Geoffrey continued. "So she shoots the arrow, right on target, then crawls out of the spy hole, runs along the passage, ducks into one of these chambers, hides the bow, and still makes it to the top of the stairs in time to meet you there?" he asked, his brows lifted.

Talebot frowned, shifting on his feet, but Malcolm seemed undeterred by Geoffrey's reasoning. "'Tis well-known that witches can fly," he put in.

Geoffrey spared him but a glance. "Do not call my wife a witch again, or I shall have to kill you," he promised softly. Then he ran a hand over his eyes, swearing viciously as his patience wore thin. Why could he not make them see what was happening here?

"The bastard who's behind this is using your own ignorance to his advantage!" Geoffrey snapped. "He's exploiting this mood of suspicion, destroying whatever gains I have made among these people and rending the alliance forged by my marriage—all by tossing about a little pitch and feathers."

Talebot, who had been studying his boots, looked up suddenly, and Geoffrey wondered if he had finally convinced the man. Malcolm, obviously, was a hopeless cause. "Mayhap it goes even farther, my lord. Perhaps someone is trying to make your wife look guilty," Talebot suggested.

Starting at the words, Geoffrey knocked his palm against his forehead. It was so simple that he could have kicked himself for not seeing it. "Of course," he whispered, his voice hoarse with excitement. Finally, they had something to go on! But the rush of triumph was brief, and he soon leaned back and groaned.

"Great," he muttered. "Now all we have to do is find out which one of Elene's enemies is responsible."

Talebot cleared his throat in sympathy, while Malcolm scratched his chin. "Does she have many?" he asked innocently.

And Geoffrey, giving way to the strain of the past weeks, laughed, so hard and long that his eyes watered.

He decided not to tell her.

After Dunstan's knights had been dispatched to their pallets, Geoffrey returned to the great chamber, where he found his wife sleeping peacefully. As he stood over her, admiring the gentle curve of her cheek and the short cinnamon-colored curl of her lashes, he realized that he could not bring himself to awaken her with the harsh news. Self-ishly Geoffrey knew he did not want to see suspicion cloud her amber eyes once more, or her hand rest upon her ever-present dagger.

Besides, his wife was agitated enough by recent events, without the added burden of knowing that someone was deliberately trying to entrap her. Geoffrey frowned at the thought, for he had heard tales of women who were burned at the stake or stoned to death on charges of witch-craft when they were guilty only of healing the sick or growing old.

Unease drifted coldly up his spine, making him stiffen. He had sworn to protect her, but he was only one man, while a crowd roused by fervor had been known to un-horse the knights trying to subdue it. And it was not only the growing ill mood of his people that worried him. This evening's arrow had come close, too close, and he had to consider the possibility that next time his enemy might not miss.

Pivoting on his heel, Geoffrey turned away from the bed with a low oath. He shuddered to think what would happen to Elene should he die, for she would be alone once more, to face the accusations of people all too ready to condemn her. He could not trust Dunstan's knights to help her, or even... Geoffrey groaned as he realized an-other bitter truth. The vengeance of the entire countryside would be as nothing compared to the wrath of his broth-ers.

With a haste born of dread, Geoffrey lit another brace of candles and took his writing box from his chest. A wise man knew when to prove himself and when to ask for help or advice, and Geoffrey was no fool. He was not going to make the same mistake Dunstan had, eschewing all aid for the sake of his pride. The threat was simply too great.

Disregarding the lateness of the hour, Geoffrey took ink to parchment and wrote to his father, haltingly at first, and then at length, of his concerns, of the danger and of Elene, for he wanted most of all to protect her. And when he was finished, he began another, a shorter, less effusive version of the message, to go to Wessex.

So immersed was he in his task that Geoffrey did not realize Elene had woken until she bent over him, her long hair falling to the knees that were hidden beneath her shift. He straightened, murmuring a greeting as he put aside his writing tools. There was no need to hide the letters from her, for she could not read them, Geoffrey realized, before flushing at his own cruel observation.

He rose to his feet awkwardly, aware of a certain strain in the air between them, but unsure whether it was of his own making. Elene walked toward the window to stare out into the darkness, and as he admired the proud set of her slim shoulders, Geoffrey found it hard to believe that this same fierce female had fallen at his feet earlier, professing her love for him.

And yet there was a new delicacy about her, a wistfulness that he had never seen before, but that made her even more beautiful and intriguing. Had there ever been a more interesting woman? Geoffrey felt sorry for all the men who were married to drab, ordinary wives, and his heart began a rapid pulsing.

She loves me.

Elene turned to him just then, extending her hands in a helpless gesture, wholly unlike her usual brusque manner. "Look at what you've done to me," she whispered. "I'm weak now, nothing more than a squalling babe."

"Nay," Geoffrey said, stepping toward her. "You're

not weak.'' He snorted at the very notion, even as he searched her face. She looked less fierce, softer, perhaps, but in no way diminished. ''You're the strongest person I know—stronger than any of my brothers.''

When she eyed him skeptically, Geoffrey nodded. ''Spoiled, pampered boys, all of them.'' And it was true. They had all been born to privilege, secure in the affection and guidance of a fair and wise parent, while Elene... He grasped her shoulders, compelled to touch her and convince her of her own worth, of the dauntless spirit that took his breath away. ''And not one could do what you've done, a woman alone, without anyone. You survived, Elene! You triumphed!''

Hearing his voice rise with the force of his belief, Geoffrey lowered it while gentling his grip. He caught her gaze and held it, pouring all his admiration for her into one look. ''Just because you have me now, doesn't make you any less strong,'' he said softly.

Making one of those soft sounds that seemed so at odds with her nature, Elene buried her face against his shoulder, and Geoffrey held her close. Resting his chin upon her head, he tried to ignore a tiny niggling of guilt, for he had left so much unsaid.

Like *I love you.*

Ever since her admission, Geoffrey had felt uncomfortable, because he could not return her heartfelt avowal. He was still uncertain, hesitant to voice the words, because Elene was so different from the wife he had imagined. And he felt a knave for thinking such thoughts. Was he being true to his own vision, or was he allowing himself be swayed by the opinions of others? The mocking jeers of his brothers returned to haunt him, now that he would make this a true marriage.

Geoffrey sighed. Somehow, he had thought that love

would be a glorious, consuming sensation that would leave no room for doubts or worries, only pure, sweet bliss. But he remembered Dunstan acting the fool, stubborn and blind to his feelings for Marion, and Geoffrey wondered if he, too, was not seeing clearly. Faith, he had been befuddled ever since his arrival here!

Drawing his wife tighter to him, Geoffrey brushed his knuckles against the heavy weight of her hair, and his body stirred. Elene obviously welcomed his response, for suddenly he felt her teeth through the linen of his tunic, biting his chest. Groaning, Geoffrey let his hands wander over the womanly curves of her body, dismissing his confusion in the passion that flared between them.

This, at least, was right.

Something wasn't right.

Geoffrey turned to scan the horizon, but saw nothing except a darkening sky. A week of unusually hot weather had dried out the wet ground, but rain was coming again. And he welcomed it, not only for the crops, but as an end to the heat that shimmered in the air, thick and ominous. If only the tension that seemed to be building daily around him could be as easily eliminated, he mused grimly.

Although there had been no further attempts on his life or cryptic warnings, Geoffrey did not believe the threat was past. Indeed, he could not shake the sense that some new strike was as imminent as the coming storm. Geoffrey sighed. Once he would have dismissed his feelings as foolish, but since his arrival at the manor he had learned to give credence to such intangibles. And lately he wondered if his very life might depend on such wariness. Oddly enough, while Elene appeared less fierce, he grew more so, as tenacious as the Wolf in protecting his home and his wife.

And so he searched his surroundings uneasily, frowning when he found nothing amiss. Overseeing the thatching of several cots, Geoffrey had intended to go on to the village and about his lands, in an effort to make his presence felt, as both reassurance and warning. He had not planned to return to the manor until supper, the midmorning meal still heavy in his belly, but that odd niggling sensation kept calling his attention back.

Waving to the workers, Geoffrey turned his mount around, staring hard and long at the manor in the distance, but he could see no armies laying siege, no telltale smoke or signs of trouble. Still, the thought lingered, driving him to retrace his steps. Although he could have given no valid reason for it, he felt a need to see that all was in order. And so he spurred his horse, not waiting to see whether Dunstan's knights followed.

Pounding through the bailey, Geoffrey felt the fool when he startled those busy at their tasks, yet he hurried on, leaping from his destrier and tossing the reins to a surprised groom. In the hall, though he found nothing unusual, his anxiety persisted. Sighing, he ran a hand through his long hair. He was imagining things, or going mad, as Elene had so often predicted.

Elene.

Abruptly Geoffrey wanted to see her, to know that she was well and truly his wife. Despite their growing intimacy, a certain distance remained between them, except in the hot, dark hours of the night. And Geoffrey felt guilty for that restraint, knowing that he could not give his heart unreservedly, while she had laid herself bare to him.

He thought too much. That was what she had told him last night, when he pinched the bridge of his nose because a headache was coming on. And then Elene, once known as the notorious Fitzhugh, had rubbed his forehead until he fell asleep, her fingers strong yet gentle, her husky voice soothing, even as she scolded him softly.

Perhaps he did think too much where she was concerned, and ought to let himself feel instead, Geoffrey mused. His heart hammered in assent, and he strode swiftly toward the stairs, driven by both eagerness and a lingering disquiet. It grew tenfold when he found the room empty, though Elene could easily be elsewhere. Tamping down his panic, Geoffrey turned on his heel and reached for the door, only to stiffen at the sight that met his eyes.

The plain plaster of the wall was marred with black, as if someone had taken a charred piece of wood—or an arrow dipped in pitch—to it. Geoffrey's breath stopped in his throat as he realized the marks formed a message, and one deliberately left for him.

Fie de Burgh. If you will not be gone, then I will.

The missive was written in huge, rambling letters, and it was signed *E Fitzhugh*. Geoffrey's brows drew together as he stepped closer. Although the signature resembled the childish scrawl Elene had once used on her marriage documents, he knew full well that she could not have written the rest of it. She was coming along in her lessons, but was still practicing her letters. And her signature. Indeed, just the other afternoon, he had watched her struggle over and over with the same words: *Elene de Burgh.*

Not Fitzhugh.

With a hoarse cry, Geoffrey cursed the lie that leapt out at him, and rushed from the room like a madman. His unknown enemy had struck at last, taking something more dear to him than his property or his life.

His wife was gone.

Chapter Eighteen

When the first drops of rain began, Geoffrey ignored them. He told himself that no matter how dark the sky, he still had plenty of time before sunset to find Elene. Whoever had taken her could not have gotten far, and yet no one seemed to have noticed any travelers leaving the manor. He had sent knights out in every direction, hoping to track her, but the ground was so dry, it yielded no footprints.

An hour later, Talebot shouted at him to go back. Rain was pouring down in great sheets, blown by the wind, obscuring his vision, but he pressed on, desperate for a sign of his wife. "We can see nothing in this!" Talebot cried.

Geoffrey simply shook his head as a fierce gust sent his horse shying. He gripped the destrier's flanks tighter and pointed to the west, refusing to let the other man dissuade him from the search. He could think of nothing but Elene, his reason deserting him in the face of his urgency, his hammering heart driving him. It was as if the madness that had seized him in the great chamber would not release him from its grip until he found her. And he could not stop to examine the motivation for his frenzy;

he knew only that pain wracked his chest with each breath he took, and his eyes smarted from more than the rain.

Ignoring Talebot's protest, Geoffrey urged his weary mount forward, only to halt once more as another sound reached him above the wind and the storm. Yanking on the reins, he turned toward the summit of the hill and blinked into the blinding wetness. The faint noise was carried to him on a sweep of chilling rain, and he saw figures cresting the slope. Kicking his destrier, he drew his sword and headed for toward them, a curse upon his lips.

Like some demon from hell, Geoffrey raced toward the mounted men, though it soon became obvious that he and Talebot were far outnumbered. Behind him, he heard the knight's urgent shout, as if in warning, but he could not understand the words, and heeded them not. Ahead of him the riders took shape, a half dozen or more, and still Geoffrey rode on. He didn't care how many there were; if they had Elene, they were dead men.

"Halt in the name of the de Burghs, whose lands these be!" he demanded as he charged into their midst, only to blink in astonishment when the leader, a huge mailed knight, swung out of his way with a loud oath.

"Geoff?" the man shouted, and Geoffrey blinked in astonishment to see a familiar face. And another. And another. Shaking his head, as if to clear it, he peered through the gloom.

"Dunstan?" he asked, certain he had truly gone mad. At the Wolf's growl, he turned to the others, dark, dripping forms that gradually took shape. "Robin? Nicholas?" Although his voice was shaky and low, Geoffrey saw the answering nods.

"Aye. We're here, Geoff," his brothers said.

"We were on our way to the manor when we got

caught in this deluge,'' the Wolf said, swinging an arm toward the angry heavens. "But what the hell are you doing out in it?"

Too weary to gainsay Dunstan, Geoffrey joined his brothers on their journey to the manor. The Wolf was eager to get out of the foul weather as soon as possible, and Geoffrey could hardly plead his case coherently on the muddy road. But once inside, he refused to change his wet clothes or, indeed, do anything but slump into his chair in the hall. Dunstan's presence meant nothing to him; the only person he wanted to see was Elene.

Heedless of the blanket someone had tossed over his shoulders, Geoffrey buried his face in his hands, despair washing over him as surely as the rain that lashed against the walls. The afternoon was passing, and he was no closer to finding her than he had been hours ago. What if she was long gone, past his borders?

And where would she be by nightfall? The memory of his wife's painful recounting of her rape made his stomach churn violently. Who had her? Someone like Avery? Montgomery was big and brutal, and Geoffrey cringed. He felt wretched, sick and weak and wholly indifferent to his brothers, who milled around, anxious and restless, while Dunstan conferred with Talebot and Malcolm.

"Geoff?" The Wolf's low growl made Geoffrey reluctantly lift his head, and he gazed sightlessly at the man who was his liege lord and eldest sibling. His other brothers hung back, as if afraid to approach him, but Geoffrey cared not what they thought. He was beyond caring about anything but his wife.

"I came as soon as I got your message. Robin and Nicholas were visiting, so I brought them with me. They can help," Dunstan said gruffly.

"Nothing can help," Geoffrey muttered. "Look out there," he said, motioning toward the window. "All the tracks will be washed away, if there ever were any. She's gone. I've failed her, Dunstan. I've failed." The last word stuck in his throat, for he had once thought himself invincible, his intellect a match for any difficulty. Now he knew differently, and the truth was bitter to swallow.

"A de Burgh never fails," Dunstan said vehemently. Pausing, as if to contain his temper, the Wolf looked away, and then leaned forward to speak more quietly. Although Dunstan had dismissed the gaping servants, the hall afforded little privacy, yet Geoffrey could not muster the energy to move. "Are you certain that someone took her?" Dunstan asked, looking uncomfortable. "She's not exactly the...uh...type to be easily overpowered."

At another time, Geoffrey would have been amused and touched by his brother's efforts at tact, but he was too defeated to appreciate such niceties. "Aye, she was taken," he whispered. "You can go up to the great chamber and see for yourself."

At Dunstan's questioning look, Geoffrey sighed, lifting a hand to wipe the dripping water from his face. "There's a message on the wall, but Elene didn't leave it." He paused, straightening in his seat. "She cannot read or write."

Geoffrey didn't realize how he had stiffened, awaiting his brother's reaction, until it didn't come. The Wolf did not blink an eye, but merely glanced toward the stairs. Then, motioning to Robin and Nicholas to follow, he hurried toward them, off to view the evidence himself. And in that moment, Geoffrey realized that he had failed Elene in more ways than one.

Dunstan didn't care if she was illiterate.

The news that Elene could neither read nor write had

made no impression whatsoever on the Wolf, while Geoffrey had carried the knowledge around with him like a heavy stone. And how many other of her faults had weighed upon him? Elene could be loud and abusive and lacking in the manners befitting a de Burgh bride. She did not always dress beautifully or wear her hair in the latest fashion. She was handy with swords and knives, but not with letters or numbers, and though he craved her, Geoffrey had used these so-called failings to keep his distance from her.

And he had hung on to them, clinging to them as if they mattered, when they paled in the face of her strength, her passion, her desire to learn, her skills with bow and blade, and the generosity of spirit that she let few others see. Would he rather have a pretty doll to wear upon his arm, or a drab mouse who never raised her voice? *Nay!* Despite all the differences between them—or perhaps because of them—Geoffrey had never cared for anyone as he did Elene. No one better educated or better behaved or better dressed had ever moved him.

Only Elene. With the realization came a pain so deep that he could not contain it, and, dropping his head into his hands, Geoffrey wept at his loss and the foolish pride that had kept him from seeing what he possessed until it was gone.

Immersed in misery, he did not even notice his brother's return. Dimly he heard a low growl, then a gruff voice calling his name, and finally he felt an awkward pat upon his back that made him shudder with renewed grief.

"Geoff?" Dunstan cleared his throat. "I saw the message, but, could she not have...coaxed someone to write it for her?"

Wearily Geoffrey lifted his head. "No," he said. "No one else knows that she can't read or write. She fooled everyone for years." *Just as she deceived them as to her true nature.*

"Hmm..." Dunstan said, as if he were digesting the information, and Geoffrey sighed. The Wolf was not known for his wisdom, but there was one thing he would understand as could no other de Burgh.

Straightening, Geoffrey met his brother's questioning gaze and held it. "I love her, Dunstan," he said.

The Wolf grimaced slightly, but to Geoffrey's everlasting gratitude, he did not try to argue the point. Taking a deep breath, he nodded. "Well, if you love her, Geoff, then that's good enough for me."

As if nothing else need be said, Dunstan walked over to join Robin and Nicholas, giving Geoffrey a chance to regain his composure. Somehow, just that small gesture of understanding, that unreserved acceptance, roused him, and he rose to his feet, drawing closer when he heard Dunstan's shout.

"Look!" his brother said. "The rain's easing off. Let's go out again. I brought six men with me, plus Robin and Nicholas. If we split up..." Already the master tactician was at work, and Geoffrey released a long, ragged breath as Dunstan's energy filled the hall.

The Wolf had always seemed bigger and better than the other de Burghs. More muscular. More powerful. And hardened by battles that the rest of them had never seen. Surely he knew more about enemies than all of them, so perhaps he could do what no one else could. Perhaps he could find Elene.

Geoffrey's spirits, deadened and lifeless, began to pulse with renewed hope. And he realized that he had not been wise to discount the arrival of his brothers. The strength to be found in family, in blood ties and the bonds of affection, was a force to be reckoned with. Had they not routed Fitzhugh himself?

Now, mayhap, they would save his daughter.

"Very well," Geoffrey said, throwing off the blanket that clung to his shoulders. "I would lend you new mounts, but the choices are few."

"I'll stick with you, Geoff, for I don't know your lands well," Robin said.

"I do, for I have long been studying these hills," Dunstan growled.

"And I, as well," Nicholas said, causing the other de Burghs to halt in their steps toward the door.

"And how is that?" A disbelieving Robin taunted the youngest of them.

Nicholas lifted his chin with typical de Burgh arrogance. "When we were here before, I rode with Simon all over the demesne. We found the priest. Remember?"

"The priest?" For a moment, Geoffrey was baffled, but then he recalled the delay in his wedding ceremony that had sent his brothers out to look for Edred. "Yes, of course. You found him in a cave," he said absently.

"That's it! The caverns!" Nicholas shouted. "I bet that's where she is. We found several of them. Simon said one was big enough to billet a group of raiders such as harried you under Fitzhugh," Nicholas added, turning to Dunstan.

Geoffrey frowned at the fierce expression that came over the Wolf. Obviously, Dunstan would be interested in exploring there for reasons of his own. "But surely whoever took Elene wouldn't stay so close to the manor," Geoffrey protested.

Dunstan gave him a considering look. "It's worth a try, Geoff. They might have seen the bad weather coming and gone to ground, waiting for it to stop."

Geoffrey's breath caught on a dizzying rush of hope. Reason told him not to expect much, but just having a plan, a direction in which to search, was heartening. He nodded, grateful for his brother's guidance.

"All right," he said. Sweeping his gaze across the three men, so alike and yet each exceptional, Geoffrey smiled. "Nicholas, you may lead the way to these caverns of yours, and just in case there is an army waiting for us there, let us all go together."

Nicholas whooped eagerly, and Robin grinned. "To the de Burghs!" he called. "To the de Burghs!"

The deluge that had soaked them to the bone earlier had tapered off to a fine rain, easily ignored as they traveled from the manor toward a fast-flowing stream, its waters high. They followed it away from the moorlands and woods, toward the rocky crags that rimmed one side of the valley, erupting into towering gray walls of stone. As they neared it, the black mouth of the cave was clearly visible, and the brothers approached cautiously, although the area was deserted. Leaving Nicholas and Robin with the horses, Dunstan and Geoffrey crept forward, swords drawn, into the gaping hole in the earth.

Geoffrey held his breath, but he heard nothing except the steady drip of water echoing from the depths below. Halting him with a hand, Dunstan knelt to scan the floor, reaching out to touch the dry, packed ground. "No one has been here recently," he said, shaking his head and surging to his feet. "But if it's as big as Nicholas says, it may have other entrances we don't know about. We can try to light a torch, if you want to look further."

Geoffrey shivered. It was colder here, within the stone, and he felt the chill through his wet clothes. The blackness yawned before them, huge and daunting, and he knew they could well spend days searching it out. Trusting to the Wolf's instincts, he shook his head.

"Nay. Let us go on," he said, though disappointment weighed heavily upon him.

Outside, they once again followed Nicholas's lead, toward the steep rise of rocks, and Geoffrey choked back a sigh. He had never explored these crags, for they had seemed of little use to him, unfit as they were even for goats. Now, he rued his carelessness, for he could well imagine tunnels below the hard surface providing a close haven for his enemies.

"There," Nicholas said, pausing to point toward one particular outcropping. "That marks the priest's hole, because it looks like a cross."

"A cross?" Geoffrey said, staring at an oddly shaped stone blurred by the rain.

"Only to our Nick," Robin said dryly.

This time, Geoffrey and Dunstan left the horses and the younger de Burghs farther back, climbing on foot towards Nicholas's landmark. If there was a path, the water had made short work of it, and they fought both mud and slippery slabs before reaching their goal. But the very same rain that made their route difficult also served them well, for the noisy drops covered their approach, should anyone be lying in wait.

Below the unusual ledge, just as Nicholas had said, they found the entrance to the cavern. It was partially hidden by summer growth, but the leaves had obviously been disturbed, and Geoffrey lowered his hand to the hilt of his sword as he leaned forward for a closer look.

Unlike the other cave, where nothing but blackness had met his curious gaze, this interior was lit by an eerie glow that made Geoffrey draw his weapon. Although he could see only dank walls, he pushed aside the obscuring branches and climbed into the rocky chamber, driven by a sense of urgency that he could not have explained.

Dunstan was right behind him as Geoffrey edged forward stealthily, following the curving face of the wall until they came full circle. At first glance, one might think the cave ended here, but the strange light spilled out of a narrow opening in the back, hinting at another chamber. With a shared look and a nod, the brothers pressed themselves close against the rocks on either side and peered into the space beyond. In the dim silence, Geoffrey heard the low, swift intake of Dunstan's breath. Then he, too, choked back a sound at the scene that met his eyes.

Flickering candles lit a bizarre interior unlike any Geoffrey had ever seen. The walls were draped with cloth, as were various seats that might have been logs or rocks or even stools, for all he could tell. And on every surface candles wavered—large ones, fat ones, slender tapers from the chapel, stubs and castoffs guttering in an errant misty draft from the entrance. They filled the cavern with the bright light of day, illuminating an elaborate shrine that was built into one corner to take advantage of a natural depression.

Geoffrey shuddered at the sight. Although an educated man of reason, a scholar who had scoffed at all of Talebot's and Malcolm's fears, now he wondered if there was a witch—or worse—using this altar for some evil arts. The animal heart left on his seat took on a more ominous aspect, and he knew a sudden stab of fear even as he hoped that whatever unnatural rituals were practiced here did not involve Elene.

Geoffrey was not sure what manner of inhabitant he expected; a bloodred demon or a cackling crone would not have made him blink. Indeed, neither would have stunned him as much as the figure he did see, moving from behind a stack of kegs, his shock of white hair instantly recognizable.

Edred.

Geoffrey jerked forward, but Dunstan held him back, pointing silently to a length of cloth lying close to the rocky floor. Pushing the wet hair from his eyes, Geoffrey squinted and stiffened as what he had thought a discarded bundle began to take on human form. His breath caught and held as he realized that the linen sack enclosed a body and, at one end, a length of cinnamon and spice fell to the ground.

It was Elene. And Edred held a dagger over her.

Geoffrey flinched, involuntarily, as dread coursed through him, and it was not until he saw the smooth length of her hair move that he at last released a chestful of air in a silent rush. She was alive, at least, but for how long? His hands itched to feel the priest's throat, even as he understood Dunstan's caution. The blade was too close to her, while they were too far away.

"Water." The voice, weak and muffled, sounded nothing like that of the fierce woman once known as the Fitzhugh, and Geoffrey shuddered. What had the madman done to her? Geoffrey's fingers tightened on the hilt of his sword, and he shifted, ready to strike as soon as he could.

"Ah," Edred grunted. "Awake at last. I feared you would sleep forever. I am not so handy with herbs as a woman, witch or otherwise, Elene Fitzhugh."

Herbs? Had he drugged her? That explained her listlessness, but the bastard might have killed her with his potions! Geoffrey's jaw clamped shut with the force of his effort to remain still.

"Water," Elene whispered again, so desperately that

Geoffrey lurched forward, only to be halted again by his brother.

"Nay. Wait until he's away from her," Dunstan whispered in Geoffrey's ear, pointing to the long dagger that glittered in the priest's hand. It was much too close to Elene, and it swung wildly when Edred turned to face her.

Geoffrey took a deep breath, realizing that this was the first time in his life that his elder brother had had to teach him patience. That jarring realization forced him to taut control, for if he made a misjudgment, Elene could die. And then he could never live with himself.

"Yes, thirst is an effect of my little concoction, but you shall have to wait. You are trussed for good reason, wicked creature, for I would not give you power over me. 'Tis time for you to relinquish your false strength, bartered with evil, and return to the fold, Elene Fitzhugh!"

Geoffrey stiffened as Edred put the blade to his wife's throat, and his knuckles ached with strain of waiting, his chest nigh unto bursting from the hammering of his heart.

"I have known of your downfall since I arrived here to serve your father. He thought it amusing to have spawned such an abomination, and would not heed me!" Edred's voice rose to a fever pitch. "Now you would work your demon craft on another, damning him, too. I tried to send him away, but he was ensnared, befouled by you, so I have taken matters into my own hands. What say you now, evil one?"

"I am not evil," Elene muttered.

"*You are!*" Edred screeched, and Geoffrey flinched as the point of the knife dipped low over her throat. "What other woman would dare use cursed language and threaten the men around her? What other would shout at her betters and murder a good knight?"

Elene's eyes narrowed. "I did what I had to do to save

myself," she whispered hoarsely. She was still groggy, Geoffrey could see, for her speech was thick and slow. "You must know that I didn't want to end up like my mother, destroyed by Father and his men. She was good and kind, and he killed her for it. He respected only those whose strength of will matched his own."

Elene paused to lick her dry lips, and Geoffrey felt as if his body were being torn asunder by her heartrending admission. "So I imitated him," she said, laughing in that bitter way of hers that was so familiar. "I acted rude and foul and cruel until he believed me. Until everyone believed me. And they all left me alone."

Geoffrey started at the revelation, for at last he understood the elemental mystery of his wife. When he first came to the manor, he had assumed her behavior was a bid for attention, when all along she had acted to deflect attention, to protect herself. And it had worked, up to a point.

Elene had made herself so frightening that nearly everyone was afraid of her, and few dared get close to her. Only Avery, reckless and desperate, had suspected the lie, but he had been proved wrong swiftly enough. For Geoffrey knew the irony that escaped even Elene herself: In pretending to be strong, she had become far more courageous than any of them.

Geoffrey shook his head, so very proud of her, and yet not so proud of himself. Although he deemed himself wise, all his learning had failed him in his dealings with Elene. He, who had been taught to look beneath the surface, had not done so. Instead, he had placed value only on those things that were outward trappings—cleanliness, and reading and writing, and habits of dress—while ignoring what was really important: strength of spirit, inherent goodness and generosity, passion and wit.

There, in the eerie dimness of the cold cavern, Geoffrey's chest ached with the force of his love for her.

But Edred was not swayed by the truth; he was far too mad. "You speak in falsehoods, though 'tis not all your doing. You are possessed, Elene," the priest said, lowering his voice as he placed the flat of the blade across her throat. "And I am the only man who can save you from eternal damnation."

Geoffrey saw Elene blink, and he struggled against the urge to leap forward. "You have fornicated with the devil, and only through a cleansing of your body can you be saved. Only by coupling with the pure of heart will you be cleansed," Edred said, his pale eyes taking on an even wilder look.

Geoffrey swallowed hard, his sword at the ready, for it was becoming all too clear what Edred wanted from his wife. And, the knife be damned, Geoffrey would not let the priest touch her. Exchanging a swift glance with Dunstan, Geoffrey leaned forward, just as Elene kicked upward violently in the air, knocking her captor off balance. Seizing the moment, Geoffrey surged into the chamber, the Wolf's howl of rage roaring in his ears as Dunstan followed close behind.

Geoffrey leapt over Elene, his sword slicing through the air and downward, to where Edred lay prone, his knife skittering away on the stone floor. "Die, priest," he said, lifting his arm, but Elene's hoarse whisper stayed his hand.

"He is mad, Geoffrey."

Surprised at such mercy, Geoffrey flicked a glance toward his wife just as Edred screamed, "You shall not have her!" Ignoring the weapon pressed against his chest, the priest heaved upward, impaling himself upon the heavy blade.

Stunned, Geoffrey shook his head. "Mad, indeed," he murmured. "May he now find peace." Retrieving his sword, Geoffrey wiped it clean on one of the many cloths draped around the cavern and sheathed it once more. Then, drawing out his own dagger, he sliced through the thick linen material that imprisoned his wife.

She sat up shakily, and Geoffrey fell to his knees to pull the rest of the offending sack from her body. Tossing it on the floor of the cave, he looked up at her and halted, struck by the memory of another time, when their positions had been reversed and she had knelt before him. Looking up at her, so rare and beautiful and fine, Geoffrey felt his heart turn over.

"Elene," he whispered roughly. She looked down at him, her amber eyes narrowed with a wariness that he was determined to remove, even if it took a lifetime. And he would begin now. Swallowing against the thickness in his throat, Geoffrey spoke the words that he had waited too long to give her. "I love you," he said, grinning at the look of stunned surprise on her face. Torn between laughter and tears, he pulled her into his arms, muttering frantic endearments. *He loved her,* and he would spend the rest of his days proving it to her. And the world.

Hearing Dunstan's low grunt, Geoffrey finally set his wife aside to help his brother wrap the dead man for transport and burial. As he leaned over to retrieve the priest's dagger, however, Geoffrey's thoughts swiftly changed direction. Straightening, he fixed his wife with an assessing gaze. "And just what did you think you were doing when you kicked that madman?" he demanded, his voice low. "You could have been killed! What exactly were you planning to do while bound in a sack?"

In response, Elene ducked and flushed, but just when Geoffrey thought she was going to lash out at him with a stream of foul curses, she lifted her head and shrugged. "Take his knife in my teeth?" she suggested.

Before Geoffrey could respond to that ludicrous claim, Dunstan threw his head back and roared with amusement. Turning to stare at his brother, Geoffrey frowned, "Don't encourage her," he muttered. Still, *he* was encouraged by the Wolf's attitude toward his old enemy.

Grinning at Elene with grudging admiration, Dunstan shook his head. "Geoff, if anyone could do it, your wife could!"

Epilogue

Geoffrey looked out the window and smiled at the view of the rolling hills that surrounded Campion, sparkling in the late-afternoon sun under a dusting of snow. He and Elene had arrived a day early, thanks to the cold, packed roads, which made traveling a little easier than the usual slush of wintertide, only to find most of the castle residents absent, out roaming the woodlands for a Yule log, at Marion's instigation.

But soon they would all gather together for supper in the great hall, and afterward in the solar, for spiced wine and Christmas sweets. It was all so familiar, and yet not so, for Geoffrey was not in the old room he had shared with Stephen, but in a guest chamber. Though small, it was far more luxuriously appointed than he had become used to during the past year, Geoffrey thought wryly, yet he had no desire to stay here, for it was no longer home to him.

His gaze slid to the massive bed, where a slender figure was curled, her long hair splayed over the pillow, and his smile widened. He had made his home with this woman, and now he would fill it with his own family, with the laughter of children they would make between them.

Sighing with contentment, Geoffrey leaned over to kiss
Elene's cheek, flushed with sleep. Although her body was
still slim, she rested more often, and he could already see
the changes caused by their child in the breasts that
strained at the bodice of her gown.

The sight stirred him, and Geoffrey was tempted to join
her in bed, but he was hoping to speak with Dunstan before supper, and Elene was deep in dreams. Leaving her
to her nap, he brushed his lips against a fall of spicy locks
and slipped away.

The hall below was bustling with activity, and Geoffrey
soon found Dunstan striding toward the high table.
"Geoff! Sorry we missed your arrival, but Marion would
not rest until we had the perfect log for the Christmas fire.
She is determined that the babe enjoy the holiday to the
fullest, though I told her the infant notices nothing except
the source of its milk!"

Geoffrey grinned, for Dunstan's pride was evident, despite his grumbling. He thought of his own child growing
within Elene, and he sobered, well reminded of his purpose in seeking out his brother. "Dunstan, after what happened this summer…well, I never had a chance to tell
you how grateful I am for what you did for me."

Dunstan made a low growl of dismissal, but Geoffrey
would not be dissuaded. "I don't know how to thank you.
Nothing I could do could ever repay you. You gave me
back my wife, my life."

Dunstan shook his head, awkwardly. "Nay. You owe
me not, Geoff, for if I remember aright, 'twas you who
got me out of my own dungeon."

It was Geoffrey's turn to shake his head. "We were all
there. I was simply the first to reach you. And it was the
youngest de Burgh who saved the day then, as well." He
glanced at Dunstan ruefully. "It appears that for all my

studies, I could learn a few things from little Nick, the most observant of us all."

"Faith, don't let him hear you, or there will be no living with him!" Dunstan protested. Then he fixed Geoffrey with a steady gaze. "I'm glad we could help, but you would have found her yourself." Holding up a hand to halt Geoffrey's denial, he continued determinedly. "Nay. Hear me out. Eventually you would have figured out the whole thing. That mind of yours has no match, and eventually you would have realized who wrote the message. They weren't going anywhere. You would have had time to find them."

Geoffrey sighed. "Perhaps, but she could have been hurt, or…" He trailed off, unable to complete the sentence.

Dunstan grunted. "I don't think that priest could have harmed her. As soon as that potion wore off, your wife would have carved him into tiny pieces!"

Geoffrey laughed, and it felt good, for he had been carrying around this guilt since the summer. Perhaps Dunstan was right, and he and Elene would have triumphed without help, but still, he was glad of the aid when he needed it. "Aye, but I see the value in my siblings," he said.

"Then we are in agreement, for I, too, have learned my family's worth many times over," Dunstan noted. As if the admission made him uncomfortable, he turned away before glancing back at Geoffrey, his expression less intense. "Now, tell me, how goes it at the manor, for it has been months since I last saw you."

"You would not recognize the place," Geoffrey said, with a wry chuckle. "I've actually caught some of the servants smiling."

At Dunstan's laugh, Geoffrey continued on, more seriously. "'Tis a different mood that prevails there, as if a black cloud has been lifted from the lands."

The Wolf's amusement fled. "You do not think the priest actually worked some...spell, do you?" he asked, looking startled.

"Nay," Geoffrey said. "There was nothing otherworldly involved. He simply used his influence and his position to sway the people, first by spreading lies about me, then, later, through intimidation and even threats of punishment." Geoffrey frowned. "He was desperate. And even those who could see he was no proper priest were afraid to speak up, for fear of retribution, earthly or otherwise."

Dunstan shook his head. "You took on a host of enemies, Geoff, and routed them all. 'Tis a chore few could have done as well."

"Ah, but look what I won," Geoffrey said. "'Twas well worth any price." When Dunstan appeared unconvinced, Geoffrey laughed and called to one of the servants. Whispering a direction to the man, he swung back toward Dunstan, just as Marion joined them, dimpled and rosy-cheeked.

"Geoffrey!" she said, holding out her hands. He took them in his own and squeezed them lightly. "I have just come from your wife, and she looks much changed," Marion said slyly.

Geoffrey nodded, unsure whether she spoke of Elene's pregnancy. They had told no one the good news, for he had insisted upon waiting until the Christmas celebration to make the announcement. Elene had, understandably, been less enthusiastic about this visit to his family, but she had agreed for his sake. Now, Geoffrey wondered if Marion had seen signs of the budding babe, but, if so, he did not want to discuss it as yet.

"I was just talking about Elene with Dunstan," he said instead, ignoring the Wolf's puzzled expression. "In fact... Ah, here it is." He motioned to the returning servant to put down his burden on the table, and bade Marion and Dunstan come close.

"What?" the Wolf growled, suspicious, as the man returned to the kitchens, leaving two dishes behind.

"Here you see two sweets, alike and yet very different," Geoffrey explained.

"Is this one of your experiments, Geoff?" Dunstan asked with a frown. "He was always trying to prove one of his studies to us," the Wolf muttered to Marion.

"A demonstration merely," Geoffrey said. "Now, look at each of the dishes. One is a milk pudding, rich, sweet and full-bodied. The other is an apple pastry, highly spiced with ginger and cinnamon and almonds, and just a little tart to the taste. Which do you prefer?" Geoffrey asked him mildly.

Dunstan eyed him as if he had finally lost his wits. "The milk pudding, of course."

"Just so," Geoffrey said with a grin.

Marion laughed and clapped her hands in delight at the comparison. "So I am a milk pudding, am I?"

Geoffrey met Dunstan's startled look with a smug expression. "I find that I prefer something with a bit more bite to it. That does not mean that I decry milk pudding, or those who like it, as well," he said, nodding graciously toward Marion.

She erupted into a peal of laughter. "Give over, Geoffrey, I think you've lost him!"

Muttering something about his brother's ridiculous book-learning, Dunstan took his seat at the high table, and Geoffrey found himself greeted by the rest of his siblings.

"Geoff!" Nicholas cried, bounding forward with his

usual enthusiasm. Robin, too, patted him on the back, while Simon and Stephen hung back, reluctant to show their affection. Reynold followed behind, his limp especially noticeable after a day in the saddle.

As they took their seats, everyone talking at once, Geoffrey wondered if he ought to go to Elene. Although she would never admit it, he knew she was anxious about seeing the de Burghs again in full force. But when he looked toward the stairs, he saw that she was already coming forward, with no other than Campion himself as her escort.

Geoffrey smiled, then sucked in a deep breath as she came into view. *She looks much changed,* Marion had said, and now he knew why. Obviously, his sister had presented Elene with an early gift, for she wore a new gown, far more distinctive than any he had seen before.

It was a deep, rich scarlet that gave color to her cheeks and clung to her newly rounded curves as did none other. Her hair had been left loose, as always, but the locks at the sides of her face had been pulled back and up, to be secured by a red ribbon. The rest fell past her hips, gleaming and smooth, yet that small change was astonishing, for no longer did any strands obscure her lovely features, her clear skin or her delicate mouth.

She looked as beautiful and ripe as a Christmas berry.

Even Geoffrey, who had admired the subtle improvements Elene made in her appearance over the past few months, was thunderstruck. His heart responded with its usual hammering, while farther down, another unruly organ strained at his braies. He sat down abruptly.

It was then that he noticed his brothers. All of them were watching Elene's graceful approach with admiration, and Geoffrey grinned proudly. At last, they were seeing his wife as a woman, and an attractive one, at that. He felt vindicated, no longer to dread their whispered jokes and crude comments or fear that his resulting fury might come between them.

But when Stephen leaned back in his chair, a slow smile of appreciation playing upon his lips, Geoffrey's amusement fled, for he recognized that look and didn't like it. Sweeping his gaze around the room, he noted Nicholas's gaping stare and Robin's interested expression, and he shifted uncomfortably, pricked by something awfully close to jealousy.

On the one hand, he was well pleased with his wife, who deserved better treatment from his brothers, but on the other hand, he felt like a man whose hoarded treasure had been uncovered by the prying eyes of the world. After all, he *always* had seen the beauty in his wife. Frowning, Geoffrey turned at the Wolf's low grunt of surprise, only to see Marion hush her husband and lean close to whisper to him. Odd, that, he thought, and then his gaze swept the table anew as a dark suspicion began to form. It was confirmed only a moment later, when Stephen, never taking his eyes off Elene, turned toward Marion.

"Have you a new attendant?" he asked in a husky tone. Laughing delightedly, Marion denied the question and stopped Dunstan from commenting with a hand on his arm. Apparently, the Wolf guessed what no one else did, and Geoffrey scowled in disgust.

None of them recognized his wife.

At the trestle tables below, whispers flew, and Geoffrey even heard one old knight's loud conjecture. "She must be Geoffrey's leman!"

Simon turned to give Geoffrey a sly look. "I thought you were bringing your wife."

"I did," Geoffrey said, annoyed.

With a gurgling sound, Simon spewed out his ale, to

the shouts and hoots and protests of the nearby brothers. Only Stephen still leaned back casually, an assessing look upon his face. "What did you do with the Fitzhugh?" he asked.

Geoffrey stiffened slightly. "The Fitzhugh is no more," he answered roughly.

"What? Did you kill her?" Simon sputtered. The look of astonishment on his hardened warrior's face made Geoffrey choke back a laugh. Even Reynold sent him an alarmed glance.

"Nay. She lives, but now she is a de Burgh." Rising to his feet, Geoffrey held out a hand to his wife. "Elene, you remember Simon, don't you?" Inclining her head in the manner of a wellborn lady, Elene nodded graciously to his brother, and Geoffrey saw six pairs of eyes swivel toward her in amazement.

"A fine addition to our family, she is," Campion said, presenting Geoffrey's wife to him. "And we all welcome her, do we not?" he asked, turning to gauge his sons' reactions. Geoffrey had the pleasure of watching all eyes move to his father in stunned disbelief, while dead silence fell over the hall.

Gradually, mutters and nods and strained words of greeting filled the air, and Geoffrey noticed that some of his siblings had the grace to look chagrined. "Good," Campion said. Then he made his way to the head of the high table, stopping to stand behind his chair. "And let me be the first to tender my congratulations."

Geoffrey grinned. His father still saw more wisely and more clearly than anyone else, and he felt an easing in his tight chest at the promise of his wife's acceptance. He nodded, suddenly unable to speak, as Campion continued. "I'm sure you will all join me in celebration of the newest de Burgh's imminent arrival. Geoffrey, don't leave your wife standing,'' he admonished.

Marion's cry of excitement was drowned out by the shouts and whoops of the brothers when they recognized the announcement for what it was, and Geoffrey noticed no furtive looks, only genuine good cheer. Seating Elene, he grinned proudly and took his place beside her, certain that the life that had seemed so bleak but a year ago could hold no more happiness.

As the shouts rose to a deafening level, Elene reached for Geoffrey, gripping the hard muscle of his arm, rather than the hilt of her dagger. She was unused to effusive behavior that did not turn to violence, but gradually the din lessened, and she was able to relax a little. It was difficult, this visit to Geoffrey's old home, thrusting her as it did into the midst of his brothers, and only the promise of Marion's presence had made her agree to come. Elene blinked, the memory of the dark-haired woman's joyous greeting still fresh, but another warm welcome had come from a most unexpected source: Geoffrey's father, and sire to the whole damnable brood.

Although all the de Burghs seemed to talk at once, when Campion spoke, everyone listened. And Elene could not blame them. Geoffrey's father was like him in many ways. She recognized the same wisdom, the same gentle man inside a warrior's body, but she was not as easy with it. Campion's eyes seemed to gaze into her very soul, and Elene had found herself holding her breath, afraid of coming up wanting in his judgment.

Apparently, she had not, for the earl had treated her with all the courtesy of his favorite son, and so she had taken his arm and let him lead her down into the midst of the others. Although Elene could not embrace them, as well, she had to admit to a feeling of triumph when they had not known her. Fools, the lot of them, she thought with a frown. And well she would like to avenge herself upon each one for their previous treatment of her.

Except for Geoffrey.

And his sire. There was something about Campion that invited loyalty—and more. Even Elene, who found it difficult to respond politely to anyone but her husband, was drawn to his still-handsome father. The earl exuded a power that was both compelling and daunting. Elene had no idea how he knew she was pregnant, for Geoffrey had sworn to tell no one.

Curious, she studied the elder de Burgh with narrowed eyes, until he suddenly looked up, just as if he had felt her scrutiny. She shivered, struck by an eerie sensation that disappeared as soon as he smiled at her. Then she felt the warmth of his gaze, so like his son's, along with a twinkle that invited her to share with him some private jest.

"This is the second Christmas that we have welcomed a new de Burgh bride and the child she carries," Campion said, sweeping a glance over the table where his sons were gathered before him. "Perhaps we shall make it a tradition." He paused significantly, making Elene wonder what he was about, before he continued. "Who among you will be next?"

Startled by the choking sounds that ensued, Elene looked around, to see the fierce de Burgh knights pale and panicked. In fact, the men who had once seemed so fearsome to her were practically quaking in their seats at the very suggestion of such an alliance, and Elene remembered Marion's mention of their reluctance to marry. Biting back a derisive laugh, Elene knew she would never see the de Burgh brothers in quite the same light again, now that she had discovered their weakness. And well she would lord it over them all.

Matching Campion's smile with her own, Elene realized that no revenge she could devise would be better than to see them all firmly in love and wed one day soon.

* * * * *

Four Bright New Stars!
Harlequin Historical™
launches its *March Madness*
celebration with these four exciting
historical romance debuts:

THE MAIDEN AND THE WARRIOR
By Jacqueline Navin
A fierce warrior is saved by the love of a spirited
maiden bride.

LAST CHANCE BRIDE
By Jillian Hart
A lonely spinster finds hope in the arms of an embittered
widower.

GABRIEL'S HEART
By Madeline George
An ex-sheriff must choose between revenge or the feisty
socialite who has stolen his heart.

A DUKE DECEIVED
By Cheryl Bolen
A handsome duke falls for a penniless noblewoman
whom he must marry in haste.

Look for all four books from four fabulous new authors
wherever Harlequin Historicals are sold.

Coming in August 1997!

THE BETTY NEELS RUBY COLLECTION

August 1997—Stars Through the Mist
September 1997—The Doubtful Marriage
October 1997—The End of the Rainbow
November 1997—Three for a Wedding
December 1997—Roses for Christmas
January 1998—The Hasty Marriage

COLLECTOR'S EDITION

This August start assembling the
Betty Neels Ruby Collection. Six of the
most requested and best-loved titles have
been especially chosen for this collection.
From August 1997 until January 1998,
one title per month will be available to avid
fans. Spot the collection by the lush ruby red
cover with the gold Collector's Edition banner
and your favorite author's name—Betty Neels!

Available in August at your favorite retail outlet.

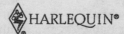

HARLEQUIN®

DEBBIE MACOMBER

invites you to the

HEART OF TEXAS

Join Debbie Macomber as she brings you the lives
and loves of the folks in the ranching community
of Promise, Texas.

If you loved Midnight Sons—don't miss
Heart of Texas! A brand-new six-book series
from Debbie Macomber.

Available in February 1998
at your favorite retail store.

Heart of Texas by Debbie Macomber

Lonesome Cowboy	February '98
Texas Two-Step	March '98
Caroline's Child	April '98
Dr. Texas	May '98
Nell's Cowboy	June '98
Lone Star Baby	July '98

HARLEQUIN®

KEY ♡ TO MY HEART

Unlock the secrets of romance just in time for the most romantic day of the year— Valentine's Day!

Key to My Heart
features three of your favorite authors,

Kasey Michaels, Rebecca York and Muriel Jensen,

to bring you wonderful tales of romance and Valentine's Day dreams come true.

As an added bonus you can receive Harlequin's special Valentine's Day necklace. FREE with the purchase of every *Key to My Heart* collection.

Available in January,
wherever Harlequin books are sold.

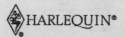

PHKEY349

WELCOME TO *Love Inspired* ™

A brand-new series of contemporary inspirational love stories.

Join men and women as they learn valuable lessons about facing the challenges of today's world and about life, love and faith.

Look for the following February 1998
Love Inspired™ titles:

A Groom of Her Own
by Irene Hannon

The Marriage Wish
by Dee Henderson

The Reluctant Bride
by Kathryn Alexander

Available in retail outlets
in January 1998.

LIFT YOUR SPIRITS AND GLADDEN YOUR HEART with *Love Inspired* ™!

Steeple
Hill™

LI298

**Look for these titles—
available at your favorite retail outlet!**

January 1998
Renegade Son by Lisa Jackson
Danielle Summers had problems: a rebellious child
and unscrupulous enemies. In addition, her Montana
ranch was slowly being sabotaged. And then there was
Chase McEnroe—who admired her land and desired her
body. But Danielle feared he would invade more than just
her property—he'd trespass on her heart.

February 1998
The Heart's Yearning by Ginna Gray
Fourteen years ago Laura gave her baby up for adoption,
and not one day had passed that she didn't think about
him and agonize over her choice—so she finally followed
her heart to Texas to see her child. But the plan to watch
her son from afar doesn't quite happen that way, once the
boy's sexy—*single*—father takes a decided interest in *her*.

March 1998
First Things Last by Dixie Browning

One look into Chandler Harrington's dark eyes and
Belinda Massey could refuse the Virginia millionaire nothing.
So how could the no-nonsense nanny believe the rumors that
he had kidnapped his nephew—an adorable, healthy little boy
who crawled as easily into her heart as he did into her lap?

**BORN IN THE USA: Love, marriage—
and the pursuit of family!**

**Make a Valentine's date
for the premiere of**

◈ HARLEQUIN® **Movies**

starting February 14, 1998 with

Debbie Macomber's

This Matter of

Marriage

on **the movie channel** ⓣⓜⓒ

Just tune in to **The Movie Channel** the **second Saturday night** of every month at 9:00 p.m. EST to join us, and be swept away by the sheer thrill of romance brought to life. Watch for details of upcoming movies—in books, in your television viewing guide and in stores.

If you are not currently a subscriber to The Movie Channel, simply call your local cable or satellite provider for more details. Call today, and don't miss out on the romance!

the movie channel ⓣⓜⓒ
*100% pure movies.
100% pure fun.*

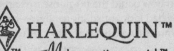
◈™ HARLEQUIN™
Makes any time special.™